The curse of a lost continent rises again!

A lost island broken by cataclysm and haunted by a dark intelligence broods alone on its bloody past. It is the lost graveyard for fleets of sunken treasure vessels. An irresistible lure for Dane Maddock and his band of adventurers, but getting there is least of their problems.

When Bones rescues a talented young programmer from a gang of mercenaries, Maddock and his crew find themselves in the crosshairs of a deadly organization that will stop at nothing to possess a priceless software program with the potential to control the world's economy.

Maddock, Bones, and the crew of the Sea Foam set out for a legendary island in the Pacific, the final resting place of a wealth of treasure vessels. Standing in their way are mercenaries, cage fighters, drug gangs, mystics, and powers beyond their understanding. But no threat is more perilous than what awaits them in the shadow of Maug.

Praise for the Dane Maddock Adventures

"Dane and Bones…. Together they're unstoppable. Rip roaring action from start to finish. Wit and humor throughout. Just one question - how soon until the next one? Because I can't wait." *Graham Brown, author of Shadows of the Midnight Sun*

"A twisty tale of adventure and intrigue that never lets up and never lets go!" *Robert Masello, author of Bestiary and Blood and Ice*

"What an adventure! A great read that provides lots of action, and thoughtful insight as well, into strange realms that are sometimes best left unexplored." *Paul Kemprecos, author of the NUMA Files*

"A page-turning yarn blending high action, Biblical speculation, ancient secrets, and nasty creatures. Indiana Jones better watch his back!" *Jeremy Robinson, author of SecondWorld*

"With the thoroughly enjoyable way Mr. Wood has mixed speculative history with our modern day pursuit of truth, he has created a story that thrills and makes one think beyond the boundaries of mere fiction and enter the world of 'why not'?" *David Lynn Golemon, Author of Ancients*

"Let there be no confusion: David Wood is the next Clive Cussler. Once you start reading, you won't be able to stop until the last mystery plays out in the final line." *Edward G. Talbot, author of 2012: The Fifth World*

"I like my thrillers with lots of explosions, global locations and a mystery where I learn something new. Wood delivers! Recommended as a fast paced, kick ass read." *J.F. Penn, author of Desecration*

"Dourado is a brisk read, reminiscent of early Cussler adventures, and perfect for an afternoon at the beach or a cross-country flight. You'll definitely want more of Maddock." *Sean Ellis- Author of Into the Black*

MAUG

A DANE MADDOCK ADVENTURE

DAVID WOOD
C.B. MATSON

Maug
Copyright 2019 by David Wood
All rights reserved

Published by Adrenaline Press
www.adrenaline.press

Adrenaline Press is an imprint of Gryphonwood Press
www.gryphonwoodpress.com

ISBN: 9781090842893

Edited by Melissa Bowersock
Cover design by Matt Williams

BOOKS and SERIES by DAVID WOOD

Arcanum
Magus
Berserk
Devil's Face
The Tomb
Cavern
Brainwash
Herald
Maug

Jade Ihara Adventures (with Sean Ellis)
Oracle
Changeling
Exile

Bones Bonebrake Adventures
Primitive
The Book of Bones
Skin and Bones
Venom (forthcoming)

Jake Crowley Adventures (with Alan Baxter)
Blood Codex
Anubis Key

Brock Stone Adventures
Arena of Souls
Track of the Beast (forthcoming)

Myrmidon Files (with Sean Ellis)
Destiny
Mystic

Sam Aston Investigations (with Alan Baxter)
Primordial
Overlord

Stand-Alone Novels
Into the Woods (with David S. Wood)
Callsign: Queen (with Jeremy Robinson)
Dark Rite (with Alan Baxter)

David Wood writing as David Debord

The Absent Gods Trilogy
The Silver Serpent
Keeper of the Mists
The Gates of Iron

The Impostor Prince (with Ryan A. Span)
Neptune's Key
The Zombie-Driven Life
You Suck

BOOKS and SERIES by C.B. MATSON

The Dane Maddock Universe
Maug

PROLOGUE

771 CE
Somewhere in the Pacific Islands

The outrigger skimmed across the aquamarine surface of the sea, driven by a group of dark-skinned men who powered the craft forward with smooth strokes. Inapo struggled to keep pace with the older men, all leaders in his village, but his mind was elsewhere.

"You are losing the rhythm, son," Gamomo, his father, said from behind him.

Inapo didn't reply, but refocused his attention in keeping in sync with the others. Of all the days for him to lose himself, it had to be this one.

"You should have named him Guifi," another man said, eliciting a chorus of laughter.

Inapo gritted his teeth. "Guifi" meant "dream." It was not the first time someone had applied that name to him.

"I was not dreaming," he said. It was almost true. "I am merely wondering about what lies ahead."

"You are about to find out," Gamomo said. "There is the island."

Inapo squinted against the glare of the sun. He could make out a forbidding silhouette on the horizon. He shook his head. It was only his imagination.

"You will be fine," his father assured, so quiet the

others couldn't hear.

Inapo didn't reply. His throat was so tight he wasn't certain he could manage the words. Instead, he focused on paddling.

Too soon, they dragged the canoe ashore on a sandy strip of beach at the mouth of a lagoon. Despite the sun beating down on his bare shoulders, he felt a chill in the air.

"What is this place?" he said to no one in particular.

"It was once part of an ancient empire," Magahet, one of the village elders, explained.

"What happened to it?" As he looked around, Inapo wasn't sure if he meant the empire or the island.

"I cannot say." Magahet took a few steps back and fell into line with the other men standing at the water's edge. In accordance with tradition, all stood in silence except Inapo's father.

"You must find this stone." Gamomo knelt and sketched an outline in the sand. "It will have markings like these atop it." He drew a series of odd, squiggly lines. "Look for this symbol." He drew a circle inside a triangle.

"Is it far?"

"It is easy to find. Over that way." Gamomo pointed across the lagoon. "Once you have found it, you will sit beside it until the sun has set."

Inapo nodded, the lump in his throat shrinking. Sit beside a stone? He could do that.

"When the time comes, you will place this around your neck." Gamomo handed him a small, golden idol tied with a cord. "And you will swim out to sea. We will meet you at the edge of the lagoon. You leave us a boy and will return to us a man."

Sitting and swimming? That couldn't be all there was

to it. "So, find the stone, sit beside it, and then swim across the lagoon?"

"When it is time." The last word came out in a hoarse croak.

Inapo frowned. Was that a tear welling at the corner of his father's eye? "How will I know when it is time?"

Gamomo flashed a sad smile.

"You will know."

Inapo awoke with a start. The stone was cold against his skin and his flesh a mass of goosebumps. He stood and rubbed his arms, trying to chafe some warmth into his skin.

He saw with alarm that the sun was almost down. What if I had slept through it? Whatever *it* might be.

He gazed out toward the open water. In the gray light he could just make out a shape bobbing in the water just beyond the mouth of the lagoon. He wondered if his father could see him from that distance, if he'd been watching his son lazing away the day of his manhood rite.

His face burning with anger and shame, he stalked toward the lagoon. He'd be ready whenever the time came to swim.

He reached the shoreline and halted. The dark depths of the lagoon made his heart race. Images flitted through his mind—dark imaginings his mind conjured to fill those unknown depths.

But those were the thoughts of a child. He was a man now.

Emboldened, he knelt and dipped a finger into the water. He'd expected it to be freezing cold, but it was tolerable. He gasped, snatched his hand back, and sprang to his feet. Something had moved beneath the surface of the water! He was certain it was not his imagination.

"What are you?" he whispered. *Think! There are many things that swim in lagoons; fish, in particular. But it had been larger. A sand shark, perhaps? Or maybe it really had been his imagination.*

His eyes searched for the spot he'd seen the flash of movement, but now there was nothing. All was calm. Not even a breeze to rustle the palms.

Dead silent.

And then it happened.

The lagoon began to... flicker. Lights like a million varicolored stars danced beneath the surface. The lagoon seemed to glow and swirl. It was magnificent. And suddenly, the iron bands of fear that had been crushing his chest melted away. This was no witchcraft. This was the work of the gods!

Smiling, Inapo took his first step into the water. It felt good.

He hung the golden idol around his neck as his father had instructed. Even for gold it felt heavier than it ought to. It seemed to pull him down toward bottom of the lagoon as he waded out waist deep and began to swim.

He kicked hard, churning through the water with powerful strokes. The lights danced all around him. It was miraculous! Soon, he was halfway across. Any fear he had felt was long gone.

He soon felt confident enough to dip his head beneath the surface to try and get a better look at the lights. The cool, brackish water stung his eyes. Something had stirred up a cloud of silt, limiting his visibility. The lights swirled in dull circles, no way to tell their source.

And then something else caught his eye up ahead. A glint of gold!

As he swam closer he realized that the object was resting on an upthrust spike of underwater rock. As the scene came into focus, he realized with horror what he was seeing.

A grinning skeleton leered up at him. Well, half a skeleton, anyway. Its bottom half had been torn away. And around the dead man's neck hung a golden idol, just like the one Inapo wore!

And then he understood. The lights were dangerous. Deadly, even! The skeleton down there might even have been someone he knew!

Terror fueling him, he began to swim with all his might. He kicked and thrashed, trying to reach open water, but something seemed to slow him down. The idol hung like an anchor from his neck.

And then the lights went out.

The water around him exploded with movement. Dark shapes all around. Something grabbed at his ankle.

All he could think of was the idol! He tore it from his neck and let it drop.

Choking and gasping, he splashed his way to the edge of the lagoon. The waters calmed. He was free!

Up ahead, he saw the outrigger where his father and the elders waited.

"Father!" he gasped. "Something…"

"The idol should be around your neck." Magahet's voice was sharp like a dagger. "Where is it?"

"I dropped it," Inapo managed, now too exhausted to more than tread water. "I think that's what saved me."

The men in the outrigger looked at one another in stony silence.

"Please," Gamomo whispered. "He made it across the lagoon."

"Without the idol," Magahet said sadly.

Gamomo began to weep silent tears. But it was not until the men began to paddle away that he understood.

"Father!" he gasped. "Please!"

But Gamomo did not look back. None of the men did.

It was over. No longer having either the strength or will to fight, Inapo closed his eyes and slipped beneath the surface.

1

New York City

Uriah Bonebrake, Bones to his friends, unfolded from the back of a gray Toyota. Like a praying mantis emerging from its chrysalis, he stretched his six-foot five frame and yawned. The Uber driver honked twice and waved before cutting back into New York traffic and heading uptown. A warm southerly breeze swept up Madison Avenue and flicked Bones' signature black ponytail over his shoulder.

He tried not to look too much like a tourist, but the iconic Manhattan skyline was like nothing else in the world. He glanced upward. Towers of granite and steel rose from the sidewalk and cut the blue August sky into a maze of lines and rectangles. Many of these buildings were nearly a century old. He could imagine the Mohawk high-iron men catching hot rivets in midair and slamming them into beams and girders, hundreds of feet over his head. Those Native American iron and steel workers had been nicknamed skywalkers for their reputed fearlessness as they worked high above the ground. *Good thing I'm just a dumb Cherokee*, he mused. *I may enjoy rock climbing, but you sure as hell wouldn't catch me balancing on a girder, way up there unless it's a matter of life or death.*

Turning south, he collided with a man in a striped suit.

"Sorry, bro," Bones said absently.

The guy started to say something, but choked it back when he noticed the breadth of Bones' shoulders. Bones ignored him and continued toward 42nd Street. Stepping off the curb, he angled his way through a pack of stopped cars. The light changed, and he had to dash for it. A chorus of horns urged him on. Bones cut through a crowd of pedestrians, almost slamming into two more businessmen. Heads down, eyes fixed on their cell phones, they could have been walking blind.

Next street. There they were, twin stone lions guarding the New York Public Library. Jessica, the librarian would be inside. *I wonder if she's waiting for me. Certainly, she must have gotten my text. But why hadn't she replied?* He decided it really didn't matter. He'd just go in and surprise her.

The library was a little bigger than he'd thought. No, a *lot* bigger. When Jessica said she was a librarian, *a reference librarian*, she'd emphasized, Bones had imagined an oak counter with green lamps. Jessica would have her long blond hair up in a bun and peer over her reading glasses to ask what he needed… he imagined.

Undaunted by lions or edifice, Bones climbed the steps two at a time and entered the cavernous marble atrium. Security check. He took out his wallet and cell phone while a gray uniform with white gloves ran a quick wand over him. At the information kiosk he asked, "Reference desk?"

Pointed fingers, vague directions, the old woman pressed a small folding map into his hand. *It's just a library, I need a map?* Bones scanned it. *Yeah, well okay, so maybe I do.* He headed down the third hall, cut right, up a flight of stairs. Sure enough, the sign read *Reference Desk.* A man in a dark blue suit sat watching a monitor.

"Hello, I'd like to speak with Jessica?" Bones waited but the man didn't reply. He rapped his knuckles on the counter. "Anybody home?"

The man's gaze slowly turned upward to peer at Bones. "May I help you?"

"I'm here to see Jessica. I have an appointment." That last bit was a lie, but what the hell?

The man blinked, gazed owlishly at him. "I beg your pardon, but we have six Jessicas on this floor alone. Which one would you prefer?"

"I don't know. Her name is Jessica and she said she's the reference librarian here."

"One of many, I'm afraid. You'll have to be more specific."

"Long blond hair?"

"Oh yes, that narrows it down."

Bones paused. Blue Suit didn't smirk or anything, but it wouldn't have taken much more to launch all two hundred and thirty pounds of Cherokee over the intervening desk—with unfortunate consequences for both parties. Bones considered that such an encounter would reduce his chances of seeing the woman in question and said, "Okay, let's rephrase things here. You are an information expert. Look at me, and then direct me to the Jessica that I would be most interested in seeing."

Blue Suit had obviously considered a similar encounter and the likely consequences because he smiled, took Bones' map and circled a room two doors farther along the hall. "Her name is Jessica Maynard, in case you never got around to asking."

The woman in question sat at a low desk, thumbing through a pile of periodicals. She looked just like she had back in April, pony tail, nicely proportioned. He stepped through the door. What's up, Jess?"

Jessica didn't look up from her work "Yes? How can I help you?"

"Well, it's me… I'm here." He held out his arms.

She shook her head. "I don't…"

"It's me, Bones. Key West, remember? You said to come for a visit. I was thinking you could show me a few more of those yoga poses."

"Key West?" Now Jessica finally looked up. She blanched and her mouth dropped open when her eyes fell on him. "Oh, my God… you came all the way from Key West to see me? I thought that was a joke."

Heat rose along the back of Bones' neck. His cheeks warmed. *You have got to be freaking kidding me.* "Dude. You specifically said 'Come any time.'"

"I also added LOL. I didn't think you were serious. Who comes all the way to New York to see someone they hooked up with for one weekend?"

"Someone who really likes your downward facing dog."

"Quiet!" Jessica hissed, making a downward motion with both hands. "Oh, my God, you can't be here." She looked around, frantic. "Just go. My fiancé is coming to pick me up any minute now."

"Fiancé? You didn't say anything about a fiancé when we were making the beast with two backs."

"It was a fling. That's all. Just having a little fun before I tie myself to one guy forever."

"You're such a romantic. I'm touched." Bones pressed his fingertips to his heart.

"I get it. I'm a terrible person. But please, just go. Oh God, if he finds out, I'm so dead."

A voice chimed in from just outside the door. "Hi, honey, are you about ready?"

Bones turned to see a generic Wall Street type standing behind him. Pinstriped suit, blue shirt, red tie, polished tassel loafers. Banker, lawyer, something like that. The man appeared puzzled so Bones helped him out.

"Yeah, we're totally done here. She was just helping me with a research project I've been conducting."

The man looked him up and down, skepticism brimming in his eyes. In fairness, Bones didn't look like any kind of researcher.

"You're a scientist?" He didn't bother to hide his sardonic tone.

"Sociologist. I study relationships, marriage customs…" He paused. "Mating habits." He turned back to Jessica. "You were a big help. Thanks for everything." He put extra emphasis on the last word.

He shouldered his way past the confused fiancé and double-timed it out of the library. He had no problem with flings; in fact, he typically preferred those, but a chick should at least have the common courtesy to let him know the score. He'd made all kinds of plans, reservations. He had to call, cancel, and rebook. *No use staying around here.* Bones reached deep into his right pocket. Wallet, keys, no phone. He patted his left pocket, the back pockets. No phone. *Holy crap*, *this day just keeps getting better.*

He'd used the phone to book his Uber ride to midtown. *It fell out in the back seat, damn, damn, damn.* Striding south on Fifth Avenue. Perhaps it was the look on his face or the growing thundercloud over his head, but people just leaped out of his way. Bones looked up.

Had he crossed Madison? Nope, this was 36th Street, what the heck? He swiveled about and looked behind him. Nothing seemed familiar. He had to find a computer, log in, and lock his phone. *The library had computers.* He started back when a faded sign in a narrow alley caught his attention. "Syber Café," it read.

"Syber, with an *s.*" He rolled his eyes as he read aloud. He could duck in there, buy a little computer time, touch base with Uber, and avoid running into Pinstripe again. It kind of looked like a place he'd frequent, anyway. A couple of well-dressed thugs loitered across the street. Broken bottles crunched beneath his shoes. The Syber Café had a stout door painted landlord green. It sported a cartoon of an old-fashioned floppy disk. Bones pushed inside.

Packed, the place was crowded with people eating, drinking, talking. Not a computer in sight. In that moment, Bones realized he hadn't eaten anything all day. *That's my problem; I'm too hungry to think straight.* Food first, he'd grab a quick bite, then see about his phone. He looked around, no open tables, not even an empty chair. *It couldn't be later than eleven in the morning. What the hell are so many people doing here?*

He caught sight of a waitress passing a tray of plates and bowls to a half-dozen eager patrons. When she straightened, he stopped her. "Say, do you have a menu?" He looked around and grinned his best Bones grin. "Okay, a takeout menu maybe? I'm starved."

The young woman eyed him up and down. Mostly up, she hardly cleared five-foot two and couldn't have weighed a hundred pounds. Short, black hair, round face, fair skin, and big brown eyes. Mixed ancestry, Chinese-American perhaps. She wore little makeup, and her nails were gnawed to the quick. At first glance he'd thought her to be college-age, but at a closer look maybe more like mid-twenties.

"We're dine-in only." She cocked her head. "I haven't seen you in here before."

"Yeah, that's why I need a menu. I'm like a shark, never forget a good meal, but I have to taste it first."

The waitress didn't change expression, as if all of her patrons were like sharks. "Over here then."

A bar stood along one wall. The waitress found him a stool and seated Bones at the last open space, next to the restrooms. She handed him a sheet and a stubby pencil. "Fill this out, both sides."

He crouched on the stool like a little kid in the principal's office. The restroom door banged open and a couple of women came out. It didn't smell nasty, *a good sign*, he thought. Bones turned his attention to the page. Two columns, multiple choice. He flipped it over. Yup, both sides. Crazy, nothing about food. *Which color do you prefer: Red, Green, Pink, or Blue?* "What the hell?" He glanced around. The young woman was nowhere in sight. *What's a guy got to do to get fed around here?* Bones glanced back at the sheet. He would have preferred the color orange, but that wasn't an option, so he circled *Red*.

Another question: *In my yard there are two trees, three roses and an azalea. How many plants do I have: None, One, Six, Three, or Not Enough Information?*

He looked up to see the waitress standing several paces away, arms folded, as if she'd known he had a question.

"What's up?"

"Nothing. I was just looking around to make sure I

hadn't wandered into a college entrance exam prep class."

She smirked, turned and vanished again.

Okay, so there wasn't any mistake. Apparently he had to jump through some hoops before he could place his order. But why? Intrigued, he decided to give it a go.

Hmm... okay, Six. Wait, wait, only three different plants. He started to circle the number three but stopped again. *Wouldn't there be like, grass or weeds or something in the yard too?*

Bones got into it. Next question, and then the next, each one with a little twist, some easy, some impossible. He filled out both sides. The waitress appeared as if she knew when he would finish. She glanced at the sheet, then at the back and said, "Oh, really?" The young woman squinted, gave him a dark look and turned to walk away.

"Yo. Do I get a menu now?"

Without glancing back, she replied, "Your meal will be out shortly."

"That makes sense." He chuckled and looked around.

People on all sides continued to eat and talk. Turning around, he could see into the kitchen. Small, noisy, it produced a constant supply of steaming platters and bowls heaped with exotic dishes. Bones amused himself watching the young woman dance in and out of the swinging doors juggling impossible stacks of crockery, cups and silverware.

The sight of all that food just made him hungrier. Fifteen minutes, nothing. Then twenty. Nothing. Not even a cup of coffee. His stomach rumbled. "Screw this. I'll buy something off a food truck."

"Here we are." His server arrived, a steaming mug of black coffee and a plate piled high. He didn't immediately recognize the dish but it smelled incredible.

He took a bite and closed his eyes, savoring the unusual flavor. He couldn't put a name to it, but the meat put him in mind of barbequed ribs on the Fourth of July. He chewed slowly, savored it, then washed it down with a swallow of coffee. Another bite. Not ribs… that was all wrong. How had he thought that? It wasn't just the meat. There was a sauce or gravy. It sort of tasted like the chicken pot pie that his grandmother used to make from scratch? No, that wasn't it either, but it was close. Still another. Squirrel gravy cooked over a campfire. No… it had sort of an Asian vibe to it.

Bones fell into the food, knife and fork. Each bite both a new adventure and an old comfortable friend. Lost in the food, he mopped up the last bits with a swab of bread that tasted fresh from the oven. Full, but not sated, he took another swallow of coffee. Strong and black, but not bitter, just the way he liked it.

He gazed around once more at the clientele; the crowd had started to thin. Two more waitresses had appeared. Dressed like K-pop stars, short skirts, bleached blond hair, they milled around handing out menus. *Menus? There must be a different crowd at lunch.* Bones took a long sip of his coffee and examined the cylindrical porcelain mug. It bore the blue outline of a seal, sitting on a stool, balancing a trident on its nose. *No, this is just crazy.* Bones spun around and peered into the kitchen. The cook, a middle-aged Asian man, grinned and winked at him. Bones grabbed his coffee mug and started for the kitchen when the waitress, *his* waitress, took him by the elbow. "You need something more?"

"Yeah, I just want to know how you did that. My favorite color? Come on. No one could learn that much about me from some silly magazine quiz."

"I'm going off shift in a few minutes. You can talk to my cook." She led Bones to the kitchen. A stout man in a pristine white apron sat on a stool smoking a cigarette. He smiled and stared at them through brown, hooded eyes, like he'd been waiting for them. He grinned and said, "You not like the food? Want to complain?"

"It was the best meal I've ever had in my life. I want to know why."

The man waggled a finger. "Why is easy. Because I can. Because I want to. Is the *how* that you are eager to know."

As they spoke, an older man stepped into the kitchen, snatched the cigarette from the cook's mouth, and began unwrapping hamburger patties. "That's Joe, don't mind him. He fixes lunch. I fix *specials*."

"Do you have a name, or do you want to go with Mr. Special?"

The man laughed. "They call me Uncle Will."

"Dude, you are a miracle worker. I'm serious. How do you do it?"

He sighed, and his grin slipped ever so slightly. "It is my niece, here. She has magic computer program. It designs recipes."

"It's a neural-network, not magic. I'm a coder, not a magician."

"Wait. You use computers and brain science to plan menus? That's not a neural network. That's a noodle network. Get it?" He tapped his temple. "Brain? Noodle?"

She rolled her eyes.

Uncle Will leaned toward Bones and muttered, "I think Sally is hacker, too. But don't say I told you."

She grabbed her uncle by the ear and gave it a playful twist. "I am not a hacker. How many times have I said?"

The cook straightened and rubbed his ear. "Ow. I meant it as a compliment."

Bones hoped the young woman couldn't reach his own ear. From the looks of it, she had a tight grip.

She looked up at him and said, "I'm a programmer, a coder. I've created a neural-network simulation that takes everyone's answers and matches them to food. Easy, not magic. Not hacking."

Bones held up the coffee mug. "And this? Your neural thingy deduced that I was a Navy SEAL?"

"I could tell you were ex-military. You have that vibe about you. SEAL was just a lucky guess."

The glint in her eye said otherwise but Bones let it slide. "Okay, fair enough. A whiz-bang computer simulation that cooks better than my mom. So what do I owe you?"

"Pay what you feel it worth." Uncle Will winked. "Within reason," he added, laughing.

Bones almost sagged with relief. He'd been ready to hand over all his cash. Instead, he pulled out three twenties. "That fair?"

Uncle Will accepted the bills, pressed them between his palms, and made a slight bow, which Bones acknowledged with a dip of his chin.

"So, what do you do with your time now that you are no longer SEAL?"

"You might say that I find lost things." Bones stopped dead. "Oh, wait, *crap*. My phone. I left my phone somewhere. I need to go online and lock it.

Damn, I was hungry and I forgot."

Sally handed him her own battered phone, an old flip model. "Why don't you just call it? Maybe someone will simply return your phone to you."

Yeah, it could happen. Pigs fly if you throw them off a cliff. He punched in his own number. Nothing. Bones waited, finally a ring, a pause, then his shirt pocket started buzzing.

Sally dead-panned, "He's good, Uncle Will. Found it first try."

He'd fumbled it in the library as he fished out his ID, finally slipping it into his top pocket. Somewhat red in the face, Bones flipped the phone shut and handed it back to her. "Thanks."

"Wait," Uncle Will said. "I ask a favor. You take Sally and go."

"What, take her? Why?"

"We have problems with these men, men with suits. You know, Wall Street guys, dangerous men. Don't negotiate, just take what they can, steal what they can't."

"Wait, isn't that what the police are for?"

Sally glared at Bones through a gap in her bangs. "Who do you think the police work for?"

Bones wanted no part of this situation, but he couldn't leave a young woman in danger.

"Please. You go now. Keep her safe. But go."

One of the K-pop twins poked her head into the kitchen. "Those creeps are back. They're asking for Sally and they brought the cops."

2

"This way, this way. Both of you." Uncle Will led them into a cramped office.

Sally grabbed a purse two sizes too big for her and slipped a thin notepad computer inside. Uncle Will pushed her in front of him and tugged at Bones' arm. "Under desk, hurry."

Sally slipped into the space behind an old rolling office chair. Bones knelt and peered underneath. She'd moved a piece of plywood and was now crawling through a hole in the office wall. He felt something shift, his phone. He slipped it out of his shirt and pushed it into a pants pocket, then wiggled through the opening.

They stood in a narrow gap between two brick walls. Old mortar oozed out like fossilized ice cream. Dark, dusty, a cold damp air pervaded the place. It smelled like an abandoned building. "Where are we?"

"C'mon, they'll follow in a minute."

Too late, a head and pair of shoulders poked through the opening. "They're in here."

Without a second thought, Bones slammed the man's head against a brick wall.

Sally grimaced. "Nice job, bonehead. You just cold-cocked a cop."

Sure enough, a standard service Glock lay just beneath his right hand. Bones tucked it into his belt. He just wasn't used to leaving a loaded firearm lying around, especially when he might be in danger. "You're right.

Let's get out of here. Which way?"

She led off and Bones followed. Almost immediately he cracked his head on a steel crossmember. A moment of stars and pain, then he heard her crunching off through the dirt and broken masonry. Shouts, a shot zinged against the brick and buzzed away in the echoing darkness. Bones ducked low and followed.

"This way." She'd jammed into a narrow slot and started climbing. Back to the wall, hands and feet pressed against the opposite brick face; he followed. Cursing from below, someone else had found the same crossmember. Bones figured he was about three stories up. It was so dark there was really no way to tell.

"Psst."

Bones looked around. A flashlight below searched back and forth. In the beam, he made out a row of bricked-up windows, trash, debris, and three men scanning the ground. The light climbed the wall behind him. "They're up there!"

Another shot, this one struck the brick so close that shards of lead and masonry scoured his neck and chin. He gritted his teeth, forcing himself to ignore the stinging pain. He felt a hand on his arm.

"Over here."

Sally crouched behind a shallow ledge to his left. Bones shifted sideways as a third shot flew up the shaft, grazing his leg, and ricocheting off some unseen obstruction above. Bones half leaped, half rolled into the alcove, pain burning along his thigh. "That wasn't very elegant," she said.

"Now where?" he asked.

"In here. It's a laundry room vent."

The flashlight beam played up and down the ledge

he'd just cleared. "Give me a second." Bones drew the Glock and squeezed off a shot into the darkness below. "That'll make them a little more cautious."

He followed, hand pressed against the wound in his left thigh. He could feel the slippery warm blood ooze between his fingers. They crawled through a square steel duct. Sally led, using her phone as a flashlight. "Be careful of the screws sticking through, they're wicked."

After about fifty feet, a dim illumination reflected off the interior. They turned right and tumbled out into a room full of laundry machines. She looked at his leg and gasped. "You're hit."

"Yeah. I should say it's only a scratch, but I guess it's a bit worse than that."

"I'll say. You're bleeding all over the place. Your face too. Quick, quick, take your pants off."

"What? It's only our first date."

"Look, I've got to bind that wound. Even if you are a tourist, you can't go running around New York covered in blood. There are some things that will draw attention even here."

Bones pulled off his shoes and slid out of his jeans. "Just hurry, they'll do a door-to-door in this building next. We've got to be gone before they arrive."

Rows of laundry baskets lined the back wall. Sally picked out an XXL tee-shirt, ripped it into strips and wrapped his leg. Bones helped her tie it off. "Not bad. You've done this before?"

"No, but I watch a lot of movies. Now empty your pockets."

Bones grunted and complied. He dumped wallet, keys, change and phone on a folding table. She stuffed his pants along with a random basket of clothing into one of the machines and set it to *Heavy Wash*. Bones fished around in the other laundry baskets and found a pair of sweats that were six inches too big in the waist and four inches too short in the leg. He pulled them up, tied them tight and scooped his belongings into a pocket. She looked him over, dabbed the blood off his face, and said, "I've seen worse on the street."

Bones peeked out the door, saw an empty hallway, fluorescent lights, six other gray steel doors. "Where to?"

"There's a stairwell all the way at the end. Run for it, I hear the elevator.'"

Bones heard it too, humming and hissing. He wasn't sure which floor it was on, but ran anyway. The leg still hurt, but it wasn't close to the worst injury he'd ever suffered. He pushed himself into a run. They reached the far end, just as the elevator doors squealed open. Sally ducked into the stairwell and Bones followed. A bullet sang past his ear and smashed through a window on the opposite wall. He crouched and returned fire. Two shots, aimed to kill now.

Two wild shots returned and a voice called out, "Man down, man down."

She grabbed him by the arm and hauled Bones up the stairs. "Climb. They'll be waiting at the bottom."

He heard pounding feet on the steel steps. "They aren't waiting. You go, I'll hold them off here." Bones' blood was up, and all he wanted was a clear shot at whoever was trying to kill them.

"You're crazy, you can't take on the whole NYPD. Come, I know the way."

Bones let her lead up the stairs. No question, she could move quietly. His wounded leg ached by the time they reached a steel platform just below the roof. Sally climbed a metal ladder bolted to the wall and put her shoulder to a trapdoor. It flipped open. "Quickly, quickly."

Bones didn't need urging. He climbed out after her. Shouts echoed up from just below. A shot rang off the ladder and spun sizzling off into the sky behind him. Bones fired a single shot back down the stairwell, aiming for the ceiling. He didn't want to kill anyone if he didn't have to. Too many complications should that happen.

"Hold on a second." Bones flipped the trapdoor shut, knelt, and closed the hasp, locking the door from the outside. "That should hold them until they find another way up."

"A way down would be nice too."

The trapdoor resounded with thuds from the inside. A bullet tore through the wooden frame, then another.

"Part of me wishes I hadn't locked it," Bones said. "Would have been like shooting fish in a barrel."

Two more shots blasted into the frame and Sally said, "A dirty cop is still a cop and you might not live to tell your side of the story."

"And even if I did, if I killed one, law enforcement wouldn't rest until they found us. Their colleagues don't know they're dirty. Let's just get away from here."

Bones followed her across the roof to the opposite edge. He looked down. Two police cars flashed red and blue in the alley below. Patrons streamed out of the Syber Café, scattering when they reached 42nd Street. She grabbed his arm. "This should be easy for an Indian like you." A gray steel pipe crossed to another building, maybe thirty feet away.

"I'm Cherokee, not Mohawk. We like to keep our moccasins on solid ground."

"Well it's easy for me, and it's the only way down unless you want to jump."

With that, she hung over the parapet until her feet touched the pipe. Arms out for balance, two steps, then she danced across without looking back. Bones peered down at the pipe. Perhaps eighteen inches in diameter, it probably carried steam or hot water in the winter. He lowered himself over and started walking. *Like a log across a creek*, he thought. *Nothing to it.*

Yet it wasn't like a log; about half way across it started to wobble. *Man, this thing wasn't meant to support a dude who weighs north of two hundred pounds.* Each step bounced the pipe a little more. Almost to the middle, his left foot slipped. Bones teetered. He stood on one leg, sixty feet above the pavement, and didn't move.

A crashing sound from the roof told him that their pursuers had blasted the trapdoor free. *Now, if they're only smart enough to be cautious.* Bones concentrated on placing one foot at a time, slowly. Half way, two more steps, the pipe started to wobble again. *Screw it.* Bones ran. Five long strides; he fairly leaped over the opposite parapet.

The young woman had the sense to stay down. Bones did as well. "I think they're on the other roof, but I don't want to look."

She signed to him. *This way.* Bones crawled after her. *Damn that hurt.* He noticed that blood had started to soak through his purloined sweat pants. He followed her down another trapdoor and flight of steps. Wood, old, the treads had worn almost to the support joists beneath them. She led him through a fire door. The floor creaked beneath a threadbare carpet. Half way down the hall, she fished out a key and opened a nondescript gray door.

Bones glanced about the room, half expecting a reception. It held a battered dresser, and a futon with neatly rolled bedding at the foot. A sink was bolted to one wall, plumbed with garden hose. A portable marine toilet sat in the opposite corner below a narrow window that illuminated the room.

A closet door stood on his right; Bones drew his Glock and indicated that she open it. Sally shrugged and pulled the door handle. A few clothes, nothing more. Bones said, "You're squatting here."

"They converted this old warehouse to upscale lofts, but no one is allowed to live above the fourth floor. Fire code or something."

"It's pretty Spartan."

"I've got half a T-1 line. It gets me 750 megabytes, wired right to the trunk."

"You can watch a lot of dirty movies with a connection like that. Kidding!" he added when she narrowed her eyes. "Now tell me, why does someone want to kill you?"

"Not me, at least not right away. They'll be after you, though. I'll explain when we get out of here."

So, exactly how *do* we get out of here?" Bones asked.

"I'll show you in a minute. Drop those sweats; I've got to rebandage you."

"I never refuse when a chick tells me to drop my pants. I'm Bones, by the way. Bones Bonebrake, at your service, in so many ways."

Sally fixed him with a long look. "That name fits. I already thought you were a bit of a bonehead. Now, to hell with the dance and down with the pants."

Seeing no other place, Bones closed the marine toilet lid, pushed his pants to his knees, and sat. Sally found a first aid kit from somewhere, with antiseptic and gauze. She peeled off the blood-soaked strips and inspected the wound. "You've lost a good sized chunk of skin, and ought to have stitches."

"Do you have a sewing kit?"

She gave him a funny look. "Serious?"

"Stitch it up. It can't hurt any worse."

It wasn't the first time someone had sewn him up, and he knew it was going to hurt like hell, but he wouldn't let it show. Instead, he focused on the sunlight playing through her high window and shut out the pain. She dabbed his leg with antiseptic and wrapped it in gauze.

"You didn't make a sound," Sally said, impressed.

"Native American trick. It's a focusing technique to block out the pain."

"Really?"

"No, I just love how white people will believe anything."

Sally grinned. "At least now you won't look quite like the walking dead. Stand up and let me know how it feels."

"Feels like crap, but it'll do. In fact, that was a good bit of battlefield surgery. Thanks."

"Just pull up your trousers, big guy, and don't get your hopes up. One more thing I've got to do." She dug a roll of duct tape from the dresser and used it to cover the bloodstain on Bones' sweats. "Now you're a tourist in torn pants."

3

"Whoever is after you will have figured out that we crossed the pipe by now," Bones said. "They may not be willing to follow, but you can bet the cops are searching this building."

As he spoke, someone pounded on the door. Sally rummaged a few things from her dresser. The pounding came again.

"NYPD, open up," a sharp voice ordered.

Bones heard a key scratch in the lock. Sally picked a few more things from her dresser and mouthed, *let's go*. The door rattled with a thud that shook the floor. It didn't yield, but Bones took the hint.

Sally dragged him into a closet packed with winter clothes. He pulled the door shut behind them while she burrowed her way to the back. Another thud and Bones thought he heard something give. Sally switched on a miniature flashlight. "It's solid core steel, in a steel frame. We still have some time. Squeeze through here, but watch your step."

She'd swung a loose board to one side, revealing a dark opening. Bones bent almost double and backed into the hole. Half way through, his foot slipped, and he nearly fell, hanging only by the flimsy wallboards. Scrambling, he managed to find a ledge and plant both feet on it. She followed, holding onto a steel rail while she reclosed the loose board.

"A hundred years ago, this building was a

warehouse," she said. "We're standing in the old man-lift."

Bones followed her flashlight beam. About two feet away, a vertical conveyor belt stood in silent decrepitude. It held a row of steel bars that vanished into the darkness below. Without another word, Sally leaned out, grabbed a bar and began climbing down. Bones followed, wondering if a hundred-year-old belt would meet OSHA requirements.

A few minutes later, he found nothing but air beneath his feet. "Drop," Sally said. Bones let go and fell almost five feet before landing on a dirty concrete floor. "Getting back up is a little trickier. In the summer, I prefer to walk the pipe."

The flashlight beam picked out an array of spoked iron wheels and rotting leather drive-belts. In one corner, an ancient electric motor lurked in dusty squalor. Bones heard rats squealing in the corners, felt cobwebs fall against his face. "You don't get many visitors, do you?"

Sally had already made her way to the far wall. When Bones caught up, she pointed to a riveted iron door and said, "That way leads up to the parking garage, but they may be watching it."

"I really want to know what the hell is going on here."

"Okay, you go ahead and stay right where you are. You gonna shoot it out with the cops? Wonderful. I'm leaving, but you stick around. You'll make a good target." She took a few steps, then turned. "Don't you get it? These cops take orders from the Wall Street suits. They don't obey any laws except supply and demand. You supply, they demand. This is New York, the big bad

City, not Mayberry. Now do you want to walk out of here or ride a gurney?"

"There had better be one hell of a thorough explanation coming very soon."

"Follow me then, and for God's sake, keep your head down."

"Why do I think you have another exit in mind? One a little less comfortable?"

"Steam tunnels. They're not used in the summer. Follow me." She squeezed behind a large upright tank and sidled through a narrow opening in the cement wall.

Bones followed, doing his best contortionist routine. He found himself in a narrow passage dominated by an array of large insulated pipes. The air was stale and dusty. He tried not to think of the asbestos dust and mold spores they inhaled. Why was he even worried about that? Maddock must be rubbing off on him.

A small chamber, dim light filtered down from a grating overhead. Traffic rumbled above. Sally skirted a bundle of rags and blankets. Bones stumbled over an empty bottle; it clattered off to one side. She led him into another passage, this one narrower than the first. Bones glanced back, the bundle of rags twitched. "Are we going to find alligators down here?"

"No alligators, the rats ate them all. Now, quiet! There's more dangerous things than alligators or rats that could find us."

Bones hung back a few paces and watched behind them. He'd had a lot of experience in tunnels, little of it pleasant. Sally brought them to another junction and was about to continue when a shadow stepped away from the wall.

"Not so fast little lady." The voice crackled like dry

paper crumpling. "Let's see what you have in your purse."

She backed away and another shadow closed in behind. "I'm thinking she's got more for us than her purse. What do you say? Want some fun?"

Bones dropped him with a blow from the butt of his Glock, then turned and took aim at the first shadow. "Tell your friend there, the one who hasn't come out yet, to show himself before I blow your head off."

Bigger than his accomplices, the man who stepped into the dim light pointed a thirty-eight revolver at Bones. Holding it inches from Bones' temple, he said, "Drop the…"

Bones struck like a viper. He batted the revolver to the side and drove his fist into the gunman's chin. The man's knees buckled and he fell to the ground. Bones drove the butt of the Glock into his temple, then returned his aim to the first man and said, "Run, before I really get pissed off." The fellow ran and Bones turned.

Sally stood frozen for a moment. "He had a gun pointed right at you and you just… took him down."

"He was a dumbass. He got too close."

"That was crazy, though. Have you done that before?"

"Once or twice. Look, I won't let anybody hurt you if I can help it. Now just get us out of here before our friend returns with reinforcements."

Sally pushed her way into another dark tunnel. Before he followed, Bones snatched up the revolver. It was an ancient Smith and Wesson police issue. He didn't want to know its history. He tucked it into his pocket, then squeezed past a cluster of pipes and followed her.

Cement walls gave way to crumbling red brick. A

small rivulet trickled underfoot. The passage made several tight turns before opening into an echoing dark tunnel. Sally stopped him. The tunnel grew lighter. Bones felt a blast of wind and heard a roar like a tornado. Twelve hundred tons of subway train flew past, only a foot from his face.

Sally put a hand on his arm. "That was a Number Seven express. The next train will pass here in exactly two and a half minutes. We have to run." She hopped off a low sill and sprinted up the track. "Watch for the third rail. It'll kill you."

Bones followed. He could do about a half mile in that time, if properly motivated. "How far?"

"Two long blocks. We'll just make it."

Taking three ties at a stride, Bones tripped over the irregular spaces. Sally had a jerky, uneven pace that looked inefficient but kept each step exactly on the center of the next tie. They rounded a gentle curve, just as Bones felt the first puff of wind at his back. The tunnel grew lighter, and he saw the station just ahead.

"This way. No, this way," Sally said. She vaulted a curb and ducked under an escalator run. Bones followed. The train blasted its horn as it thundered past him.

In a great hissing and squealing of brakes it rumbled just inches from where he stood. "Come on," she said, "we've got to get out of here before the trainman calls security."

"Wait, take this." Bones handed Sally the old revolver. "The Glock is bad enough; this thing is too obvious in my pocket. At least, on top of the bulge that's already there."

He smiled to show he was joking but Sally wasn't having any of it. She made a sour face and slipped it into her purse. They followed a crowd of departing passengers up the escalator to the terminal.

"Here we are." Sally spread her arms wide. "Grand *bloody* Central Station. Can you believe this place is one of the top ten most visited tourist destinations in the world?"

Bones had to admit he'd always liked Grand Central, especially the main concourse with its barrel vaulted ceiling, celestial mural, and beax-art chandeliers. As he admired the architecture of the historic building, he caught a whiff of the menu from one of the terminal's eateries. He took a deep breath and let it out slowly, allowing the accumulated tension from their fight and flight to dissipate. "You hungry? All that running made me work up an appetite. I'm starved." He looked up at the massive clock face adorning the central atrium: three thirty. "How time flies when you're running for your life."

"Relax, big guy. We'll be good unless you decide to shoot someone else. Let me show you the second-best food in New York." She led him outside, down the block, and around a corner. "Here."

Bones looked about; nothing resembled a restaurant. Sally stepped up to a box-van with a window in one side. "Do you want mustard?"

"A roach-coach? You're kidding."

"I know what I'm about. Here," she held out a hotdog on a bun. "No mustard, try it."

Bones took a bite, then another. The bun was light, but not doughy. *The meat?* Bones tasted it again. *Like veal?* "Okay, I'll admit it. You know your food. Hell, I'd eat another."

He ate two more. When they'd finished, Sally stood

and smiled at him.

"There, you've had the best of New York: you got in a shootout, stopped a mugging, explored the sewers, climbed a building, rode the subway—sort of. Am I a great tour guide or what?"

Bones managed a grin. "It's not exactly what I was looking for, but it wasn't boring."

"Why did you come here anyway?"

"I came to visit the library."

Sally quirked an eyebrow. "Right, you certainly look like the library type."

"Well, a librarian, okay? I was inside. Here, I can prove it." Bones patted his shirt pocket. "Damn, I had it right here." He rummaged in the other pockets. "It was right here where I stuck my phone."

"Not a library card, I hope."

"No, a map of the second-floor reference section. It must have fallen out in the restaurant when I crawled under your uncle's desk."

"Then they'll know you were at the library. They'll check the security cameras."

"Worse, it had Jessica's room marked; they'll talk to her and get my name."

"Jessica? It all comes clear now, big guy. She would be named *Jessica*. Let me guess, blond, dim bulb, big…" She cupped her hands in front of her, "here. Says things like 'Oh-my-God' and 'that's everything.'" She paused. "Wait, wait, she told you to bugger off. Right? Otherwise you'd be with her."

"You had to have been there… but I really think we should get moving."

"They'll be watching the trains," she said, "and the airport's off limits. Where would you go, anyway?"

Bones racked his brain. Even if he could get someone he could trust at a high level of law enforcement on the case, that would only initiate an investigation. That was typically a slow, laborious process, and might not help them in the short term. What they needed was to get out of town quickly, to somewhere they could stay without risking getting onto the grid.

"I've got a friend stationed at Little Creek, in Virginia Beach. He's got a cottage that I use sometimes. We get down there, we're home free."

Sally nodded. She didn't seem to smile much, but a nod was good. "Then we'll walk. You got any cash?"

"A couple hundred and change."

They set off south on Park Avenue. Taking his arm, she said, "*Louis, I think this is the beginning of a beautiful friendship.*"

Bones paced along beside her. She stretched it out, New York style, and they made good time. "Stock market will be closing, and the early commute will begin. Keep your head down and don't gawp around so much."

Bones had other things on his mind besides sightseeing. Sally seemed to have a plan, and she knew the territory. He let her take point. Bones maintained a subtle watch for followers, police, or anyone else taking undue interest in them. The Glock thumped in his pocket like a grocery cart with a bad wheel. He stopped her at the next crosswalk. "Is there a thrift store or something around here?"

"Used clothing? No, but good idea. We'll get you some real pants."

She cut several blocks to the east where rows of small storefronts sold electrical equipment, plumbing parts, and tools. They stopped at a janitors' supply. "In here, you should find some work clothes that'll fit."

Bones picked out a pair of khaki trousers and a web belt. He found a plain white painter's hat and a pair of cheap safety glasses. Sally looked him over. "Okay, I don't see tourist here, I see Rikers Island fugitive. Lose the hat." She found him a yellow plastic bump cap. "Now I see a maintenance worker headed downtown for a drink."

They cut over to Third Avenue and followed it to Bowery Street. Every few blocks the neighborhood changed. Italian, Russian, Korean, little shops lined the streets selling anything and everything. Each change of neighborhood was presaged by the delicious aroma of food wafting through the air. One of these days Bones was going to take a week off and eat his way through Little Italy and Little China.

Eventually, they reached a neighborhood of Asian restaurants. Sally led them onto a brick alley, and up a short flight of steps. "We stop here for tea."

They both squeezed into a narrow booth with an old-fashioned mahogany table. A wrinkled little woman appeared shortly after, and Sally dashed off a few words of what Bones took for Chinese. Tea arrived in a light green pot, along with a plate of almond cookies. "I take it we have a reason to be here?"

"Best tea in Chinatown. But that's not it. We came here to get inspected, just sit tight and try not to shoot anyone."

Bones fidgeted while he sipped his tea. As with the menu in the café, she was right. It was excellent. Pale green and flavorful, it had just the right blend of bitter and aromatic. Bones took another sip and relaxed... a little. "You said you were going to explain later. Now's a good time…"

"I pissed some guys off. They want my recipe book. It's complicated, okay?"

"Seems like the wrong guys to mess with in New York, the big bad City."

Sally ignored him and opened her notepad computer. It had a kickstand and a detachable keyboard. Her hands danced across the keys like little pink spiders; she looked, snorted and danced on. After a few minutes Sally glanced up at Bones. "The Syber Café is gone. They burned it out."

She spun the screen around so he could see it. New York Times web site, *Local Eatery Burns – Exhaust Fan Blamed.* Bones scanned the article. "And your uncle?"

"I don't know. Sent him a text, but no response."

"So, anything about the shooting?"

"No. I'm checking the police logs now, but they're a little harder to get into."

"You're hacking the New York City Police Department?"

"I'm not a hacker. There's just ways to find out stuff and I sometimes use them."

Bones slumped back in his seat. "What are we doing here anyway?"

"I told you, being inspected. They haven't asked us to leave yet. That's a good sign."

At that moment the little old Chinese woman reappeared. She squinted at Bones and exchanged a few words with Sally. Bones waited. The woman said, "Two hundred."

Sally stared at him for about a three-count and then said, "Well, pay the woman."

"For what?" He didn't wait for the snotty answer but

pulled out two big Bens. The woman looked at both sides of each bill. "Fresh off the Xerox. You won't find better copies anywhere."

Sally kicked him under the table. The old lady sniffed, put two black poker chips on the table, and shuffled away. Bones picked one up, turned it over. Nothing unusual.

"Bus tickets," Sally said. "Special ones."

4

Key West

For what must have been the hundredth time, Dane Maddock thanked some nameless marine engineer for designing *Sea Foam* with a stand-up engine room. He straightened his six-foot frame and wiped a shock of blond hair from his eyes. "So how bad is it, Doc?"

Calvin "Doc" Jacobs mopped the sweat from his deeply tanned brow, took one more look down the open injector port and said, "Number three hole has a broken ring and the liner's shot. If we just slip in a new kit, I'd say you'll get five-hundred hours before you lose another cylinder."

"Six new pistons and sleeves then. How long?"

"Two weeks to get the parts, a week to button her back up, say another two weeks if I have to mill the bolsters."

"A month and a half then. What's the bad news?"

Doc named a figure. It seemed fair, but still it was a hell of a lot of money. Maddock, as he was known to his friends, considered his mechanic more of a wizard than a doctor. From a shop no bigger than a single car garage, he kept the yachts and fishing boats of Key West cruising the Gulf with clean stacks and white wake. Maddock sighed and nodded. "Do it."

Sea Foam had twin Cat diesels. Fifteen hundred horsepower, they drove thirty- inch wheels, through a pair of Twin Disc three-fourteens. Eighty feet long, she could hit hull speed at twenty-eight knots. But *Sea Foam* was an expensive mistress, and a thirsty one too. Maddock knew he had to keep the money coming in to feed his baby and to pay his team. To do that, he needed salvage jobs. Special salvage jobs. Maddock and his crew combed the seas for lost gold and silver.

He and his team were good at it. Pros, they excelled in cutting the right deal, scooping the easy loot, and then leaving just enough behind to make the locals think they'd horned in on the prize. Low-profile, no one complained, and everyone scored a handful of silver that Maddock had "missed."

Sometimes he made out, sometimes he didn't. The past few months had run a little lean. Then, two days ago, the starboard engine began blowing black smoke and Maddock knew that *lean* was headed toward *hungry*. He'd given his team some much needed time off, and called Doc.

Now, standing on the pier, he wondered if he shouldn't just take on some contract work that paid hourly, but kept the books in the black. He immediately laughed. His crew, with one exception, loved adventure, and if he was honest with himself, so did he. Still, a bit of financial stability would be welcome.

The call came in as Maddock walked toward the parking lot. Maddock frowned when he saw Bones' name on the screen. He'd gone to New York to meet up with a girl. If he was calling Maddock, something must have gone awry, or else he'd be… otherwise occupied. Maddock considered letting it ring through to voicemail, but he was curious to see how bad it was. "No, I won't make bail for you," he answered.

"Not bail. Not yet. It's complicated. Hold on and let

me explain."

"Holy crap. Just let me sit down first." Maddock turned and climbed the steps to Toni's Dockside, the local watering hole. Toni, a brown-skinned Jamaican with a trim, athletic figure, long hair, and big brown eyes, brought him a Dos Equis without asking. She winked and flashed a grin at him before moving on to another customer. Maddock nodded his thanks. He liked Toni. A few years his senior, she was friendly, insightful, and easy on the eyes.

"All right, Bones. Problem, emergency, or global disaster?"

"I don't know yet. We're on a bus, headed for Virginia Beach."

Maddock listened while Bones described his situation. A few bits of information seemed missing, but he knew they'd come out eventually. "You said *we…*"

"Yeah, the waitress and me."

"So, not Jennifer? The woman you hooked up with down here?"

"That was Jessica. She had other plans. Namely, she's planning to be married."

"And you've already hooked up with someone else?" Maddock wasn't surprised. His friend went through women like a salesman goes through Buicks. "So, when do you arrive?"

"We didn't hook up. We just managed to run afoul of the same people. We go to Atlantic City first and stay about six hours. Then we cut across at Cape May and head south on the Eastern Shore. Driver says eight a.m. It's a gambler's bus, they've got a few seats in front for show; the rest is pai gow tables and blackjack. No one asks questions."

Maddock circled back to the shooting. Something seemed odd. "They started shooting right away? Are you sure you had no warning?"

"I'm positive. Someone said: 'they're up there,' and *bam*, I got winged."

"And you knocked out a cop, too."

"It was later, but yeah. Well, I guess he was a cop. He didn't flash his badge. I don't know."

"What have you gotten yourself into?"

"No freaking idea. You want to help me figure it out?"

Maddock considered the situation. He could probably get Bones and Sally safely to Key West, but there was a good chance the people who were after Bones would look for him there.

"I think we need a better understanding of Sally's situation and the capabilities of her software. Do you think she'd share with one of our guys?"

"Maybe if she got to know them, but maybe not even then. She doesn't know who to trust."

Maddock made up his mind. "Okay, hunker down when you get to Virginia Beach. You'll be safe there. I'll grab some backup and meet you."

Maddock ordered another beer and considered his options. There had been a time when he would have told Bones to go solve his own problems. He might have even taken some satisfaction in watching the big man squirm. Those days were long past, and now Dane Maddock and Bones Bonebrake were like brothers.

A little crisis could be okay, he told himself. *It could take all our minds off busted boats and slender rations.*

Maddock thumbed a different number on his mobile. Willis Sanders picked up second ring.

"Maddock, tell me we're back in business," Willis answered. "I knew ol' Doc was a genius. Packing my gear now, boss. See you on board in an hour."

Willis was a former Navy SEAL who had served with Maddock and Bones. He was as loyal and hard working as they came. Always ready for a treasure hunt or an adventure.

Maddock stopped him. "Hold on. It's not that. I need you to be my shore-captain for a few days. Got to go bail Bones out of another pickle. Give Doc a hand and get Matt to help. I'll be back as soon as possible."

"If Bones is in trouble, you sure you don't want me to come along?"

"At the moment I'm going to say no. I think I've got it covered."

Willis didn't complain, that wasn't his way, but Maddock could hear the disappointment in his voice. *Crap, the sun hadn't set and already he was letting his guys down.* He thumbed the next name on his list. Six rings before Corey Dean picked up. "Yeah? What gives, skipper?"

"I've got a little rescue mission. Thinking maybe you should come along for this one."

"A rescue mission? Are you sure you want me?" A tech wiz, Corey was the brains of their operation, while Willis, along with Matt Barnaby, a former Army Ranger, provided the muscle.

"Bones is already on the scene. I need your techie brain."

"Fair enough. I'll pack."

Maddock booked two for the morning flight out of Key

West. Connecting in DC, they could get to Virginia Beach by early afternoon. He booked a car, too. *On second thought, I should get a van.* Toni cruised by his table once more. *She's a walking advertisement for cutoffs.* He nodded and held up a finger. Another Dos Equis joined the two empty bottles on his table.

Willis strolled in and straddled a chair. Not quite as tall as Bones, still he was a large man, heavily muscled, with a shaved head and dark brown skin.

"Matt ain't coming," he said without preamble. "Dude has actually got a date."

"Is he sure it's not his cousin this time?" Maddock asked.

Willis laughed. "I think he's running her through Ancestry.com just to make sure." Another member of their crew, Matt had recently hooked up with a woman at a friend's wedding, only to discover she was a distant relation. Of course, Bones had turned that into, 'Matt hooked up with his cousin.' Matt's protests that they had only fooled around a little had not helped.

Willis waved to Toni who nodded, knowing his standard order well.

"From the look on your face, you've got bad news to share. Give it to me straight."

"*Sea Foam* is down for at least a month, Bones is running from the cops, and we're getting a little low on operating cash." Maddock took another long pull on his bottle. "How are you at flipping burgers?"

"That's nothing. We've seen worse."

Toni cruised by and brought Willis a Corona. Both of them watched her retreat behind the bar. "Hey, man, wake up. Most guys spend their lives tied to a desk or driving a forklift or something. Just look around, look out there." Willis pointed across the harbor where the sun was painting the western horizon in hues of orange and gold. "Ain't no one that wouldn't trade their best days for your worst."

Maddock nodded. "Most guys don't have friends like you and the guys." He looked out again at the sunset, breathed deeply of the warm breeze that blew in from the Gulf, and came to a decision.

"I'm glad there's one optimist in our crew. We'll find a new score, something big. Hell, I'll mortgage the condo if I have to, but we'll get back out onto the water."

"That's what I'm talking about." Willis slapped the table. "Next round is on me."

Maddock forced a smile.

"You still look like a sad sack."

"Sorry," Maddock said. "Just wondering exactly how much trouble Bones has gotten himself into."

5

Corey hadn't asked many questions. He'd seemed a little surprised when Maddock had asked him to come along, and not Willis or Matt, but he'd been pleased. The man was quiet, not as outgoing as the others in the crew, but he was steadfast. As their tech specialist, he usually kept to the background. Still, Maddock had watched the man work miracles with balky equipment and unreliable data. Besides, he counted on Corey's calm demeanor to balance Bones' impatience.

They found their friend holed up in a little white cottage just off a broad sandy beach. He met them outside. Still limping slightly from his wound , Bones walked around behind a low dune. A few families were out on the beach, but the scene was quiet. Bones shook his head sadly. "They call this place Chicks Beach and look, nothing but middle-aged moms and their kids. Not that I have anything against moms, but that's more Corey's speed."

"Screw you, Bones," Corey said, grinning.

"Where's Sally?" Maddock asked.

"Sleeping. We haven't been here long."

"Any more idea of what you've gotten us into?"

Bones shook his head. "Not entirely. There wasn't any privacy on our bus so we couldn't talk. I think I've managed to convince her that the two of you are trustworthy. She said we'd talk when we were all together." He lowered his voice. "I actually thought about calling Jimmy, but you know how he is."

Maddock nodded. "My thoughts exactly." Jimmy Letson was a former comrade in the Navy, and an accomplished hacker. He was also pushy and abrasive. Not the sort of person you'd want to help ease a frightened person out of her shell.

They entered the cottage to find Corey examining a thin notepad computer.

"I wouldn't touch that, Dude. If she sees you screwing with it, she'll go off on you. I'm not kidding."

Moments later the bedroom door opened, and a young woman stepped inside. She was short and wore a wrinkled black hoodie about four sizes too big, black tights, and slip-on deck shoes to match. She glared at the three men in turn, and her eyes came to rest on Corey.

"Okay ginger, what were you doing with my computer?"

Corey blanched and ran a hand through his short, red hair. "Just looking."

"Let's keep it that way." She snatched up her computer, glared at Corey, then her demeanor softened. "Sorry. I'm not usually such a bitch. Well, people say I am, but I have good reasons."

Maddock smiled. "No worries. I'm Dane Maddock, but everyone just calls me Maddock. This is Corey Dean, our technical specialist."

She pursed her lips, still eyeing Corey with suspicion. "You're the cavalry? I was expecting someone more… thuggish."

"That's what I'm for," Bones said.

"That's little comfort, Bonehead." She turned to Maddock. "Okay, Murdock. What's the plan?"

"Maddock."

"Whatever." She stopped, squeezed her eyes shut for a second. "I have, like no manners. I'm Sally Smith."

"Good to meet you. Tell me about your magic program."

"Her noodle network," Bones said.

"It's not magic. I told Bonebrake, it's a computer model, a neural-network with some enhancements of my own."

"It's a predictive model. It took your personal preferences, combined it with other variables, like the time of day, and predicted what you would like to eat at that moment."

"I still think it's witchcraft," Bones said. "That thing works too well."

"Wait," Corey said. "If it's really that effective, there's potential to use something like that to predict all sorts of consumer behavior, sociological issues. Hell, I don't know, applied properly you might could predict the stock market."

"Yeah, well that is exactly what these guys do when they aren't shooting at Bonehead and me. Their buddies on Wall Street have models of their own. The lot of them spend all day trying to get one millisecond's jump on each other. My model is different; it's based on people, not the market. It doesn't track stock movement, it tracks peoples' reactions to the movement. It even takes into account variations in reaction due to external factors: socioeconomic, political, fluctuations in the market, even the weather."

Maddock thought for a moment, trying to imagine

just how many people would kill for such a program. "That's pretty expansive. How far out can it project?"

"Days, sometimes more." Sally looked around. "Do you understand now? Well I didn't. I was stupider than the lot of you put together doing shots at a fraternity bash. I used it myself. Just to pay off my student loans and to have a little walking around money," she added.

Corey gave a wry grin. "And the *Sith Lords* of Wall Street felt a disturbance in the force."

"Did they ever. I had to vanish. Fortunately, my uncle Will needed a waitress. I've been hiding out at the Syber Café ever since. Working for cash, keeping off the grid."

"So, they tracked you down to the café and bribed some cops to bring you in. Rather, to take you into custody and make you disappear. You're already off the grid, so it's no great risk to them." Maddock said. "You'd disappear, and suddenly a fresh crop of billionaires would pop up on the Street. Why didn't they just buy the model from you?"

"These guys don't like to buy what they can steal. And they sure don't want to leave a source of future competition out there. Besides, I'm not terribly inclined to sell."

"And you're sure it wouldn't be safe to just cruise on back to Key West and hang out with us?" Corey said.

Bones shook his head. "They probably know who I am." He told of his trip to the New York City Library, most of it anyway. "That map must have fallen out of my pocket back at the Café. I figure they've talked to Jessica by now."

"And how much would she have told them?"

"She's got my number, but I don't think she knows

my last name, or even my actual given name. And we never really left the beach." Bones paused. The others stared at him. "Well, it was dark, okay? We were discrete. I was anyway, and she…"

Sally broke in. "Okay, we get the picture. There are also bound to be fingerprints and drops of blood you left behind. Now that you've assaulted a cop, the department will investigate. Any chance you're in the system?"

Bones nodded. "Not for anything too bad, but it amounts to the same thing."

"Can you tell us who, exactly, is after you?" Maddock asked.

"I can. Pym Investment Trust, a particularly rapacious hedge-fund managed by Augustus Pym Senior. Augustus Junior handles the dirty work. They are a criminal gang masquerading as investment bankers. That raid yesterday had Junior, as everyone calls him, written all over it." Sally spent the next few minutes telling how she'd been yanked out of class at Colombia by campus police and handed over to a private security force. "They called themselves field agents. A bunch of Russian mercenaries, I can imagine what kind of *field work* they do. I spent two wonderful hours with him, locked in a closed office. I won't bore you with the details, but he made it *painfully* clear that I wouldn't leave there alive without first giving him access to my models."

Bones said, "Then you broke a chair over his head and escaped."

"No, he had me on a sofa. I had to wait until he was close, very close, and um… occupied. Then I bit a chunk out of his ear. He started screaming, one of his agents opened the door, some grunt with less between the ears than you. While he was attending to Junior, I bolted. I don't think Junior made it clear to his underlings that I was to be a semi-permanent guest. Not the most trusting fellow. Neither is his dad."

"Does anyone else know about you and your program? Any other groups like Pym?"

"Doubtful. There's so little trust within that organization I'd be shocked if anyone aside from Junior knows the full story. Rumor is he's looking to screw over his old man first chance he gets, and my program could make that happen. In any case, the company would want to keep it under wraps. If word leaked out, they'd have competition."

"So, we cut the head off of the snake," Bones said. "Or heads. Deal with the Pyms and Sally's safe."

"I could look up Alex Vaccaro," Maddock said. "Get the FBI on the case if she's still with the bureau." Alex Vaccaro had helped them out of a few jams in the past, but it had been years since they'd spoken.

"But that would only initiate an investigation," Corey said. "That can be a slow, laborious process with an uncertain outcome."

Maddock nodded. "So even if we can get help, we need to get you two to safety for the short term."

"Or we just take the two of them out?" Bones offered.

"We're not assassins."

"I know. Just talking out of my ass."

"You might could get to Junior," Sally said, "but dad is a different matter. Although, like I said, I'm not certain he knows I exist."

"Here's what I think," Maddock began. "We get the authorities on the case. If it's not Alex, then there's bound to be a friend of a friend who will get the ball rolling. If nothing else, that will draw Pym's attention."

"That's a start, I suppose," Sally said.

"Have you tried hacking… I mean, digging into Pym's system? Maybe find some incriminating evidence that could help shut him down or at least keep him at bay?"

"Not really. I'd risk drawing attention to myself."

"We've got a friend we can put on the job. He's trustworthy and capable. He'll let us know if he can't do it without drawing attention, but it's worth a try."

"Jimmy?" Corey asked. "Why not me?"

Maddock grinned. "I've got another job for the two of you." He looked from Corey to Sally.

Bones caught on immediately. "That's what I'm talking about," he said. "We've got a massive database of possible lost treasures."

"*Who* has a database?" Corey asked.

"Fine. It's your database. You tell her," Bones said.

"We're treasure hunters. I'm constantly adding new data: myths and legends, geographical data. The only predictive capabilities I have relate to shipwrecks and the effects of currents and extreme weather on location. But if we could apply your system to my data…"

Sally's brow furrowed. "So you wanna get rich, too. Is that it?"

"We just need a good reason to get out of Dodge for a while. Treasure hunting is what we do. Of course, if it paid the bills, I wouldn't mind."

"I assume this is more than a simple matter of you choosing a treasure and I predict where we find it."

"Exactly. It needs to be obscure, in a remote location, but with a high probability of success."

"Meaning we shouldn't go after something stupid, like the Loch Ness Monster."

The three men exchanged amused glances, but Sally was already in gear. She retrieved her laptop and fired it up.

"Okay, ginger," she said to Corey, "I'm going to make some tweaks on my end. You work out how I can access your data. We'll also need to start trawling the web in case I find something better than what you've got."

"I've got almost a terabyte of info," Corey said. "A veritable treasure trove, so to speak. I just hope you have enough computing power in that little tablet of yours."

"Want to lay a bet on it?"

"Dinner at the restaurant of the winner's choice after this is all over?" Corey asked.

"Deal."

They shook hands and set to work. Swapping instructions at a rapid-fire clip, tossing out terms and acronym, making suggestions and rejecting the others' ideas.

Bones turned to Maddock. "Remember that TV show called *King of the Nerds*?"

Sally rolled her eyes. "Yeah, why don't you try doing something useful, like making me a nice cup of coffee?"

"How do you take it?"

"Like you—big, strong, and nothing else in it."

Bones chuckled and retreated to the kitchen while Maddock grabbed his phone and headed to the front door. His first call was to the last known number for Alex Vaccaro—a cellphone. To his surprise, it was her that answered.

"Dane Maddock. What are the odds you're in

trouble and need a favor?"

"You wound me," Maddock said. "I'm calling in a tip."

"Would you happen to be tipping me off about someone who is giving you trouble?"

"Are you psychic?" Maddock asked.

"No, you're just predictable. When did I last hear from you?"

"I called you when the Dolphins beat the Redskins."

"Three years ago you called me to gloat, and you didn't even talk to me. You left a voicemail. Christ, who uses voicemail anymore? You call if you want to talk, text if you want to leave a message."

"I get it. I'm a crappy friend. I'll do better. But can I at least tell you what's going on?"

"Shoot."

Maddock outlined the situation as succinctly as he could.

"I've heard of Pym. The Bureau is aware of him but as far as I know, he's never been accused of any crimes. Wouldn't shock me though. We can take a look at the local precinct where the café was located, mention his name, stir the hornet's nest a little. That should get his attention."

"Which makes it imperative that Sally and Bones are kept safe. They're the only witnesses to the incident," Maddock thought aloud.

"Exactly," Alex said. "You're on your own there, I'm afraid."

"I can handle it."

"Good. I'll do what I can, but it would help if we had something, anything, to incriminate him."

"I've got a plan for that, too," Maddock said.

"I don't want to know any details. Just, get somewhere safe and I'll keep you posted."

Maddock thanked her, then made a call to Jimmy Letson. As usual, his friend berated him for only calling when he needed a favor, although that wasn't strictly true where Jimmy was concerned. In any case, he agreed to cyber sniff around Pym in exchange for a bottle of liquor.

Maddock's third call was to Willis.

"What's up, Maddock?"

"How's it going down there?"

"Matt and Doc are still ripping the guts out of our starboard engine. How about you?"

"We're working on a plan. Any signs of trouble down there?"

"Yeah, I was going to call. I heard from one of the bartenders at Sloppy Joe's that there's been two guys nosing around, looking for someone named Bones. They don't know his real name or anything else about him, but Key West is small and Bones stands out. I'm sure they'll track him down sooner or later. I was thinking Matt and I would crash at Bones' place and try to catch them in the act."

"No," Maddock said. "Better to avoid these guys if we can. Besides, I'm lining up a job. You and Matt get ready to move out. Tell Doc he's in charge, then grab the uplink, the coms, the side scan sonar unit, and our data recorder. We'll want our scuba gear, but forget the tanks. Box it all to travel."

"Will do." The pleasure in Willis' voice was evident. The man hated inaction. "Where's this job?"

"I hope to know by the time you get here."

6

Key West

Matt straightened slowly, stretched, and knuckled the small of his back. *It's not that I'm getting old*, he told himself, *I'm just tired of crawling around under diesel engines.* Manifold, turbocharger, water pump, and idler pully all stood in a neat stack aft of the engine compartment. Doc had unbolted the shaft and mounts. Now cylinder block and reverse gears all stood twelve inches above the engine bed. Doc had gone up to get another hydraulic jack.

Matt heard voices on the dock. *It's after ten, who the heck is coming around this time of night?* He slipped up the ladder and crept along the deck, instinct telling him to remain out of sight. Just beyond the rail, he could hear Doc arguing with someone. Years of Army Ranger training and a fair number of firefights had taught him to keep his head down and wait for the moment.

Doc started to shout, then silence. Matt knew he'd tried to warn him of something. On his belly, he scrambled forward of the boarding ramp and crouched behind a stanchion. He felt a reassuring weight in his back pocket, then remembered it was only a large crescent wrench. *Better than nothing.*

A shadow stormed up the ramp and turned toward the engine hatch. Matt clocked him with the wrench and dragged his limp form out of sight. A quick shakedown yielded a fancy combat knife and a nine-millimeter

Makarov pistol.

Silence, the growl of rub-rail against dock fenders, then a voice called out in a Russian accent. "Aleksey, what are you doing?"

Matt stepped up on the ramp. He had about the same build as Aleksey, close enough to make the other hesitate. In the dim light along the pier, he made out two shadows. One, thin and wiry, had to be Doc. Matt slipped the Makarov from his pocket and thumbed the safety over. "Your friend is a little busy right now, can I help you?"

"You are Bonebrake?"

"That dude? I couldn't be that ugly if I tried."

"Okay, smart guy. I need cooperation, or your friend dies."

Matt crouched and aimed at the shadow. "That would be very stupid, comrade. I've got a better shot at you than you have at me. You'll die, your buddy's about to die, and your boss will be very upset."

Matt felt the pier vibrate and started to turn when a beefy fist smacked into the side of his face. The blow stunned him and another sharp strike to his wrist sent the Makarov skittering across the timber decking. Matt recovered and charged into his assailant, but the man equaled him in size and weight.

A flash, and a bullet dug into the pier, throwing chips and splinters into the air. The other yelled, "Ilya, *stoeteya*, stop!" Matt took advantage of the moment to tackle his opponent about the knees and drive him to the deck. He drew the combat knife and held it against the man's neck.

"Not so fast."

He felt a pistol barrel against the back of his neck.

"Not fast for you, either. Maybe you let him go, so I don't spatter my brother with your brains."

The man beneath him began struggling; Matt pressed the razor-sharp knife edge hard against his throat. "Shoot me, and you kill your brother as well."

"I think I take that chance."

Matt leaned forward and pressed a little harder with his knife. He whispered, "Don't move comrade. We'll soon be together in Hell."

"Hell ain't half full, bro. Why don't I just make it three?"

Matt froze. He recognized that voice.

Willis Sanders emerged from the shadows, pistol leveled. "If you think there's any chance I'll miss," he said to the man threatening Matt, "I promise you're wrong."

"Willis," Matt breathed, "where's Doc?"

"I didn't see him. All I see is y'all having some kind of party."

Still holding a pistol to Matt's head, Ilya said, "Maybe we make deal, yes? Maybe no one visits Hell tonight."

"Ain't going to be no talking. Toss your weapon in the drink." He inclined his head toward the water, the moon glinting off his shaved scalp.

"Wait, I talk, you listen. My brother goes first. Hands up, no tricks. Then your friend and I walk down the pier. You follow. We get in car and leave. You let our friend off later."

Willis shook his head. "I got another idea. I shoot you right now, Matt takes care of your friend, and we head out to sea and drop y'all's asses in the gulf stream."

"You might drift all the way to Ireland before

somebody finds you," Matt said. "At least, whatever parts of you the sharks don't eat."

Ilya must have known he was beaten, because the pressure of the pistol against the back of Matt's neck was suddenly gone. A moment later he heard a small splash. The pistol striking the water.

"I will cooperate," Ilya said.

Matt nodded. "It's about time. I'm tired of smelling this guy's stinking breath." He rose to one knee, but kept the knife pressed against Aleksey's throat. "Now roll over, nice and slow." The man complied. "Hands behind your neck, fingers laced together. And don't try anything brave. My buddy is very good with a handgun."

He stood and turned toward Ilya in time to see the man shift to the side, putting Matt between himself and Willis, and draw a snub-nosed .380.

"You are stupid man. I will…"

Whatever he was intending to do, they never found out because, just then, a dull thud broke the silence and Ilya slumped to the ground. A very wet Doc stood holding a bloody jack handle.

"I had to jump in the harbor to get away from this clown. Do I have to fix everything for you guys?"

Matt grinned in relief. "Your timing was excellent."

Willis knelt and checked the fallen man. "You didn't kill him, but I might. What about silent Sam there?"

Matt said, "Duct tape. You wouldn't happen to have some in your van, would you, Doc?"

Between Willis and Matt, they managed to bind the Russians and wrestle them into the back of a gray rental sedan.

Doc said, "I don't want to see what happens next. I'll close up shop and call it a long night. You two may need to disappear."

Willis shook his hand. "Thanks, man. We got this one. I'll get Matt out of your hair. Just take care of lady *Sea Foam* for us."

Matt had fished a set of keys out of Aleksey's pocket. "I'll drive, you think. What should we do with these guys?"

"We could hand 'em over to the cops, but they've got to be connected to the guys who are after Bones."

"Who are also cops," Matt said. "No telling how high up their connections go or how expansive they are." He paused. "How about Tam Broderick?" Tam headed up a CIA task force called the Myrmidons.

Willis shook his head. "I don't know, man. Last I heard, things are touchy for them right now. The higher-ups are keeping a close eye on her. Making sure they don't do anything outside their purview. If we bring these guys in, she won't be able to give us special treatment."

Matt gaped at Willis.

"What?"

"Did you just say 'purview'? Where did you even learn that word?"

"Screw you, man." Willis scratched his chin, thinking. "How about we just dump 'em back in the mangroves somewhere."

"There's salt water crocodiles in there. We might end up with manslaughter charges."

"They're little ones; they wouldn't eat much. Even if they did, who's gonna find the bodies?"

"True. As long as we deal with their clothing and personal effects, there won't be anything left of their bodies by the time nature gets through with them."

Through the back of his seat, he could hear the Russians thrash and kick. Chuckling, Matt drove them down a dark coral road. Loose stones rattled and pinged off the wheel-wells and their captives continued to struggle and moan in protest. Matt finally pulled over in a remote area.

"This look like a good place?"

"Good as any," Willis played along. "Let's see if our friends have something to say before we do it."

The men had lots to say. Much of it was profanity, but the rest confirmed what Maddock had already related to Willis.

"Yeah, here's the plan."

Just after midnight Matt and Willis were cruising north on the Seven Mile Bridge. The moonlight danced on the dark water that swept out to the horizon in every direction. The windows were down, refreshing gulf air filling their nostrils. "In the Air Tonight" by Phil Collins was blaring on the radio. Willis turned to Matt and shook his head slowly.

"Got a problem?" Matt asked. "Don't tell me you hate this song, because I'm not sure we could stay friends."

"No, man. It's just… cruising at night to this song. It's kind of a white people cliché, don't you think?"

"You've used the words purview and cliché in the same evening. Are you studying for the SAT or something?"

Willis replied with a laugh and an upraised middle finger. He reached over and switched the channel on the satellite radio, and "Informer" by Snow filled the car with a reggae rap beat.

"This is what you want to cruise to?" Matt marveled.

"What the hell is 'licky boom-boom' anyway?"

"Ask your sister. I showed her last time she was in town."

Matt rolled his eyes. "You're such an asshat."

Matt passed a couple of traffic cams, then pulled over on a deserted stretch, just long enough for Willis to hop out and toss the Russians' wallets and cellphones over the side. Once on their way again, Willis dialed Maddock and put him on speaker. Four rings and Corey picked up.

"Where the hell are you guys?"

"Corey?" Matt said. "What are you doing with Maddock's phone?"

"He and Bones crashed. Sally and I are sitting here parsing a complex data set."

"Parsing? Is that what you nerds call it?"

"Don't try to be funny. You're not Bones."

Willis laughed. "You telling me you find Bones funny?"

"Fair point."

Matt drove while Willis filled Corey in on the events that had transpired in Key West. "So, then we dumped them off at the emergency clinic, pushed the button and ran like hell."

"Camera?"

"Not with Matt's MagLite shining in it."

"Did you get the gear we need?"

"Everything is in the back. We caught Doc just as he was closing things up. He helped us with the gear, and whoa, he laid a new toy on us. Said it might come in handy."

"Can't wait." Corey sounded distracted.

Matt spoke up. "So, we're going to wipe this car

down and leave it somewhere safe, then we'll head your way. Can you find us a discreet flight? Someone who can take our gear, too?"

Corey agreed and clicked off and Matt settled in for another three hours of driving. They'd planted the discharged pistol on Ilya. He'd have residue on his hands that would be hard to explain. Worse still, no ID and no good reason to be in town. It had taken a lot of convincing to pry that Makarov away from Willis, but cleaned and stashed in the trunk, it would further implicate Aleksey and his brother.

They wheeled into Fort Lauderdale about four a.m. Not wanting to be caught on security video, they parked the car in a lot behind an abandoned grocery store a few blocks away from the airport. They wiped it down, stashed the keys in the glove compartment, and locked it up. It looked to be a decent neighborhood. Hopefully it would be discovered and returned to the rental company in short order.

Their belongings were stowed in two large Pelican cases of gear. Equipped with handles and wheels, their fiberglass shells were made to take some real abuse. They slipped through a hole in a fence and cut across a vacant lot to a nearby apartment building. From there, they called a car to take them to the airport.

"Nothing suspicious," Matt said. "Just a couple of local residents catching a lift."

By the time they reached the airport, Corey had come through with flight arrangements, and they dozed in the terminal until departure, then slept again on the flight. It had been an exhausting night, and they arrived at their destination still weary and aching.

Maddock was waiting for them at baggage claim.

Matt slapped him on the shoulder and Willis said, "Just what we needed. A Sherpa."

Maddock grinned. "I'm just glad to see you both made it safe. Doc called this morning. He'd filed a police report about unknown parties shooting at him on the pier. I don't think the *Brothers Karamazov* are going to give us trouble for a while."

Matt shook his head. "I wouldn't count on that. Whatever hornet's nest Bones has stirred up, they mean business."

Maddock explained their plans on the way back to the beach house. "Corey and Sally are trying to gin up an expedition for us. Something that will get us out of the country."

Matt shook his head. "Leave it to Bones to put us all in mortal danger over a girl."

7

Virginia Beach

When they reached the cottage, Sally and Corey were peering at the computer screen, eyes locked on the display. Bones was crashed out on the couch and greeted his friend with only a casual wave. Sally paused long enough for introductions while Corey ignored them completely.

"I don't like this, not at all. It's not converging," Corey said.

"It's been like this for hours," Bones said. "Riveting stuff."

"Corey spending hours on a computer?" Willis asked. "The only surprise is that it's not porn."

Corey didn't reply, such was his focus on the task at hand. "Sally, what's it doing?"

Sally sat down and punched a few keys. The numbers stopped scrolling. "The iterations are diverging," she said. "We're missing something."

"Yeah, you tossed half our data." Bones said.

"Your ridiculous conspiracy theories, you mean. C'mon, alien machines from Atlantis? Templar plots? A magic sword from the stars? Give me some credit."

"You can't toss the data," Maddock said. "Look, we're trusting in you and the capabilities of your program, no matter how far-fetched it might sound. On top of that, we're risking our asses to keep you safe. At least do us the courtesy of trusting us in return."

Sally shook her head in resignation. "Okay, I'll give it a try." A few clicks, several commands, then the numbers on the screen began to scroll again. "I don't see how any of that will help," she said. "It's likely to go unstable and trip the limit switches."

Silent, like cats at a mousehole, they all watched the screen. Maddock was almost sure Corey held his breath. Only he and Sally had any idea what it all meant.

After a few minutes, Sally stood up. "It doesn't look like it's gonna crash the system quite yet. I'm going to scare up some food."

She disappeared into the kitchen and soon, the delicious aroma of baking filled the air. When she next appeared, she was bearing a tray of muffins.

Maddock took a bite of his and sank back into his chair as a symphony of flavors filled his mouth. Blueberry, dark chocolate, a hint of honey. "This is amazing. You take this food bit seriously."

Matt nodded in agreement. "I've paid seven bucks for a muffin that wasn't half this good."

"Glad you like it. Food is sort of my thing. When we first arrived, I entered a list of available ingredients into my program, along with a few other details." She cast a meaningful glance at Maddock, who was too busy trying to stop himself from downing the rest of the muffin in a single bite. "It popped out a few recipes."

"You could make a killing opening a bakery," Matt said. "Hell, come down to Key West. You'd put everyone out of business."

"Maybe, once Pym's been dealt with. Of course, I'd need a place to stay."

"My lap is always available," Bones said.

Sally smirked and Maddock didn't miss the furtive

glance she cast in Corey's direction. He had a feeling she preferred brains to brawn.

"Corey's got a spare room," Maddock said.

"Yeah, but it's full of My Little Pony stuff," Willis chimed in.

Sally's face lit up. She turned to Corey. "You're a brony?"

"What's that?" Corey asked, still focused on the screen.

"Oh. Never mind." Her fair cheeks went red. "Anyway, I love cooking. Look at how happy a simple muffin has made you."

Maddock couldn't disagree. He wasn't a foodie but what she'd prepared was exceptional.

"I could make a million dollars with my software and spend all my time looking over my shoulder, or I could do something simple. I prefer spreading joy in tiny ways."

"That's what Maddock said on his honeymoon," Bones said.

Sally's eyes narrowed. "Oh. I didn't realize you were married."

"Widower," he said.

"Oh. I'm sorry." She sounded like she really meant it. Perhaps the young woman was finally letting her guard down.

"Thanks. It was a long time ago."

Corey pushed back from the table, turned, and broke the awkward silence. "Take a look at the screen. I think we're in the groove."

Sally took his place. "It's stable. I think it might converge. Say two, two and a half hours and we'll know."

No one spoke. The hiss and rumble of waves filled

the night air. A large kitchen clock ticked away the seconds. The minute hand was broken, but the hour hand indicated one-thirty. Maddock dozed in his chair until Corey shook him awake.

"The simulation self-terminated. Want to come see the results?"

Maddock rubbed his bleary eyes and tried to clear the cobwebs from his mind. "For sure."

"Sally is plotting the results right now."

He looked over her shoulder. Random spots began appearing on her computer screen, each one little bigger than a punctuation mark. After about five minutes, splotches began forming small nebulae of colors. In answer to his silent question, Sally said, "Chaotic attractors. Each cluster is its own domain. The interaction of those marks will determine the final locations."

Maddock nodded, more for his own benefit than hers. "How long before it's finished?"

"Another half hour to plot, say fifteen minutes to collapse the domains. We should be looking at results by daybreak."

"Then I'm going out for a run, anyone want to join me?"

Corey demurred, Matt and Bones still slept, but Willis had been pacing about and peering out the windows. "Yeah, you're on man. I want to see you run off some of that pizza you've been munching."

They both headed for the beach. The moon, nearly full, retreated in the west, throwing a little light on the sandy stretch before him. Maddock opened it up and let the stress of the previous days burn off in his calves and upper legs. Willis kept pace, long strides eating up the ground beneath his feet.

Another mile, and the runners passed beneath a highway bridge, made another thousand yards, and fetched up against a chain-link fence. Maddock waited, chest heaving, heart pounding.

Willis folded his arms and gazed through the fence. "Check it out," he said, "SEAL City, otherwise known as Little Creek Amphibious Base, home of hell week."

Maddock had caught his breath. "Don't remind me. We were in San Diego for that one, and it was bad enough."

"Could you do it again, Maddock?" Willis asked. "You think you could take a full course of SEAL training and not ring out?"

"I don't know. I like to think we've been through worse since then. I didn't ring the bell then, and I've never regretted it."

Willis gazed up at the night sky, thinking. "I don't regret my service, but some of the things we had to see and do…" He shook his head. "I think I could do it again, but I don't want to. I enjoy our new life too much, even when things get hairy. Now, let's get the hell out of here before some MPs get all excited about us lurking around at four in the morning."

As they jogged back, they speculated about what sort of treasure Sally and Corey would come up with. "I don't know what to expect," Willis said, "but I'm curious to see what sort of answer her Magic Eight Ball is going to shake out. I hope it's somewhere close to a beach."

"You live at the beach."

"Exactly. I had enough city life and cold weather growing up in Detroit."

"We didn't really talk about those guys who came

after you in Key West. What do you think? Russian mafia?"

"Probably mercs, ex-Russian Army mercenaries. I managed to get a little info out of them. They wouldn't come out and say, but I'm sure they're working for this Pym Investment Trust."

"You think they'll track us down here?"

Willis made a face. "Depends on their resources. With the right sort of connections, they could find a record of our flight, but how would they know to come to this cottage?"

"I don't know," Maddock admitted. "Maybe it's that SEALs thing kicking in. I think we've been here too long."

They finished their run in silence. In the distance, the Cape Story lighthouse flashed its warning to sailors.

When they reached the cottage, Maddock grabbed Willis' shoulder and pointed to a thick stand of shrubs about fifty yards beyond the cottage. "Hold on. Let's recon a bit."

They hunkered down out of sight and watched the cottage. After about ten minutes, Willis began to fidget. Still, Maddock waited. A car came by, cruising slowly. Gray sedan, its license plate light was out. He watched it pass. Distant brake lights and moments later, the same gray sedan returned.

When it had left, Willis let out a loud sigh. "You think it's Pym?"

"I guess it's time to make a move, just to be safe," Maddock said.

The two waited a moment in case the sedan made another pass, then bolted for the cottage. Maddock slipped inside, but before he could speak, Sally beckoned.

"It's finished the correlations, come look at this."

He stepped up behind her and studied the display. A hundred dots of various sizes peppered the screen. The larger dots were orange in the middle with yellow areoles that faded at the edge. At the far right a large blotch glowed brick red in the center. Bones and the others looked on, while Sally explained. "We're seeing a grid of longitude and latitude. It wouldn't really go on a map, but it does cover the earth."

Willis put a finger on the screen. The display moved, and Sally smacked his hand away. "Sorry, yeah… okay, I won't touch, but you're saying each of these is a treasure?"

"They could be."

Corey said, "So look up eighteen degrees north latitude by eighty-eight degrees west longitude."

Sally zoomed in on the plot. A small orange dot swelled into prominence on her screen. "Right there?"

"Just off Ambergris Caye. That's the one treasure site I didn't give you, but there it is. I have to admit this particular application of your program works just as we hoped."

Maddock scratched his chin. "Can we zoom out and then look at each one in turn? See which is the most promising?"

"I can do you one better," Sally said. "A visual representation of the quality of each hit, taking into account not only the size of the treasure, but the likelihood of it being real and undiscovered."

She brought the entire screen back into view and then tilted the perspective. Suddenly, each of the dots became a tiny pointed mountain. Each that is, except the large red spike that towered over the others.

Willis gasped. "Damn, man. That's got to be the Mac Daddy of all treasures."

"Keep your pants up, boys. It's just a data anomaly, a cusp in the algorithm that accumulated hits."

"Don't break my heart," Bones said.

"Look, we'll check the coordinates. I'll bet it's nothing but wide blue ocean out there." Sally opened another screen and brought up *Google Earth.* A few keystrokes zoomed them across the Pacific. They descended somewhere west of Hawai'i and fell like a meteor toward the ocean below. At five hundred miles up, their view stabilized and all six of them stared at a scattered archipelago of tiny islands.

Bones said, "Get closer, get closer. I want to see this thing."

She zoomed them down to about thirty thousand feet. One island grew, then became three rocky islets surrounding a perfectly circular lagoon. Maddock said, "Where is this place?"

Sally turned on the place-names and read, "Maug."

8

Bones peered at the screen. "What the... Oh, I get it, 'Guam' spelled backwards. Good one. You had us going like a bunch of recruits on induction day."

Corey shook his head. "No, that's a real place. Zoom us back so we can see where it is." Sally scrolled back and soon a chain of islands came into view. "Stop right there. Look that's Guam down at the bottom, then Saipan. Then here, about four hundred miles farther north, is Maug."

Maddock nodded, eyes locked on the screen. If the results could be relied upon, the program indicated that this island was a literal treasure trove. "If that's not an anomaly, we can't *not* go."

Willis said, "That's a double negative, Maddock."

Sally began clicking, jumping from screen to screen faster than Maddock could follow. "It's got to be legit. Value estimate is off the chart, as is the probability rating." She clicked again. "And the danger rating."

"What's dangerous about it?"

"The program doesn't work that way. It trawls available information and gives you probabilities. It doesn't write an encyclopedia entry. We'll have to research this site and see what we can learn."

"You can do that along the way," Bones said.

The others nodded.

Sally stared at them for a moment. "You're just going to dive in? Pun intended." She wiped the hair from over her right eye.

"Every treasure hunt comes with a certain amount of risk," Matt said. "Besides, we're already in danger."

"Speaking of that," Willis began, "we should have been gone already. Me and Maddock saw someone scouting around outside."

All eyes turned to Maddock. "Yeah, we saw two guys in a rental car snooping around when we came back. We all need to bug out."

"Are you sure?" Matt said. "How in hell did they find us so quick?"

"It's got to be me," Sally replied. "They must have a way of tracking my login. Of course, they'll only know the vicinity, not the exact house. At least, not right away."

Bones patted his purloined Glock. "Just two? Maybe it's time to deal with them permanently."

"You know, Bonehead, I was just starting to like you, and you want to play gunslinger. Do you think Pym is fooling around? You make a couple of Pym's agents disappear, it won't matter if you hide it from law enforcement. He'll send everything he's got after you, I'm sure of it. You'll just be stirring up an anthill."

Bones turned to Maddock. "So, what do we do?"

Maddock considered. "The guys in that vehicle weren't exactly being discreet, were they?"

"You're right. They wanted us to know they were there," Willis agreed.

"Which means another attack is coming from somewhere else," Bones finished. "I'm going to take a look around while you all make ready to bolt." Before anyone could object, he slipped out the back door, returning ten minutes later with a grave expression on his face.

"Two snipers hiding in the dunes, one just to the north, another to the south. A dude with a bulge under his coat, and I don't mean his package, out for a very early stroll on the beach, but never wandering too far away. And there's a boat offshore that I don't like the looks of."

"Did they see you?" Sally asked.

Bones flashed her a pitying look but didn't bother to answer. Few people could move around unseen the way Bones could.

"Plus the two men in the car," Matt added. "I don't like the odds, especially when we have only a few handguns at our disposal."

Maddock took out his phone and scrolled through the contacts.

"Is this really the time to update your Grindr profile?" Bones asked.

"Screw you, Bones. I've got a plan." He tapped out a text message describing their situation and waited for the reply. It came almost immediately.

Sounds fun.

"Everybody grab your things and keep away from the windows."

They all huddled in the corner of the living room, waiting. Five minutes passed. Then ten.

"So now how much longer?" Matt asked.

Maddock raised a finger. "Wait for it…"

All fell silent. The sounds of early risers driving to work drifted over from the street. A flight of helicopters headed out from Little Creek on their morning patrol rumbled through the air. Maddock heard the usual whine of outboards off across the Chesapeake channel.

And then the *whoomp* of chopper blades drew closer, grew louder until it sounded like it was on top of them.

Sally looked up at the ceiling. "What did you do?"

Through the gauzy curtains at the back of the house they saw a helicopter set down on the beach just behind the cottage amidst a cloud of sand. Armed, uniformed men poured out, some taking up positions on the beach and others dashing toward the cottage.

Bones whistled. "Would you look at that? The dude on the beach is running for it like his life depended on it, which it probably does. And that boat I was wondering about? Headed out to sea."

Matt rushed to the front window and peered out. "A couple of guys just bolted from the dunes and piled into a gray sedan. You did it, Maddock. They're running like Bones from a committed relationship."

Steps on the porch, and then a sharp rap at the door.

"United States Navy! Are you in there, Maddock?"

A broad grin split Bones' face. "I know that voice!"

Maddock opened the door to see a solidly built man grinning back at him. The fellow was a bit shorter than Maddock, but built like a tank.

"Am I ever glad to see you," Maddock said.

"Cooch!" Bones cried, hurrying up to shake the man's hand.

"That's Chief Cooch to you, Bonebrake."

"Racist," Bones said.

The man stepped inside and closed the door behind him. Maddock introduced him as Casey Couture, nicknamed "Cooch."

Cooch removed his helmet, wiped the sweat from his brow, greeted Willis with a bro hug, and shook hands with the others.

"Those are some cool scars," Sally said, pointing in turn to a pair of scars on either side of the man's forehead, just at the hairline. "If you don't mind my asking, how did you get them?"

"That's where they removed my horns when I was a kid," Cooch said, laughing. "Mom always said I was a devil."

"How did you manage this?" Matt asked.

Cooch laughed. "What do you mean? We're just practicing urban tactics. Securing a residence. Nothing out of the ordinary."

"I can't believe you got here so quickly," Maddock said. "That's impressive even for you."

Cooch shrugged. "I get a lot of leeway when it comes to keeping these guys sharp. I'm known as a bit of a bastard so no one argues with me too much as long as I get results and don't stray too far afield."

"I owe you big time," Maddock said. "The Red Sox are playing in DC this year and I've got a friend who can score dugout seats. That is, if you're still a Sox fan."

"Still a fan? Now that we're finally good? You bet your ass I am."

Sally groaned. "I'm a Yankees girl."

"I'll pretend you didn't say that." Cooch winked.

"Still playing guitar?" Bones asked.

Cooch nodded. "Punk band and a cover band. Even recorded an album. It's called *The Starry Robe Sessions*. I'll send you a signed CD if you like."

"A CD?" Sally asked. "You play those on a Victrola, right?"

Cooch chuckled. "I don't know whether to laugh or cry." He turned to Maddock. "How is it you keep running into trouble with shady characters? You living the James Bond life?"

"I'm Bond," Bones said. "I always get the girl. Maddock is M. Corey is Q. Matt is Moneypenny."

"Hey, now!" Matt protested.

"And I'm the redshirt who's just here for diversity's sake," Willis chimed in.

They spent a few minutes catching up, then Cooch and his men stood guard as they piled into the van Maddock had rented and headed to Dulles.

Maddock didn't breathe a sigh of relief until they were safely on board the plane. Matt and Willis immediately nodded off. Bones was highly amused by his seating assignment, 36C, which he proclaimed loudly was also his favorite cup size, drawing a disapproving glance from the woman seated next to him. She was attractive with long brown hair, blue eyes, and a light tan. Bones tried to engage her in conversation, but she was engrossed in a Dodge Dalton adventure novel and had no time for Bones. Meanwhile, Corey and Sally huddled over their laptops, trying to research their destination, and bickering like an old married couple.

Maddock smiled and closed his eyes.

Just let us get safely out of the States and we'll be fine.

9

New York City

Amadi hopped his battered bicycle over the curb and sped down Water Street. *Old building with a bird*, his cousin had said. Recently arrived from Ethiopia, Amadi had joined his extended family in New York. Now, delivering packages twelve hours a day, he made enough money to send a little back to his mother in Addis Ababa.

There is no old building with a bird. Amadi glided between stopped cars, glancing down each canyon he passed. *No old buildings, only cliffs of steel and glass*. He hopped another curb and stopped at Maiden Lane. People rushed by, mostly suits. Amadi felt invisible, an obstacle like a lamp-post or trash can. There was power in that invisibility, and there was loneliness.

He searched up and down the echoing granite canyon. From the corner of his eye he caught sight of a battered window air conditioner. *What devilishness is this?* Back from the street, behind a shiny new bank lobby, seven stories of old red brick rose from the sidewalk. Double-hung windows adorned the brick wall. Half of them sported the rusting grill of an air conditioner. *Such a place does not pay five hundred dollars for a delivery.*

Amadi pedaled a block farther, cut across to Front Street, and cruised down the opposite side. He passed a marble entrance in the algae stained brick. Above the stone lintel, it bore a heraldic shield with the outline of a bird's head and the motto, *Tekeli Li*. Amadi allowed himself to coast between the parked cars and traffic. *Whatever I have in my backpack, it will certainly get me arrested or killed.*

Behind a delivery van, he stopped to consider his options. He could run now and take the consequences. He'd run from Ethiopia and didn't want to run again. He could return to his cousin and claim he never found the building, but that would be a lie, a lie to his family. Finally, he chained his bicycle to a rack and walked two blocks back to the marble doorway. *Invisible man.*

Up a short flight of granite steps, through a swinging glass door, Amadi sweated all the way. Not daring to look back, he glanced at the thick manila envelope in his hand: *Happy Dragon Imports*. "Devils," he muttered.

Through a second glass door emblazoned with a smiling green dragon, he stopped at a plain wooden counter. Years of wear and cigarette burns showed on both sides of the worn top. A smiling Asian woman took his package and handed him an envelope. The young man counted out five crisp new one hundred-dollar bills.

Amadi dashed back out to the sidewalk, careened around the corner, flew up Water Street, and sprinted another three blocks to a coffee shop. "Triple espresso, milk, sugar, yes please." He peered out a window, watching. Suits walked by, no one remembered the invisible man and he never returned for that bicycle.

Augustus Pym Senior felt the pneumatic cuffs tighten on his immobile legs. He counted to five, knowing exactly when they would deflate. Beneath his back, the motorized chair subtly realigned his lumbar support and adjusted the seat elevation. He took the moment to perform a few isometric exercises on his arms and shoulders. Pym had no delusions about his age or infirmity, but he was not about to surrender to either of them.

He turned his attention to the envelope sitting on the polished birch slab that served as his desk. Pym savored the moment. A twitch of his head and the chair docked itself against the block of wood. Inside the envelope, he found a smooth gray packet. Carbon fiber, it was locked with an electronic seal. Pym opened it with a command to his chair and spilled a stack of aging documents out onto his desk.

Bonds, bearer bonds denominated in the tens of millions. *Sometimes the old ways are best.* He leafed through the pile. Most of these securities had been issued over seventy years ago and few had their coupons still attached. Still, like cash, bearer bonds were always worth face value to the person who held the paper. Thirty-seven sheets, they totaled one point nine billion in U.S. currency.

Almost two billion, still a tiny drop of what had been lost when Hurricane Sandy plowed into New York. His team had been among the first to enter the flooded vaults below the Depository Trust Company. No one knew how many bundles of securities they had managed to smuggle out in those first few hectic days. Unfortunately for his team, none of them had survived for long afterwards.

Pym replaced the stack, re-locked the packet and returned it to his desk. The bonds would go to Zurich.

There they would be witnessed by an underwriter and stored in a vault. Pym Investment Trust would never need to liquidate these securities. Instead, they would collateralize a series of long-term loans. Minutes later a young woman swept in, retrieved the packet, and disappeared.

He glanced down at the tiny clock on his chair. Twelve-thirty. His son would be coming up now. He tracked the elevator on another small screen. Four, five, six, seventh floor it stopped.

Augustus Pym Junior, Auggie to his father, Junior to everyone else, much to his son's chagrin, crossed the thirty feet between the elevator doors and his father's desk. "So much for our mercs. Lost them! Gone! What do I do now?"

"You know the rule," Augustus said in a tired voice.

"I know. I'll never be a true leader until I can sort out my own problems." The younger Pym took out a cigarette and placed it, unlit, between his lips. He muttered curses as he paced to and fro across the Italian marble floor.

It was one of Augustus Senior's rules—anything Auggie took upon himself, it was up to him to see it to completion. The elder Pym didn't even want to know about it. It was Auggie's problem. His mother had been too soft on Auggie growing up. Of course, Pym knew the real reason for that, and it grated at him after all these years.

"Okay," Auggie said. "In general terms. What do you do when your mercenaries run away without firing a shot?"

"That would depend on the circumstances."

"A bunch of Navy SEALs showed up."

"Ah!" Pym nodded. "I wonder if perhaps you forgot the rule, 'Know your enemy'?" When his son didn't reply, he went on. "Did the background checks you ran on your targets turn up any connection to the Navy?" Auggie didn't meet his eye. "Did you run background checks at all?"

"I did on one of them. Doesn't matter anyway. They're gone and I have no idea where they've run."

Pym Senior was fast losing interest in his son's failings, as well as the rumors of Auggie's scheming. He closed his eyes and pressed his fingers to his temples. *Patience,* he told himself. *He's your son, but at least he's not your blood.* He opened his eyes and twitched his head. His motorized chair undocked from the desk and rolled on silent tires across the room. It stopped in front of an illuminated case.

"Do you see this statue? It's carved from ivory that was harvested from the tusk of an elephant no longer found in Africa. It has been embellished in gold and precious stones over the past thousand years. But in one night—one bloody night, the Khmer Rouge looted and burned its monastery. Now this thing of rare beauty is mine."

"What the hell does that have to do with anything, Pops? I've seen that ugly bit a thousand times." Junior spread his arms and spun on his heels. "I'm sick of all this bloody crap you've surrounded yourself with. What good does it do anyone?"

The old man kept smiling at the illuminated case. "Behind you is an original Monet. In 1992, I purchased it from the Saint Petersburg Hermitage museum. That painting cost me a case of good vodka and a high-quality reproduction. Such were the times in Russia after the fall.

With the right contacts you could buy anything."

"I still don't get it."

"Don't you?" Pym asked.

Junior paused, removed the cigarette from his mouth, and rolled it between his fingers. Then his eyes lit up.

"With our contacts all around the world, depending on where they go, I might actually stand a chance of running them down."

Pym nodded. Perhaps there was hope, if scant, for Auggie yet. "Exactly. Let them run. There is no city, no jungle far enough that our network can't find them. I would track your targets, will wait until they are far from any help, then fall on them with an overwhelming force."

His son smiled, a faraway look in his eyes. "And I'll be there when it happens."

10

Guam

The tropical heat and humidity soaked Maddock to the bone. He felt like a damp dishrag. Even indoors it was uncomfortable. He nursed his beer, a draft of questionable origin, and watched Bones and Willis patrol the pool tables and slot machines. Rebuffed so far in all their attempts to hire a ship, they were making the rounds of the most unsavory joints they could find, hoping to make a connection with someone who liked money and wasn't risk-averse.

The sky had clouded up and a warm rain began to fall as they arrived at the *Kokonut Klub*. Maddock had no idea how Bones had found this place, but it fit the bill. On a small stage near the back, two emaciated young Korean women and an androgynous guitarist struggled through a variety of local hits. He could barely hear them above the shouts and laughter nearby. Someone must have cranked up the slot machine volume, because they rang and flashed like fire alarms on a submarine.

Two men slipped through a curtained doorway on the left. Maddock noticed them immediately. They had the look of sailors—calloused hands, leathery skin, scars. More than that, he was a sailor himself and he knew instinctively these men took to the sea in some fashion. He followed, only to be stopped by a gigantic man.

"Twenty dollars."

"For what?"

"You want to watch cage fight? Twenty dollars."

"I've got a five." He held out the bill and it disappeared into the man's massive palm.

"One fight, then you go."

Barring a quick finish to the next fight, he ought to have enough time to find the sailors. He squeezed through a mixed crowd amidst a rain of shouts and curses in English, Spanish, and what he presumed was Chamorro, the local tongue. He even noticed a man screaming in Japanese; probably a descendant of a World War II soldier.

At the center of the room stood a rough cage of welded rebar and rusty chain link fencing. Two men were warming up, waiting to be introduced. Maddock noticed immediately that there was a significant disparity in size between the two. Definitely not a sanctioned bout. Not his problem. He had a task to complete.

He looked around for the two men he'd seen entering and spotted them speaking with an attractive woman, tall with brown hair and blue eyes. She wore a snug-fitting blue and white striped shirt that accentuated her curves. Something about her seemed familiar. As he approached the trio, he heard her speak sharply to the men and they walked away, heads low. Strange.

"I know you," the woman called. "From the plane."

Now he remembered. Smiling, he approached her.

"Yeah, you got stuck seated next to my friend."

"He wasn't so bad. Just likes to show off a little. Drink?" Before he could reply, she waved to a young man in the corner who hurried over carrying two bottles of beer. She paid him and he bowed to them both.

"Thanks. I'm Maddock. Dane Maddock."

"Lyn Askew." They shook hands and then she raised

her bottle. "Cheers."

"Cheers." They clinked bottles and drank. It was a golden lager with a hoppy aroma and just the right balance between sweet and bitter. He nodded approvingly.

"Bochkareve Svetloe," Lyn said, noticing his reaction.

"A Russian beer?"

"It's popular here for some reason."

Maddock took another drink.

"So, how does the line go? What's a nice girl like you doing in a place like this?"

Lyn laughed. "I'm hardly a nice girl. As for what I'm doing here, I love sports. Especially football, but I like all kinds. I did sports photography in high school and thought about doing it professionally, but the sea called to me."

"What's your football team?" Maddock asked.

"Carolina Panthers. Yours?"

"Miami Dolphins."

Lyn gave him a sympathetic pat on the arm. "Sorry to hear that."

Inside the cage, the two fighters were being introduced. The larger man, called Mako, received the louder cheers by far.

"I hate that guy," Lyn said. "He's the house champion. Dirty fighter, and never fights anyone his own size." She turned and locked eyes with him. "Same question back at you. What's a clean-cut guy like you doing in a seedy dive like this?"

"Actually, I'm looking to charter a boat for an expedition."

"Interesting. I'm in the chartering business. Tell me

the details."

"We want to take a dive trip up north. You know, the northern islands, Pagan, Agrihan, Asuncion. Places people don't often see. We need something seaworthy, comfortable, and dependable. Maybe eighty feet or so."

Lyn pursed her lips and eyed him before speaking. "You and your friend Bones don't look like dive tourists. Neither does the guy you two came in with tonight. You look like a pack of mercenaries."

"We were in the service together. Navy. We still dive."

Lyn nodded. "Let's talk about Pagan then. Funny you should mention that island. I've got friends there that grow some of the best weed west of Maui. Might that be what you're after?"

Maddock chuckled. "I won't say I've never availed myself, but you'll have better luck with Bones and Willis." He inclined his head toward the outer room.

In the cage, the fight had begun. Mako circled his opponent, hands held low. His opponent flicked a jab that just missed, but Mako didn't flinch.

"Maybe you're federal agents?" Lyn asked.

"We're not feds or MPs. The truth is, we're treasure hunters. And not to be rude, but can you help us out or not? Because, if you don't want the job, I need to keep looking."

Lyn smiled. "I overheard enough of your group's conversation on the plane to figured that you're treasure hunters. I just wondered if you'd tell me the truth." "We're seldom popular with the locals. People tend to think of us as grave robbers."

Inside the cage, the smaller fighter, emboldened by Mako's passive approach, attempted a combination. The first blow caught Mako on the cheek, but Mako's counterpunch was lightning-fast, and stunned the smaller fighter. Just like that, technique went out the window and the match became a brawl.

"The most important thing about *Lark* is that she's the only boat that will take you to the northern islands during typhoon season."

"How much can you pay?" Lyn asked. They haggled as they watched the fight.

Mako landed a right hook that dropped the man to the floor. Before he could push himself back up, Mako kneed him in the head, knocking him out cold.

"Knee to the head of a grounded opponent!" Maddock shouted, as Mako straddled the fallen fighter and rained down blows to the back of the head.

"I told you," Lyn said. "Dirty fighter." She sighed. "Your offer is fair, but I don't know. It's a dangerous time of year. I'm only considering it because I need to make a run to Pagan anyway."

"What if I added twenty percent…" Maddock began.

"It's not the money."

"… of any treasure we find."

That gave her pause. She bit her lip and stared at the cage where Mako was dancing around to a cacophony of cheers and boos. As he dodged beer bottles hurled by a few disgruntled fans, two attendants entered and dragged his unconscious victim away by his heels.

Lyn turned to him. "Tell you what, I'll…"

Maddock felt a hand on his shoulder. It was the big man who guarded the door. "Remember the deal. One fight. Now you go."

"Can I give you a few more bucks? I'm having a nice conversation with the lady."

The man grinned, enjoying the tiny measure of power he held at the moment.

"Too late. Should have given me the twenty."

"I can give you twenty now."

The man shook his head. Up in the cage, Mako was circling, shouting challenges to men in the crowd. Maddock gathered that this was the point in the evening where the fighter took on all comers for a cash prize.

"The only way you stay is if you fight Mako."

"I'm not fighting anyone."

"You strong guy," the man insisted. "Ten dollars to enter. You win, you make a hundred. A big Ben Franklin!"

Maddock shook his head and turned to Lyn, who was smiling.

"I'll make a deal with you. You want to charter my ship, you fight Mako."

"Are you crazy?"

"I like the fights. Come on, you don't have to beat him. Just give it the old college try. I'll even cover your ten dollars. But my cut is twenty five percent." She locked eyes with Maddock. "You won't find anyone else to take you north this time of year. I promise you that."

Maddock stood, sighed, and turned toward the cage.

"I'll fight," he called, raising his hand. A man in a cheap suit spotted him and beckoned him into the ring.

Bones and Willis wandered in as Maddock stepped up to the cage door.

"Maddock! What the hell are you doing?" Bones called.

Maddock slipped off his shoes and socks and tossed them to his friend. "Chartering a boat." With that, he stepped inside.

The crowd jeered as Maddock stepped inside and began to limber up. The volume fell as he stripped off his shirt, revealing the years of scars that marred his back, torso, and arms. They were reassessing him.

Suddenly, it seemed everyone was waving cash about, laying bets. From the corner of his eye, he saw Willis getting in on the action, apparently taking bets from all comers.

Maddock stepped up and eyed Mako. Not quite as tall as Bones, but just as muscular. When his eyes locked with Maddock's, the man screamed in rage. He turned and pounded the bars. A skinny young man in a striped shirt beckoned him to the center of the cage. He would be no help if things turned dirty.

The referee shouted something to Mako, who nodded, then turned to Maddock.

"Ready?"

Maddock nodded. "Let's do this."

The referee forced a sympathetic smile. "Fight!"

This time, Mako did not circle and counter. He charged across the cage, leapt into the air, and threw a Superman punch. Maddock dodged it easily. Mako rolled to his feet and charged in again, throwing a wild haymaker.

Maddock ducked it, drove an uppercut to Mako's ribs, then shoved him away. He followed with a leg kick that his opponent failed to check. Mako smiled and shook his head.

Grandstand all you want, Maddock thought. *I know you felt that.*

Mako remained aggressive, headhunting with every strike. But Maddock was too skilled, too quick, and understood how to control distance so that all the punches fell just short of his chin or winged past his head. Again and again Maddock countered with body punches or kept Mako off balance with leg kicks.

That's how you take down the larger fighter. Chip away at his base.

Mako was growing tired and a glint of desperation flashed in his eyes. He drove forward, faking a takedown attempt, but came back up at the last second and aimed a knee at Maddock's unprotected groin. Maddock was expecting it, and pivoted so he caught only a glancing blow. Still, it hurt like hell.

Gritting his teeth, he clinched, pressed Mako against the cage, and punished ribs and thighs with powerful punches and knee strikes. The big man felt every one of them, letting out a pained grunt with each blow. He pawed at Maddock's head and then thrust a thumb into Maddock's left eye.

Maddock shouted in surprise and pain, and Mako broke loose of the clinch. Maddock circled away, trying to clear his vision, and took left to the jaw for his trouble. But there was little power behind the blow. Mako was wearing down.

Mako charged like a runaway train. The big man smashed his head into Maddock's chest and slammed him back into the cage. The impact rattled Maddock's teeth. Shrugging it off, he turned Mako against the cage and replied with more punishment to the body. Steroids and meth likely fueled his opponent. The man would feel little pain, but his breath now came in ragged gasps. As Maddock pressed his weight into Mako's chest, the bigger fighter spat out his mouthpiece and tried to bite Maddock's ear. Maddock released his grip and pulled away in time. *They didn't offer me a mouthpiece* He looked at the referee, who shrugged and waved him toward Mako.

From the other side of the cage, he heard Bones shout, "Sweep the leg, Johhny!"

Mako seemed to have gained his second wind. He flew at Maddock in a whirlwind of punches. Most missed or were blocked, but a few landed. Maddock's ears rang and he felt blood trickling down his cheek from a cut near his eye.

The crowd was howling for Maddock's blood. Mako grinned wildly, raised his arms above his head, and stalked toward Maddock, who held his ground. Mako leaned in, leering, and screamed something incomprehensible. He must have forgotten he had lost his mouthpiece because he seemed genuinely surprised when Maddock knocked his front teeth out. He screamed in rage, but Maddock was already on him. A right to the jaw stunned him; a left elbow strike split his forehead; and a right cross turned his legs to rubber.

Maddock couldn't help himself. He held out one hand, palm-up, and blew across the top as Mako collapsed in a heap. There were plenty of cheers, but many more boos. Apparently a lot of people had bet on the champ. In the midst of the chaos, he saw Willis collecting his winnings from disappointed gamblers.

The man in the cheap suit slunk into the cage and pressed a crumpled hundred dollar bill into Maddock's palm.

"You fight again?" The man asked hopefully. "Take on all comers. I give you half."

"No, thanks," Maddock said. "I need another beer and some rest."

"You wait til things calm down."

For a full ten minutes, the pandemonium made Maddock grateful he was safely locked in a cage. Eventually, as bets were settled, Bones and Willis shouldered their way up to the front.

"I leave you alone just once and look what you've gone and done," Bones said as Maddock sat on the steps outside the cage and tugged on his shirt, socks, and shoes.

"Was that really the smart thing to do?" Willis asked. "Not that I mind. You won me some cash." He patted his pocket.

"I didn't have a choice. It was the only way we could hire a boat."

"Yeah," Bones said, "what was that about?"

Just then, Lyn arrived.

"Bones, Willis, meet our captain."

11

Maddock felt the deck rock gently beneath his feet as he stood on board Lyn's boat, *Lark*, at its mooring in Apra Harbor. In the distance, the sparkling blue Philippine Sea danced beneath the Pacific sun

Lark turned out to be a converted LCM-6 landing craft. Twin four-hundred horsepower Detroit Diesels pushed her about twelve knots in good weather. "She was built during World War Two and survived the Battle of Saipan," Lyn said. "These old hulls weren't made for speed, but they can sure take some punishment." Accommodations were Spartan but sufficient. "Plenty of room," Lyn said. "I've got two settees in the cabin and six bunks in the doghouse below. My own crib is up in the wheelhouse where I can keep an eye on things."

Maddock drew on his personal credit to fuel *Lark* and provision her as well, along with ten fifty-five-gallon drums of diesel that nestled just forward of the doghouse. He also sprang for a ridiculous amount of Spam, purchased at Lyn's insistence. She claimed it made for valuable currency in certain remote islands. Sally made sure they had a few luxuries like toilet paper, laundry detergent and bleach. Matt and Willis went over the engines and changed the oil and fuel filters.

Willis crouched in the engine compartment. He wiped his hands on a rag and said, "Damn look at these old monsters. They ought to be in a museum or something."

"We should be in a nut house or something," Matt said, "just for leaving the harbor in this wreck."

It took most of that day to ready *Lark* for sea. A typical landing craft, she had a forward ramp that could be lowered, and a well deck just behind the ramp for cargo. At some time, *Lark* had acquired a cabin and upper level bridge for navigation. Maddock peeked inside. A compact galley and laundry occupied one side of the cabin. To the left, a settee and small dinette provided cramped quarters for eating. Just below the cabin, a portion of the cargo well had been converted into a doghouse with bunks.

Bones and Lyn had left to scour the island for available scuba tanks. Maddock was packing the remainder of their supplies when he noticed a scraggly character watching from the dock. Rail thin with a stubble beard, he could have been thirty, he could have been fifty. The man invited himself onboard and said, "So, you're Lyn's new crew, huh?"

Maddock introduced himself and said, "I didn't know she had a crew."

"That's because you're from off island. You don't know our Lyn. I've crewed her. Lots of guys around here's crewed her. A big hombre like you'll do her just fine. *Ha!* Lyn always likes it when she gets a nice crew."

"I'd tell her you stopped by, but I'm not sure I caught your name."

"Jim, Jungle Jim. Best dive master on the island. You remember the *Concepción* up on Tinian Channel? Well, they took tons of silver and gold off that wreck, and I found it."

Maddock resumed carrying boxes on board. When Jungle Jim showed no sign of leaving, he said, "I'll bet that made you pretty rich, all that gold."

"Not a damn bent penny. I first dove it back in '82 but no one would listen to a kid. Five years later, a bunch of pecker-necks come and grabbed all of it."

Maddock took a different tack. "Say, uh… Jim. Why don't you help me with some of these boxes while we talk?"

"I'd like to, but I've got to run. There's this rich guy what hired me to take him out fishing or something. You be good to Lyn and her *Lark* now. I'm gonna be keeping an eye on you."

Jim had just left when Matt returned with a handful of spare injectors. "We ran these Mike-boats in the Gulf. Blow an injector, and she'll go through fuel like a C-130 on takeoff."

"Where's Willis?"

"Hunting up fuel filters and, check this out, crowbars. That's another staple you better keep handy."

Lyn drove a rusty Toyota pickup. She and Bones showed up a half-hour later. "Look who we found lounging at the hotel," Bones said.

Corey climbed out of the back. "I knew you would come for the Pelican cases sooner or later. Besides, they have decent beer and good wi-fi."

Willis returned shortly toting an oversized cardboard box. He peered in the back of the Toyota and said, "Damn you guys cleaned this place out."

Bones beamed and hooked his thumbs beneath imaginary suspenders. "Twenty high-pressure one-thirty-threes, three thousand pounds of nitrox in each. We're going to Disneyland, boys!"

Maddock caught Lyn as she was stepping on board. "I ran into a friend of yours today. Jungle Jim, he said to say *hi*."

She squinted. "Did you tell him anything?"

"No, he just wanted to talk."

"Well, that little creep is my main competition. He's a hundred and fifty pounds of bad news. Seems he's hooked up with a nasty outfit lately. Hanging around with a bunch of goons—Russian mafia or something, well-funded too." Lyn glanced back at Corey. "So, what's this about Disneyland?"

Maddock didn't want to discuss their entire situation. "A joke. Where we're going when we get rich and all."

"Well, as long as I get my cut."

"Twenty-five percent and a thousand pounds of canned Spam, just like we agreed."

"Who's got a thousand pounds of Spam?" Willis asked.

"We do. Here's Sally coming down the pier with it right now."

As he spoke, Sally arrived on the passenger side of a beat-up Isuzu flatbed. A stack of cardboard boxes rattled around in the back. A local kid drove. Tousled black hair, no taller than Sally, he helped them load the cartons in the forward well. "Looks like another Pagan run, *Mama*. Remember me when you return."

Lyn winked and blew him a kiss. Maddock said, "I think all of Guam must know where we're headed by now. So much for lying low."

Bones nodded. "Let's leave tonight. if we clear the island before sundown, we can make Saipan by daybreak."

Now, with twin diesels rumbling beneath them, Maddock and the others gathered in the cabin to hear

Corey's report. They shared a cramped chart table that doubled as a dinette. Maddock glanced back at the cabin door to make sure they were alone. "Lyn's at the wheel," he said, "and I don't expect her to come down until we're clear of the island. We need to make some plans. Corey, what's the news?"

Their chief information officer bent forward with both elbows on the table. "Not everything is as it seems… it seems. I got into the police records; they don't quite agree with what we've been told." He looked at Sally. "Your uncle's café burned out. Grease fire, they say. A completely different report covers police raids on two buildings adjacent to the café, drug busts. Now get this, nothing in there about police officers down. No shots reported. Nothing about Bones and Sally."

"So, Pym's dirty cops haven't tried to get their colleagues involved," Maddock said. "That's good."

"Why wouldn't they use all the resources at their disposal?" Matt asked.

"Pym must have them doing all sorts," Sally said. "They don't want anyone honest looking too closely at what they're up to." She bit her lip and looked at Corey. "What about my uncle?"

"No word, yet," Corey said. "He's definitely not listed as dead. I'm sorry Sally, I just can't say."

Sally blanched, but kept her expression blank. "Will would lie low and wait. He escaped Vietnam; he's a survivor."

"So, what do we do now?" Matt asked.

"I move we stay with Plan A," Bones said. "There's this *ginormous* treasure out there, we know where it is, and we've got the stuff to get it."

Maddock said, "If we follow through on our plan, it

will keep us out of sight for a while longer. I'd second that motion."

"What about the danger rating?" Matt asked. "You two learned any details about the island?"

Corey shook his head. "Not a thing. It's bizarre. All the reports of shipwrecks around Maug, and there are countless reports, are all secondhand. We couldn't find a single record of a sailor or passenger living to report what had happened. Just tons of last known locations, ports of call where they never appeared. Best guess is there's some crazy currents or weather patterns in the area. But we're in a modern ship." He paused, looked around. "Sort of."

"Nothing at all?" Maddock asked.

"I found records of some archaeologists trying to get funding for an expedition there, but no details. A Japanese outpost from way back. No information on that. Also, a few references to a Mama-Lani."

"Is that like a pina colada?" Bones asked.

"I think she's a native wise woman or storyteller or something. Lyn might know of her."

"We ran off without firepower," Willis said. "What'll we do if the natives get restless?"

Bones grinned. "We toss Sally into a volcano. Isn't that what they do in the movies?"

"I don't think I meet the requisite qualifications if you know what I mean."

"No, I think you should elaborate," Bones said.

Sally made a face. "In your dreams."

"I wouldn't worry," Maddock said, trying to get everyone re-focused. "I checked around earlier; our good captain has a small arsenal up in the wheelhouse. But we should take inventory. Willis, what did you and Matt bring from *Sea Foam*?"

"Oh, man, you've got to see this." Willis dragged one of the Pelican cases to the middle of the cabin and turned the tab-locks. The lid popped open. "We got ourselves a drone." He brandished a device that looked like nothing more than a fat spider. "And, check this. It's got multi-spectrum LIDAR imaging, courtesy of our good buddy, Doc."

Corey bent closer. "This will give us high resolution bottom profiles in a variety of water depths."

Sally said, "Can we import the data? I could run a multi-spectra profile for bottom anomalies."

"Will somebody just get them a room?" Bones said.

Willis grinned. "It's all Greek to me but have at it boys and girls."

Maddock looked in the case. "In all this excitement, did you happen to bring our dive gear?"

"Oh, yeah. Masks, fins, BCs, the works. We got the side scan for bottom profiling, a hundred yards of line for the 'fish,' and our satellite uplink."

Bones said, "I think I saw a few cases of beer come on board; we've got food and a place to sleep. Not much more that I need. I'll just run up to the wheel house and see if Lyn wants some help." With that, he slipped out the cabin door. Maddock heard his tread on the ladder outside.

Shortly after, the cabin lights began a rhythmic flicker. Matt looked up. "We got electrical problems already?"

Maddock grinned and shook his head. "She's switched on the auto-pilot. We won't be hearing much from either of them for a while."

Maddock crashed on the settee; the others chose

bunks in the little doghouse. They passed the island of Rota in the dark before Bones came down and woke his friend. "Want to take a hand at the wheel for a spell?"

"Yeah, you look all tuckered out."

Above, Lyn snored peacefully in a dim cubby behind the helm. Bones showed Maddock the throttles, radar and auto-pilot. "That lever engages and disengages the steering motor. Old-school, but simple as a hand grenade. Keep the engines at eighteen-hundred. Marine radio is on sixteen. Radar works okay, but watch for small boats; they don't appear until you're right on top of them."

Maddock checked their compass heading and paged through a chart book by the red lights of the instrument panel. The radar screen showed Rota about five miles astern. He flicked it back to a two-mile range. Nothing visible. They'd pass the island of Tinian at sunup.

As his eyes adjusted to the darkness, Maddock made out more detail on the water's surface. A long swell followed them from the south, noticeable, but not uncomfortable. Far to the west, thunderheads flashed on the horizon. He wouldn't be surprised if they passed through a rain squall before reaching Saipan.

After a few hours at watch, the following sea strengthened, and the auto-pilot struggled to keep their course. He disengaged the drive and turned it off, taking the wheel himself. *Lark* was not the most sea-kindly craft and clearly did not behave well with the waves off her stern. Maddock settled into the rhythm of cutting slightly east at the trough, then correcting west as the wave rose up behind them. The night passed quickly, and as the island of Tinian crept onto the radar screen, the sea settled back to a gentle roll.

He didn't hear Lyn get up but felt the woman's hand on his shoulder. "We could put *Lark* on auto-pilot for a while…"

Maddock glanced over. Intimately close, her high cheekbones and generous mouth glowed in the red instrument lights. He grinned. "I'm afraid I'm spoken for, so let's keep this professional." That wasn't exactly true. He and his fiancée, Angel, were broken up at the moment. He'd briefly had another woman in his life, but she'd given him the shaft and gone over to an organization that had tried to kill him.

"As you wish. Let me take the wheel then. You can crash in my cubby until we reach Saipan."

Maddock did feel tired. He rolled into her bunk and drifted off to the grumbling engines, and the gentle roll of the waves.

12

Sally awoke when *Lark's* diesels wound down to a low murmur and she felt the surge as their wake overtook them. A gleam from the portlight above told her that the sun was up, and they must be nearing Saipan Harbor. Matt and Willis still slept. She climbed up to the cabin and found Bonebrake sprawled on the settee like a hunting dog returned from the chase. She paused to admire his sleeping form. She wasn't into him, but there was no denying he cut a fine figure.

She slipped out the door and paused on the aft deck. No rail stood between her and the glittering water. So casually dangerous, here where everyone simply took responsibility for their own safety. With a shrug, she climbed the steep ladder and stepped into the wheelhouse.

Lyn stood at the helm, while Corey fiddled with some piece of equipment. From the high vantage they could see all of Saipan rise in rolling green hills before them. A row of hotels stood at the water's edge, their guests still sleeping off a day of swimming, gambling, and lounging in the sun. Sally wondered which world was truly hers: comfort and safety, or hazard and excitement?

Movement behind her. She turned to see Maddock rise from a tiny cubby and rub his eyes. "Maddock? You spent the night up here too?"

"Yeah." He rubbed his face. "Bones got tired, so I

took over for him."

Lyn grinned like a well-fed tiger. Sally shook her head. "I'm sure you both got a good workout."

Maddock's eyes went wide and he gave a quick shake of his head. Sally had to laugh. Finally, he forced a smile and said, "I guess each in our own way, we did."

As they rounded the outer buoy, Lyn pulled the throttles back a notch and let their momentum carry them into the harbor. The radio squawked, and she responded with a few words. Corey looked up from his tinkering. "You'll need a new antenna before this GPS will work."

"We'll tie to the fuel dock and top off our tanks. But I don't want to spend any more time here than we have to. If you can get it in an hour, great. Otherwise, the Love Boat sails without you."

Maddock said, "I'll go handle the lines."

Corey followed, saying something about coffee and breakfast. Sally stood at the bridge, suddenly awkward, watching Lyn's expert control of engines and rudder. "You must do this a lot. I mean, two powerful motors. How long have you done it?"

"As long as I can remember. Come here, take the wheel and I'll give you some pointers."

Lyn insisted when Sally demurred. Reluctantly, she took the stainless-steel helm in hand as the tall woman stood behind her. "Now we're going to dock right there where that guy is standing. The trick is to come in with a little momentum, then play the engines against each other. Port, starboard, back and forth, let them do the work."

Lyn took Sally's right hand and placed it on the smooth throttle levers. "Now reverse starboard like this and wheel over. Now reverse port."

Sally felt like a little kid again steering the family car from her father's lap. Behind her, Lyn instructed her, and soon she felt like she was getting the hang of it.

"Now throttle in neutral and wait," Lyn said.

They bumped the dock a bit too hard and Lyn crashed into her.

"Crap," Sally said.

"That was your first time, wasn't it?" She winked. "I mean, docking, of course."

"Great. I'm surrounded by jokers."

Lyn cocked her head to one side, and to her credit, didn't smirk much. "In all seriousness, you did well. You've got the moves. We'll keep practicing. You'll get your turn at the wheel."

Down below Sally could see Bonebrake securing the lines. Maddock stood on the pier arguing with someone. Moments later, he was in the wheelhouse. "We've got a problem. Seems that *Lark* slipped out of here without paying her fuel bill a few months ago. Now I've got to pay in full, and in cash. That wasn't part of our deal."

Lyn said, "Okay, deduct it from my share of the treasure. You're the one who figured I was broke. Why are you surprised?"

"Twenty percent. You're down to twenty percent or we take our thousand pounds of Spam and leave right now."

Sally made a face. "Do you know how ridiculous you both sound?"

"You are a hard man, Dane Maddock." Lyn pursed her lips and eyed him intently. "Someday maybe I'll find out how hard."

Maddock ignored the innuendo. "It's a couple of

grand, I can't get that much from an ATM and it's two hours before the banks open. I'll get some cash then, but we won't be out of here before noon."

Corey said, "There's a marine supplies shop just up the road. I'll go pick up the GPS antenna."

"Just don't mention who it's for," Maddock said. "I don't want to be paying off half the island."

Lyn nodded. "Probably a good idea. I'll talk to the dock-master up there and tell him he'll get paid if he keeps his mouth shut. Oh, and don't mention to anyone where we're going. Special permits and everything. We just don't need the hassle."

Sally didn't feel like hanging around. "I feel like stretching my legs. Mind if I come along with you into town?"

They managed to flag a cab just outside the port gates and headed for Garapan, the main tourist center. Sally noticed that most of the people she saw were more of her own stature, and closer to her own complexion. The cabby explained. "We are *Chamorro*, the original inhabitants. My ancestors lived on these islands for thousands of years before the Spanish came. After that, the Germans, then the Japanese, and now the Americans. In a thousand years, we'll still be here. I wonder about everyone else though."

He pointed out the bank building. As they entered town and dropped them both off near the casinos. Garapan looked to Sally like any other small island town. Clustered about the hotels and casinos, it had a shopping nucleus at the center and commercial districts on the perimeter. The bank was not yet open so Sally suggested a walk on the beach.

They passed several early-risers, hotel staff mostly,

and found themselves on a deserted beach. Sally took off her shoes and dug her toes in the sand. "I guess you and Bonebrake are used to this sort of atmosphere."

Maddock maintained his usual quiet manner. "Yeah. We see a lot of sand and saltwater."

She watched him from the corner of her eye. For a man with such a dangerous background and risky career, the man seemed oddly introverted. A young jogger passed them. Tall, blond, high cheekbones, she looked Slavic, probably Russian. Sally watched Maddock watch the ponytail as it bobbed by. He turned and grinned at her. "Go put your foot in the water."

"Why?"

"Just do it."

She walked to the water's edge and waded out. "My god, it's warm... like a bath."

"Takes some getting used to. Come on, let's go walk through town, what there is of it."

They passed a variety of restaurants and outlet stores. Sally peered at designer purses on display. "They're good, mostly fakes... but look at those prices; I could find cheaper stuff in New York City."

Maddock walked along looking at the upper floors. "Interesting, this one is a Chinese brothel, and across the street it looks like a Russian brothel, but there's no Japanese establishment anywhere."

"It's here, you just won't see it, sailor. They're far more discreet."

Maddock checked his cell phone. "We've got time for a cup of coffee," he said. "Maybe we should take our last good meal before we leave civilization."

Just down from hotel row they found an espresso bar with outside tables and home-baked pastries. Sally ordered a cinnamon roll and a cappuccino. The roll was huge, and she could swear it was still warm. The cappuccino was served in a proper white bowl with just the right touch of foam. She settled back and watched Maddock gulp his Americano.

"So, what's your friend's deal? In terms of relationships, I mean."

The man checked his phone again. *Umpteenth time,* Sally thought, *worse than some New Yorkers.*

"He's a good guy, but he changes girls like some people change underwear."

A pang of disappointment washed over Sally. "Really? He doesn't seem the type."

Maddock looked up. "Really? He's just so… in your face with his flirting I didn't think it was possible to miss."

Sally understood. "Not Bones. Corey! What's his deal? Has he got some cute cosplayer back home? Tell me he doesn't live in Mom's basement."

Maddock laughed, shook his head. "No. He's got his own place. Doesn't date much. Too shy."

Sally nodded. *Challenge accepted.*

At straight up ten, the bank doors opened, and Sally followed Maddock inside. He spoke at the counter for a while. The teller shook her head. Maddock spoke again, and the teller glanced at a security guard.

"Come on, Sally. We've got bigger problems than I thought." Maddock was out the door before she could react. She caught up with him at the curb. "Quick! This way. Don't run, and don't look back."

Sally followed across the street, through a parking lot, and around behind a two-story apartment. Maddock grabbed her arm and pushed her toward a flight of stairs.

"Up, up."

Quick footsteps in the alley, and the security guard stepped out just as someone peeled away from the curb and swerved into the morning traffic. He paused to write something on a pad and walk back to the bank.

Maddock shook his head. "Someone has frozen my account and put a fraud alert out on withdrawals."

"They'll know we were here," Sally said. "We've got to leave now."

"Can't do it. Not without fuel. Say, you wouldn't happen to have a spare thousand or two, would you? I'll cut you in for Lyn's five percent."

"Not a chance, sailor boy."

"Well, I know my guys don't have it."

"I've got an idea. Something I haven't done in a while but I'm pretty good at it." She paused, enjoying the bemused expression on Maddock's face. "You've got to ask yourself one question: *Do I feel lucky?*"

"All right, Dirty Harry, what's the plan?"

"Just stroll toward the casino. I'll catch up."

To her surprise, Maddock didn't argue. It was nice to have trust placed in her from time to time. Of course, if he knew what she was up to, he might not be so trusting.

She wandered into a nearby gift shop and began to browse, letting her eyes sweep across the rows of kitschy souvenirs and gifts. The cashier was an inattentive young woman who had eyes only for the screen of her smart phone. In no time Sally had swiped a cap and two sets of fake prescription glasses. She paid for a pack of breath mints, but only because the cashier's purse was sitting open next to the register and it gave Sally the opportunity to swipe her wallet. Sally tried to engage the cashier in polite conversation, but the girl pointedly turned her back and returned to her phone, which was reason enough, Sally determined, to help herself to a knockoff *PINK*-brand shirt.

Maddock didn't recognize her when she caught up to him at the Island Girl Hotel and Casino.

"How do I look?" she asked, turning around for him to admire her change in appearance.

"I like the glasses, but the girly shirt and hat make you look younger and frankly kind of bubble-headed. I prefer the brainy version."

She resisted the urge to ask which version Corey preferred.

"So, what's the plan?"

"Here, you take this." She handed him the cash she'd taken from the cashier's wallet. "Go inside and play a few games until I catch up with you. And you need a disguise." She tousled his hair and handed him a pair of John Lennon glasses.

"Where did you get all this?"

"I've lived on the streets at times, and I've developed a few skills. Don't worry about it. The credit card company will cover the losses," she waggled a purloined card, "and I've got a plan for returning the wallet with the cash. Just play along."

Maddock shook his head. "I thought I was leaving the criminal element back on the boat when I didn't bring Bones along. But all right. I don't see that we have much choice."

As he turned to head for the casino, he warned, "Keep your eyes peeled. The guard from the bank is wandering around with two other guys. Whatever you've got in mind, it better be quick."

"Then quit talking and start gambling."

As Maddock wandered over to the slots, she walked up to the cashier's cage, giggling and winking at the old man behind the counter. "I don't know how much I have left on my card," she said.

"How much you need?" the man asked.

"Three thousand," she said. It was a gamble. She had no idea how much available credit the woman might have. "All black chips."

The man swiped the card and shook his head. "Declined."

"I'm so sorry. I might have brought the wrong card. Can you try it again for two thousand?" She hated the faux-sweet persona she'd adopted, but it was working on the old man.

"No problem, sweetie." He swiped the card again. This time, he smiled. "All good."

Sally accepted the chips, then slipped quietly into the crowd. She first headed for a nearby gift shop where she purchased a few small items, mainly because she wanted the gift bag. Back at the casino, she caught sight of Maddock, still at the slots. Hopefully that would keep him busy for a while. Not wanting to be spotted together, she wandered the floor for a while. Most of the men paused to check her out, but a few creepers, older white guys, American to a man, called out invitations to join them, calling out lewd invitations and asking if she wanted a daddy. These were the men to whom she paid the most attention, as she was more than happy to relieve them of cash and chips.

"Go back to the 1970s, you creeper," she muttered as she sashayed away from the last man, who had told her one too many times that she reminded him of his niece. He was now $100 lighter, but given his drunken state, he was unlikely to miss a few twenties from the wad of cash he'd tucked into his pocket.

She texted Maddock to check his whereabouts. He replied that he'd won $200 at the slots and was now running it up at the blackjack table.

Sally grinned. He didn't know his gambling was a mere distraction. Why not let him have his fun, at least for a little while? She sat down at a slot machine and watched Maddock play a few hands. Maddock was steadily gaining. As Sally watched, he doubled-down on a pair of eights with four hundred dollars riding on each card. A small crowd gathered to watch the action. He tipped the dealer with a chip and she hit him with a nine and a seven. He waved her off. She hit out the old woman next to him, then turned a king to her own five and hit herself out with another king. The crowd let out a collective sigh. Maddock pulled his winnings over to him, tipped her once more, and stacked four more chips on the table.

Sally looked around the casino. From the corner of her eye, she saw three bulky men cruising through a bank of slot machines, headed in the direction of the blackjack tables.

She sent Maddock another text. *Bank guard and friends are here. Need to act fast. I'm at your five o'clock. Don't acknowledge, just grab the gift bag next to my seat, and go cash out.*

Maddock replied with a thumbs-up. A minute later, he strode past her and scooped up the gift bag. She heard his grunt of surprise when he felt its weight and realized what was inside.

These dummies think of me as a little girl. Maybe they'll finally change their minds.

She met him a short distance away a few minutes later. Maddock was grinning from ear to ear.

"How did you manage it?" He grimaced as she explained what she'd done. "So, we basically stole it from that cashier."

"No, a bunch of it was stolen from drunken perverts. And don't worry about the cashier. She'll report the card stolen and get the charges reimbursed. Actually, give me $200." He handed over the cash and she tucked it into the girl's wallet. "Now she'll actually come out a little bit ahead." She handed the wallet to Maddock.

"What's this for?"

"One last bit of stealth. Go back to that t-shirt shop and drop this into the girl's purse."

"What if she sees me?"

Sally laughed. "You were a Navy SEAL and you're worried about being spotted by a shop clerk?"

Maddock smiled. "Point taken. I won't be a minute. Stay close and keep an eye out for the Russians." He turned and melted into the crowd.

Sally followed him, or at least, headed in the same direction. The man actually could vanish when he had a mind to. The t-shirt shop was just ahead, so she moved off to the side and kept an eye on the front door.

She smelled him a second before he grabbed her roughly by the arm. Cheap cologne, the kind that stung your eyes and burned your nostrils. She was already in motion when he grabbed her.

Sally spun in the direction in which he pulled, adding the momentum to the force of her blow. She drove her elbow into the jaw of the man she recognized as one of the bank guard's cronies. The blow snapped his head to the side and he spat a curse.

"Su-ka!"

Living in an international city, she'd been called a bitch in many languages, including Russian, so the word was familiar. She clawed at his eyes, but he turned his head and her nails raked his shaven scalp. She followed with a knee aimed for the groin that he blocked with his hip. Sally tried to jerk away, but she could not break the grip he had on her arm. God, the man was strong!

She landed a side-kick to the knee, which actually made him wince, but it wasn't strong enough to do serious damage. She balled her fist but froze when she realized he was smiling down at her. He wasn't threatened by her. He found her amusing?

"Oh, hell no," she hissed.

The man frowned and then…

A fist struck him in the temple with a splat like raw meat hitting the counter. Her assailant collapsed.

"You all right?" Maddock asked, rubbing his fist.

"I was just getting started."

"No sign of his friends?"

Sally shook her head.

"Good, let's get the hell out of here."

They made their way back to *Lark* without catching sight of the Russians. She kept a lookout as they topped off her tanks and Maddock recounted the story of their exploits.

"I'm telling you, it was all her," Maddock told the other crew members.

"Doesn't surprise me," Corey said.

Sally hated that her heart skipped a beat when he said that. What she hated even more was how Maddock's approval warmed her heart. She was beginning to feel like part of a team. That wasn't her.

When they were finally back on the water, Corey wandered up.

"Hey, I was wondering if you'd like to go over some of the treasure data together."

"Look, I'm not one of your crew, or whatever you guys are. You can handle it yourself."

Not quite sure who she was angry with, Sally turned on her heel and stalked away.

13

"So, Pym is on to us." Bones cracked his knuckles as he gazed out at the water. "That is not what we needed."

Lyn stared at the compass a moment, waited for the needle to come to rest, then pulled in the auto-pilot. Without looking up, she said, "Who the hell *is* Pym?"

Bones said, "A minor complication we ran into back in the States."

Sally snorted and rolled her eyes. "She needs to know. She's in on this now."

"In on what?" Lyn demanded. "I was hired for a job; not to stick my nose into the middle of trouble."

"We didn't do anything wrong," Sally said. "Pym's a businessman who really wants to steal my invention."

"Invention? Do you have it here with you?"

"It's not that kind of invention."

Lyn turned her attention to the gauges, bumped the port engine up a few revs, then said, "Okay, we're clear of Saipan. I think we can spare a few minutes to clear the air. Fill me in on the details."

As Sally explained the situation, Lyn's cheeks grew redder, her expression darkened. When Sally had finished, Lyn gave her head a shake. "You should have told me. I'd have taken the job anyway, but you still should have told me."

"Fair enough," Maddock said.

Lyn cocked her head. "Speaking of details, you've been vague about where you want to go after Pagan. I know you want to search for treasure in the area. Where, specifically?"

"You're taking us to a nearby island called Maug," Maddock said.

Lyn's face blanched and she took a step back.

"The hell I am! You can all swim there. But I'm not going."

Maddock said, "That was the deal. We'd finance your little trip to Pagan and cut you in on a quarter of our find. But you had to provide the transportation for our dives. You agreed to it."

"Because I never dreamed you were talking about Maug. It's cursed, dangerous. A lot of dumb people have gone to Maug and never come back."

"And that's why there's still something left to find." Maddock caught himself leaning forward. He straightened and said, "So tell me, say we don't go, and you return to Guam just as broke as the day you left. What then? How long before the marshal seizes *Lark* and sells her at auction?"

"And what makes you so sure there's something on Maug worth risking our lives for?"

Maddock looked at Sally who grimaced, then nodded.

"It's not easy to explain," she began. "We have done extensive research that suggests there have been multiple disappearances of ships laden with treasure around Maug or in the immediate vicinity."

"Exactly! Disappearances! I don't want to be another one."

"We're talking old-school stuff," Maddock said. "Wooden sailing vessels."

"I don't like it," Lyn said. "Did your research suggest

what dangers might be waiting there? I mean, there's got to be a reason no one goes there or likes to even speak about it."

"Not a thing," Sally said. "Not a single myth or legend. Just a whole lot of treasure." She said the last bit slowly.

Lyn nodded. Obviously coming around.

"The only thing even close to a story I could find associated with Maug was the name Mama-Lani. Does that mean anything to you?"

Lyn nodded. "I know of her. She lives on Pagan, which just happens to be the first stop I need to make. Tell you what. You talk to her and after that you still want to go, I'll take you. But now I want fifty percent."

"Twenty five percent. That was our original deal. I'll pitch in the fuel."

"Not one iota less than thirty."

Maddock nodded and held out his hand. "Deal. Thirty percent."

They shook on it.

"Dane Maddock," Lyn said, "you'd better not get me killed."

The Pagan run proved to be a day and a half of slogging into a strong northwest swell. *Lark* rode up on the waves, then plunged into the troughs, sending sheets of spray from her flat bow-ramp. The forward cargo well was self-draining, but sometimes it would take on so much water that the little ship rolled dangerously with every wave. Lyn had to constantly throttle back and let the well drain before proceeding.

"Why don't we just sink with all that water?" Sally

asked.

Lyn explained that *Lark* had flotation tanks along the sides and a double bottom under her well. "She won't sink, but too much water makes her unstable. I'd hate to roll over."

That night, Bones, Maddock, and Matt took turns at the wheel. Lyn would get up at times to check their position and watch a chain of small islands pass on the radar screen. "They are all volcanos, you know. Even Pagan is a big old volcano and it smokes and belches sometimes. Wiped out the only airstrip a few years ago. Still, some of my boys hang out there." She grinned. "Don't ask me why."

"Honestly, I don't want to know," Maddock said. "Just let's not linger. The further we get from Saipan, the better I'll feel."

A series of tropical rain squalls passed the next morning, and the wind swung around from the south. Sally entertained them all by subjecting them to her questionnaire, then entering the responses into a new program she was developing that was supposed to predict their future love lives. Lyn, she proclaimed, would marry a man of the sea and live out her life in the islands. Willis had a girl waiting for him, but he would have to search for her, whatever that means."

"Is there a girl waiting for me?" Matt asked.

"There's someone waiting for you, but I didn't say it was a girl."

Matt spewed a mouthful of beer onto the deck. "Wait, what? I mean, it's not like it matters but does your computer really think I'm gay?"

"No, it just chose not to predict the gender of your future partner," Sally said.

Bones reached over and clapped Matt on the shoulder. "Just make sure he's not Army or Air Force." He paused. "Or Marines, for that matter. I might could stomach Coast Guard, but he'll have to wear a life preserver at all times."

Matt laughed. "Funny. But seriously, I mean, I hooked up with your sister…"

The silence that fell over the group was sharp and sudden. Corey and Willis appeared shocked. Matt wouldn't meet Maddock's eye. Neither would Bones.

Lyn reached out and took Sally by the hand. "I think we should give these guys some privacy." The two hurried away, leaving the four men sitting in silence.

Maddock felt as if he were encased in a soundproof booth. No, not soundproof. A dull roar was building in his ears. The back of his neck itched, and his ears burned. He tried to speak, but his throat was suddenly dry.

"I'm sorry, Maddock," Matt said. "I made them promise to let me tell you myself, but then Isla screwed you over in Madagascar and that really wasn't the time. And by the time it felt okay to tell you, it had been way too long. And it was just one time."

Maddock turned to Bones, who hung his head. "Sorry, man. Angel made me swear and Matt kept promising he'd tell you."

Maddock felt numb all over. As if the world around him wasn't quite real. One of his oldest, closest friends… and his fiancé, make that his ex… And his best friend kept the secret? What the hell was he supposed to say about all of that?

"I don't think it's a good idea for me to talk to you right now," he said to Matt. "Either of you," he added for

Bones' benefit. "Just stay out of my face."

The men gave him a wide berth for the rest of the day. The women were quite the opposite. Sally gave him a hug, which was more affection than he'd thought the young woman capable of, and Lyn actually managed an entire conversation with him without hitting on him, which he found disappointing at the moment.

Pagan appeared as an orange blob on the radar about midnight. By three in the morning, it dominated half the screen. Maddock was on helm duty. He pulled the throttles back and disengaged the auto-pilot. Lyn appeared beside him wearing a short kimono, open to reveal ample cleavage.

"Looks like we've got a little time till daybreak. Want to get back at your ex?"

Maddock actually considered it, but deep down he knew it was a bad idea.

"We're about five miles offshore. According to the GPS, our destination is three more miles up the coast. So, probably not enough time to do it justice."

"That's way more time than you need, Maddock." Bones eased his bulk through the wheelhouse door, carrying two mugs of coffee. "Sorry, didn't know you were here," he said to Lyn.

"And yet you brought me a cuppa anyway," she exclaimed, taking the cop from his hands.

Maddock waved away the cup Bones offered him, even though the rich aroma called to him like a siren's song. It wasn't often that Bones felt genuine contrition for any extended length of time, but when he did, he was tractable and rarely argued. Might as well take advantage of it while he could. Besides, Maddock was still pissed.

Lyn took a sip, closed her eyes, and let out a moan filled with possibilities. "Coffee, hot and dark. Not heaven, but the closest you're likely to get,"

Daylight arrived as a pink glow that outlined a conical mountain. It steamed in the morning air. Lyn, now fully dressed, guided *Lark* into a small cove. They dropped an anchor off the stern on their way in. Bones paid out line as *Lark* grounded against a beach of coarse black sand. Willis and Matt scrambled to the bow and lowered the ramp, spinning the winch handles that planted the steel plate firmly on the shore.

"My boys won't be up yet," Lyn said, "so stay with the boat while I go roust them. We don't want anyone getting too jumpy and grabbing guns right now."

Maddock walked down the beach and watched the sunlight bathe the mountainside above him. A faint southerly breeze just barely trembled palm fronds inland. It brought the moist, fecund jungle aroma of Pagan with it. When he returned to the boat, four grinning Chamorro men stood next to Lyn like acolytes guarding their priestess. "Welcome to paradise," she said.

Bones swung his large frame down into the cargo well and stepped off the bow-ramp. Hand out, smiling, he introduced everyone around. Maddock noted with approval that his friend had pushed the Glock into the back of his pants and pulled his shirt down over it.

In turn, Maddock introduced himself and said, "Let's not get too sociable. They need to unload their Spam, so we can get out of here."

Lyn pointed out that he had agreed to meet someone on the island. Maddock nodded. "Willis, you supervise.

Nothing leaves that isn't in one of those sealed cartons. Matt, take a look at that port engine, it didn't sound quite right as we came in."

Corey said, "I'll see if I can get that uplink working. It would be nice to hear from civilization again."

Lyn spoke with one of her Chamorro "boys." He shook his head and pointed at Sally. They argued for a minute, then she said, "Javier claims that Mama Lani will only talk to a girl, or a young woman." She grimaced. "I guess I don't qualify. Sally goes with us."

Sally nodded and brushed the hair away from one eye. "I was going anyway."

Maddock took stock of their party. Likely more of Lyn's "boys" remained out of sight, watching, rifles trained. The whole program stunk of "setup." Still, they weren't going to leave without visiting this Lani character. Matt brought out a worn rucksack. "Water, first aid kit, bug repellant."

Maddock shrugged the pack over his shoulders. "Lead on then, Javier. The sooner we do this, the sooner we're out of here. Sally, follow Lyn. Bones, you take the rear."

"That's what she said."

"Just don't today." Maddock snapped. "All right?"

"Yeah."

Their guide led them up the volcano by a steep path that wound north along its flank. They crossed a grassy clearing and passed the immense decaying carcass of a World War II era B-29. Farther ahead, jungle and brush gave way to a hillside of broken lava rock. Lizards scrambled across the red boulders and disappeared into a thousand crevices as they approached.

The sun climbed higher and Maddock felt the sweat

soak his back between his shirt and pack. Finally, Javier called a halt. Shaggy black hair, army surplus shirt, he didn't stand much taller than Sally. Maddock passed him a water bottle. "How much further?"

Their guide grinned. "We are here. Mama Lani awaits."

Here turned out to be a deep depression in the hillside. Javier scrambled over the rocks, hung by his hands, and dropped a few feet. Lyn helped Sally down, lowering her by her arms. She followed, along with Maddock. He saw Bones' dusty shoes dangle for a moment before his friend thumped down on a patch of packed earth.

"Lava tube," Lyn said. "This island is riddled with them."

Maddock peered into the gaping black tunnel before him. It exhaled a cool breeze that smelled vaguely like a burnt match. "We didn't bring flashlights."

"Mama Lani does not allow electric light," Javier said. He picked up a torch and lit it with a disposable lighter. "There is oil enough for twenty minutes. You must return before that time."

Maddock said, "You're not coming with us?"

"Mama Lani will speak with the girl. She may allow you to listen, but she does not love me." Javier laughed and continued, "I will wait here for your return."

Bones said, "That's one fussy mama. Why is she so special?"

Lyn pointed at the torch. "Just shut up and go, big guy. I'll explain when we have time."

Maddock took the light and nodded to Bones. His friend made a quick sign with his hands in return. *I'll cover our back.*

The four of them followed a faint path into the darkness. As for illumination, the torch served more as a beacon than a light. Maddock picked up only shadows and vague outlines ahead. The lava tube was shaped roughly like a flattened ellipse with some areas of breakdown that nearly filled the chamber. He pushed the guttering torch ahead of him as they crawled past the latest obstruction. Bones caught up with the group shortly after and said, "Lyn, how well do you know these 'boys' of yours?"

Maddock couldn't read her expression by the flickering light, but he heard the hesitation in her voice when she replied. "They are business partners, of a sort. Most of them are wanted on one charge or another in the southern islands. I bring them supplies and they give me, um… merchandise in return."

Bones said, "If I wanted to rig a kill-chamber, that pit back there would be ideal."

"One problem at a time," Maddock said. "How much further, Lyn?"

"I don't know, I've never actually seen Mama Lani. But she is a legend all over the islands."

Sally said, "We are totally screwed. There's nothing in here but bats and idiots, and only the bats know it."

"We play this out." Maddock said. "Let's move on."

The tube climbed from there, matching the slope of the volcanic cone that spawned it. The trail they followed cut between fallen boulders and zig-zagged where the ground grew steepest. "Someone has come this way," Lyn said. "And look, I think I see light up above."

Maddock saw it too. He scrambled up a boulder and stepped into a dim chamber. Bones stopped to boost Sally over the same rock. "Watch your hands,

Bonehead," she said in response.

Walls of broken rock rose vertically to converge on a glowing mass of green vegetation. Over a hundred feet of ferns and dripping stone walls separated them from the surface. Water filled a basin on their left and gurgled away down a crevice, finding its own path to the sea.

The others joined him, staring in awe at the towering chamber before them. "It's like a cathedral," Sally said.

A that moment, a flock of birds burst from the far side, circled over their heads and shot through the opening far above. A thin, reedy voice said, "Who seeks the Mama Lani?"

14

Bones had known boredom many times in his life, but sitting and watching somebody sit in front of somebody had to top the list. And Sally had been sitting before the old crone for a long time. Of course, it wasn't entirely her fault. Any moment of inaction was a moment for Bones to feel guilty about keeping Angel's story… Matt's secret… from Maddock. Hell, Maddock was his brother in all but blood, but Angel was his sister, and Matt one of his best friends. It had been a no-win situation so he'd trusted his gut. Screw Maddock if he didn't get that.

Tired of exploring his feminine side, Bones refocused on Sally. He watched her shift and fidget on the stone slab in what seemed to be Mama Lani's home. At a distance the old woman looked strange, featureless.

Lyn leaned over and whispered in his ear. "Think we could get Sally to hurry up?"

Bones shrugged. He gazed at the fern-covered walls around him. A pile of broken rock climbed almost twenty feet up the opposite wall. A little higher, a fracture line angled up one side.

Lyn nudged him in the ribs. "Your boss wants us."

"Come on," Maddock called. "Sally is waving us over."

The three scrambled up on the stone slab and sat a respectful distance from the old woman. Even up close, she resembled nothing more than a tree root, or some grotesque stalagmite all covered in dirt and moss. Sally said, "Mama Lani is tired, but she's told me some things that you need to know."

The old woman raised a withered finger and pointed it at Maddock. "You, Dane Maddock, are known to the Ma'óghe, the Eternal One. You have meddled in so many things of this earth, and not of this earth. Now you come to disturb its slumber, and I wonder why." She next waved at Lyn. "And you, daughter of the wind, priestess of chaos, you know better than to seek the Ma'óghe, yet still you come."

Mama Lani shifted where she sat. Bits of earth tumbled from her back in a miniature landslide. She glared at Bones. "Of you, I have no good words. You were charged with the care of this child, and now you have dragged her into a storm of treachery that none will survive. How does that make you feel?"

Child? Sally mouthed, frowning.

Bones started to answer, but Mama Lani raised her hand. "Say nothing. I will pronounce your fate and then you must depart. Through this girl, I have read your hearts. In there, I see nothing but blind determination and stubborn will. I cannot change your minds, but I can tell you this, the Ma'óghe will test you, it will judge you, and that judgement will be your doom. Now go and do not return."

Sally wobbled to her feet; Bones put a protective arm over her shoulder. "Come on, I don't think she likes us very much."

Maddock dropped off the edge of the slab and turned to help Sally down. Bones jumped off beside her. Lyn said, "Hey! What about me?"

Bones held out his arms. "Take a leap of faith."

Sally said, "...Only in the leap from the lion's head

will he prove his worth..."

Lyn hopped down. "Yeah, I saw *The Last Crusade*, too. The girl died. It wasn't pretty."

Maddock said, "Okay, we listened to Mama Lani. She wants us to go see her Ma'óghe, her Eternal One. Any ideas what we do next?"

"Well, I do not like the idea of walking back out the front door," Lyn said.

Their torches had burned out shortly before they reached Mama Lani, meaning they had no light with which to safely find their way back. The man who had told them they had twenty minutes' worth of oil had either made a huge mistake, or he had lied.

"Even if we managed to scramble down in the dark, there are too many nasty things that could happen if we return to that pit."

"There's another way out," Bones said. He looked up.

Sally and Lyn spoke in unison. "You're kidding."

"He's not," Maddock said. "I think it's climbable." He shrugged the pack off his back. "Everybody, drink some water. We'll refill the bottles at the top." Maddock unbuckled the straps and loosened them. "Sally, you'll wear this."

"And the empty water bottles will cushion my impact, I'm sure." She glared at him between strands of hair.

"No impact, you're not going to fall." Maddock crossed the straps over her chest, pulled them tight, and tied the ends across her stomach. "It's not a proper climbing harness, but we'll make it do."

Bones watched the process. "I get it. I'll be her skyhook if she needs one. I've seen her climbing around in abandoned buildings. She can handle it."

"You're forgetting someone," Lyn said.

"Nope, I'm counting on you to lead," Maddock said. "You've got the reach and I'll be right behind to help."

She rolled her eyes. "And they say that chivalry is dead."

Bones looked over his planned ascent route again. The first ledge should be easy. They'd have to traverse around to pick up a vertical crevice. About fifty feet up, it crossed the fracture line he'd noted earlier. Things could get tricky after that. He craned his head back. There might be a bit of an overhang near the top.

Lyn worried him. She was Maddock's concern on the climb, yeah, but Bones had chosen the route. He went over it again. Too many unknowns; a climbing instructor would be insane to drag a novice up that wall. Free climbing, too. But the alternative was more dangerous. He kicked himself for not carrying a MagLite, as usual, but he hadn't thought he'd need it on his trip to New York. He turned to Maddock and saw the look of determination in his friend's eyes. Maddock got stubborn and a little reckless when he was angry. He'd insist on making the climb. Bones shrugged.

"Last one to the top has to bunk with Willis after he's eaten chili."

Lyn headed up the talus slope. Loose rock rattled down as she climbed. "Call it out if something falls," Bones said. "It's bad enough we don't have helmets."

Lyn worked her way out onto the ledge. "This sure isn't National Park Service standard."

Maddock followed a few feet behind. "Just concentrate on your handholds. Move one limb at a time, foot, hand, foot, hand. Whatever you do, don't use your knees."

Bones watched Lyn creep along. *She certainly had the reach*, he thought, *but that tremor in her left leg didn't look good.* He waited until Sally had climbed the talus slope before starting up. She followed Maddock out onto the narrow shelf of rock. And Bones stayed right behind her. *Could he grab quick enough if she slipped?*

Sally closed the gap between herself and Maddock. As Bones suspected, her urban adventures had prepared her well for climbing. Lyn wasn't saying much. She usually would have had some smart remark by now. He hoped that his friend noticed as well. They all concentrated on finding handholds and staying on the ledge. Maddock was speaking to Lyn in a soft voice. Bones heard a few words about the next move, where to put her feet. Then he said, "Stop looking down, Lyn. It's only going to get worse."

As they neared the vertical fissure, Maddock said, "Just keep moving. We'll take a break at the top."

Sally stopped as Maddock wrapped his left arm around Lyn and bunched a fist in the crevice. "Now you reach up and do the same, if you can't find a hold, just wedge your fist between the rocks." He guided her left foot into the crevice. "Same move, jam your foot in there, get some traction, and up. Right hand, right hand… there you go. Now right foot and up."

Bones signaled Sally to wait. Lyn made about fifteen feet up the wall before her foot slipped. She slid back into Maddock. They clung there for a moment, then he said, "Get another grip, put your foot on my shoulder, now I can't stay here forever, so keep climbing."

Maddock's soft even tones, better than any threats or banter, kept the woman climbing. Bones figured they were over thirty feet up the crevice when Lyn froze. Looking up he saw her left leg spasming up and down like she was riding a tricycle.

"What's happening?" Sally asked.

"Sewing machine. It happens. Even experienced climbers get freaked sometimes."

"Lyn's scared?"

"Hell, I'm scared. I've never lost anyone on a climb and I don't want to start here."

After a few moments, he saw Maddock put a hand on Lyn's leg. His friend said a few words. He saw her look up, reach, pull, scramble, and reach again. "Come on girl, you're next," Bones said. He gripped the crevice with one hand and reached the other behind Sally, hoisting her up shoulder high. She stretched as far as she could, took hold of the rock and pulled herself up. Bones stayed right behind her.

Sally managed to scale the fissure with little trouble. As they both neared the top, Maddock called down, "What's keeping you?" He and Lyn sat on a small ledge. Sally joined them, and Bones followed.

He couldn't see how far the ledge went, but it was as good as he'd hoped to find. Lyn grinned at him. "I haven't gone splat yet."

"You're not going to either. Not on my watch. So, what are you waiting for?"

Maddock said, "We're admiring the view. Lyn thinks she can spit from here and hit Mama Lani."

"I didn't say that. You're no gentleman after all."

Sally said, "Get a room or keep going."

Bones helped Sally stand. "What she says. We've got to keep going."

They made it fifty feet across the rock before their

ledge turned into an overhang. The fracture zone presented plenty of handholds and footholds, but they were traversing along an open face. Bones had to admire Lyn, she seemed to have swallowed her fear and put her mind to the climb.

They made almost a hundred feet of horizontal progress, and at least another thirty feet up when Lyn reached a patch of ferns clustered around a rivulet of brown water. She reached in, grabbed, then pulled her hand back calling out, "Rock."

A cascade of dirt and pebbles rained down beneath her, followed by green swirling fronds. She reached again, extending her leg as far as she could. Pulling, Lyn put weight on her foot, only to have a larger section of cliff fall away.

Bones froze, too far back to do anything. The woman shrieked, and her hand pulled free. She slid, kicking. Maddock seized her by the shirt.

Lyn whipped both arms around and grabbed him by the wrist. For a moment, they hung there. Sally scrambled down the rock face like a spider monkey. She caught Lyn's belt and heaved. Between the two of them, they managed to drag her kicking and weeping back to a dry cleft in the rock.

Sally dangled from her perch; Bones saw her waver, and realized she only hung by one hand. He didn't think about the next two moves, but reached down, seized her by the pack, and curled her over his head like a hundred-pound dumbbell. She grabbed rock and climbed.

Maddock called down just above. "Rotten rock. We can't go any further that way. It looks like only fifteen feet more to the lip; we need to climb."

Sally worked her way upward. "Go as far as you can,"

Bones said, "but don't push it. We'll be right behind you."

Sally muttered something back, but Bones had already dragged himself alongside Lyn. She clung to the rock like a starfish at low tide. The woman's face pressed against the rough lava as if she would burrow into it. Her shoulders trembled, and Bones heard her breath come in ragged gasps. He said, "You're okay, you did well. Maddock is coming down to help."

She gasped and her voice broke. "I can't breathe, I can't breathe... Oh God, I looked down. I'm so dizzy." Between her words, Lyn's breaths came like shouts, like cries of desperation.

Maddock positioned himself at her right side and said, "Try to relax and tell us what you saw Lyn."

"Falling, falling, water and leaves and rocks all falling so far." Lyn didn't gasp quite so hard as she spoke. "Mama Lani was there, under her ledge. She looked up and smiled a curse at me. I saw her."

Maddock said, "You are doing fine. We're right here, and we're not going to leave you. You can breathe again, can't you?"

Bones looked up. Sally had stopped about eight feet above them. "You don't have to wait. Keep going."

"I'm stuck. There are no more handholds."

"Relax," Bones said. "Do you know how many women dream of being alone at close quarters with me and Maddock?"

Lynn managed a tight smile. "You're more annoying than I thought."

"Well, you're stuck with me now. C'mon, there's a grip just six inches above your left hand. Reach for it."

She pushed with her right foot, reached above her

head, and grabbed a rock crevice. "That's a lot more than six inches."

"I hear all the girls say that. Just keep going. Pull up, there's a cavity in the rock about two feet higher."

Maddock scrambled up to Sally, while Bones stayed with Lyn. Above them, Sally began working her way to the right and climbing higher. "There are bubbles, holes in the lava rock over here."

"Go for it," Bones said. "Sally's found us a ladder." He grinned and waved his friends on.

Maddock felt open cavities in the lava rock beneath his hands. He held back and let Lyn pass. Before finishing, he took one last look down. In the misty darkness below, he could swear he saw the old witch smirking up at him.

Maddock hadn't climbed another two feet before Sally let out a high pitched scream. Heedless of the drop, he scrambled up the cliff face. Sally had frozen in fear.

"Tarantulas!"

15

"**Giant tarantulas!**" **Sally** shrieked. "Hundreds of them!"

Maddock and Lyn both raced up the rocky slope. When they reached Sally, Lyn doubled over in a fit of uncontrolled laughter. "Get it together," Maddock said.

"They're just crabs," she said between gasps, "harmless land crabs."

Bones ran up, pistol drawn. He stopped in confusion, staring first at Lyn and then at Sally. She bounced from one foot to another at the edge of a dense jungle of palms and underbrush. All about her, an array of hairy, multi-legged shapes jumped and twitched and clattered. Some were no bigger than rats, while others were the size of bulldogs. The smaller ones crawled about her feet as Sally danced and shrieked. The larger creatures stood their ground, or advanced slowly.

Lyn ran to Sally's aid. "These are coconut crabs. They should be afraid of us."

Maddock grabbed Sally's backpack and pulled her away. "Look at those claws," he said. "They could snap your bones like a pretzel stick."

Lyn stepped forward and waved her arms. "Shoo, go away before I boil you and eat you." She seized the largest crab just behind its body. The creature hissed. Flinging it at the other crabs, she kicked a third out of her way. "Come on," she said. "This is just getting too weird."

The woman dodged between two palm trees. As she

did, a huge brown shape dropped from the fronds. Instinctively, Bones whipped out his Glock and blew the crab in half. As his shot echoed off the mountain, ten thousand birds rose shrieking into the air. Bones stared a moment at the claws that twitched at Lyn's feet.

"I swear, it was going for your throat. Somehow I just knew."

"Mama Lani must have called them," Lyn said, quickening her pace.

"What? On the phone?" Sally asked as the others followed.

"Don't discount it," Maddock said. "Think about the torches. They would have known how many we'd need to get safely there and back. Theirs wouldn't be the first culture that exacts a high price for sharing their knowledge."

"Why give you the knowledge at all if they're just going to kill you?" Sally said.

"I imagine the strong survive," Bones said. "That way they weed out the unworthy."

"Fair enough," Sally said. "But that's a far cry from a priestess or whatever she is having a way of controlling monster crabs. It's impossible."

Bones was about to share a few thoughts on what was and was not impossible, but Maddock beat him to it.

"You don't need to believe it right now; just go with it. We'll discuss it when we have more time."

"Speaking of more, here come the crabs again," Lyn warned, pointing to movement off to one side. "We need to get out of here."

Maddock gazed about at the surrounding chaos of rock and jungle. "I'm not so sure I know exactly where 'here' is."

Sally pointed at an opening in the palms and lianas. "It looks like a big rock, or a hilltop over there. Maybe we can see something from the top." She shuddered and looked up. "Besides, nothing can fall in our hair if we're standing on that rock."

Bones squinted in the direction she pointed. "I'd like to look at that, too. It's got kind of a strange shape."

Maddock was intrigued by the rock himself. "We might be able to spot *Lark* from up there, if anyone's up for another climb."

Bones had already set off, picking his way between the trees and thick undergrowth. Sally and Lyn fell in right behind him. Maddock took one last good look at where they started before following the others.

The whole setup just smells fishy, he mused, pushing through the branches and leaves. *Lyn has more going on than smuggling a boatload of pot.* He worried briefly about Willis and the crew before remembering the small arsenal Lyn kept in the wheelhouse. They could hold their own, he knew. Maddock hustled over a patch of bare ground to catch up with the others.

Bones had halted in front of a sheer rock face. Creepers and lianas clung to its surface like a vertical garden. Whole trees jutted out from crevices and dark cavities in the looming cliff face. Something that looked almost like a path led up to its base. There, a black opening could be seen through a veil of leaves and vines.

Lyn balked. "You do not expect me to go in there. One filthy cave is enough for today."

"Sounds like Maddock in Tijuana," Bones said, trailing off at the end and casting Maddock a side glance.

Maddock walked up and pushed some of the vegetation aside. "This is no cave; this stone has been cut and laid by hand." He peered closer at the rock. "And look here, some kind of symbol, a circle inside a triangle. There's more, but it's so badly weathered I can't make it out."

Bones stared up at the wall in awe. "It's a temple. A giant temple built on the side of a volcano."

"No." Lyn backed away. "I mean it. You will *not* get me to go inside."

Sally crouched low and crawled under the vines. "This goes all the way through. I see a faint green illumination on the other side."

Lyn hugged herself. "Am I the only sane person on this island? Let's go load my cargo and get the hell out of here. Even Maug is starting to look good."

Sally wormed her way a little further into the opening. "I think we were supposed to find this place. Mama Lani sent us here for a reason."

"Yeah, she hates our guts," Lyn said. "Remember the crabs?"

"Maybe they were just herding us in the right direction."

Bones started ripping vines from one side of the entrance. "I think we can fit through here."

Maddock grinned at Lyn. "Why don't you just stay outside and guard our backs?"

"And miss watching all three of you fall down some bottomless pit? No, I'll come along."

By the time Maddock crawled through the curtain of leaves, Sally had explored almost a hundred feet beyond. A pale green glow lit the interior. He watched her silhouette move against the shadowy background.

Lyn squeezed past the vine-covered entrance. "Couldn't possibly be anything dangerous in here. No way."

Bones grunted and came through behind them. "Where's Sally?"

"She's up there," Maddock said. "I just saw her a minute ago." He called out, but no answer.

Bones hurried into the dim passage. He tripped on a fallen stone, cursed and kept going. Maddock followed, avoiding most of the larger debris. They both halted at a green rippling pool. It glowed from within, throwing bizarre shadows across the vaulted stone ceiling. Sally's pack lay right at the edge. Bones snatched it up; a few empty water bottles fell out and clattered on the rocks.

Once more, Maddock called. His voice echoed for several seconds before vanishing into the surrounding darkness. No answer, no sound but Lyn's gasp as she approached the pool.

"I've seen something like this before." She inched closer. "It was at Nan Madol--the stone ruins on Pohnpei."

"Lemuria," Bones said. "Holy crap! Are you telling me we've found another remnant of the ancient Lemurian Empire?"

Maddock peered around in the gloom. He ought to be more excited about this find, but he was concerned. "That's great, but where's Sally?"

Entranced, Lyn kept staring into the opaque green water. Her voice flat, almost hypnotic, she said, "Sally is gone—you will not see her again."

"What the hell does that mean, Lyn?"

"I saw… I once saw a man fall into a pool like that. He never came out."

Before Lyn could finish, Maddock had shrugged out of his shirt and kicked off his shoes. He grabbed Bones by the arm. "If I'm not back in three, get Lyn the heck away from here."

On impulse, he almost dove in, but something strange about the green fluid halted Maddock at the edge. He sat and lowered his feet into the glowing surface. The ripples danced about, throwing the chamber into a glittering green chaos. He took a deep breath and slipped off the rim of cut stones.

The rock scraped his back as he slid below the surface. Maddock fell almost five feet before he could twist and grab a handhold. The green fluid was hardly more substantial than air. With no idea how deep this pool was, he climbed down the side. Blind in a sea of light, he had to grope among the rocks for every move.

After almost a minute, his feet reached a sloping bottom. Soft and springy, it crunched like centuries of leaf-litter in a virgin forest. *I'm hunting rabbits in the dark*, he thought. Well into his second minute, Maddock wondered if he should try calling. He didn't dare inhale the fluid; any breath lost would be unrecoverable. He shuffled around trying to find his bearings. A moment later, something grabbed his foot.

Maddock jumped in surprise, lost his balance in the tangled mass, and fell. His outstretched hand grasped at the first object he touched. Smooth, round, rough-edged holes, he recognized it as a human skull. The rest could only be bones. A small voice: "Help me."

"Sally?" Half his breath, gone in one word. His heart pounded, not in fear, but straining for oxygen. The grip on his ankle tightened. Maddock reached out, took the hand in his and helped her to her feet. She wrapped him with the strength borne of uncontrolled panic.

Maddock broke free and pushed her away, but she

clung to his arm like a squid on a dying fish. Pulling her along, he plunged through the clutter of bones. The wall, he had to find it. Up, the only way out was to climb the littered slope and scale the rocky wall. *No air.* Maddock knew he was about to pass out but feared that breathing any of the green fluid would doom them both. His hand touched the rocky surface, he reached behind Sally and boosted her as high as he could.

Maddock's chest heaved, fighting to breathe— anything. The universe of green that had surrounded him began to fade. He felt the rock slip from his fingers. *What was it again he had to do?*

Lying on a bed of soft grass, breathing the cool dawn breeze wafting from a garden of ten thousand flowers, Maddock watched a flock of scarlet birds cross the sky. *There was something…* The flowers swayed on their tall stems and a swarm of tiny insects buzzed about the garden. He sat up. A handful of the little bugs clung to his skin. Maddock brushed them off, but like flies they returned. Tiny feet, scratching, itching. They crawled in his ears, buzzed about his lips and landed in his eyes.

Maddock slapped and jumped, but they only flew off to return tenfold. He rubbed his arms and face, crushing them by the thousands. Something bit his foot. Centipedes as big as garden snakes swarmed about his ankles, eating the tiny carcasses he'd crushed.

Dancing, jumping, he shook the creatures from his legs and trampled them beneath his feet. In an instant, a dozen large rats sprang from the undergrowth and began devouring everything they could find. Maddock couldn't think. The rats jumped waist high, crawling up his back. He knocked one squealing into the air only to see it land in the jaws of a large black wolf. Just as six more wolves faded into view, an enormous orangutan swung down from above and seized him about the waist. *Something. He had to do something… climb, that was it.* Rough tree-bark beneath his fingers, Maddock followed the orangutan up into the shadowy branches above.

"*Come on, Maddock. Wake up.*" He heard the voice but couldn't figure what was so urgent. Someone smacked him in the face, then again—harder. Maddock let his eyelids flicker open. A world of green twilight, Bones knelt over him. In the background he heard a woman's voice. "The still girl isn't responding."

Maddock remembered, *he had to find Sally.* His voice came as a whisper "Did you get her?"

"I think this one will live," Bones said. "You with us, buddy?"

"I'm not sure. Did you get Sally?"

"Yeah, she came crawling out like some kind of creature from the green lagoon."

"She's alive?"

"Unconscious."

"How—how'd I get…?"

"You don't think I would have left you in there? Really—you thought that old pal?"

Maddock's head spun. There? *In the garden with the animals? No, in the pool, the pool without water, looking for Sally.* "Bones, that's not water in there."

"No crap it's not water. Were you breathing it?"

Maddock sat up and tried to stand. The hall spun as he straightened. Bones grabbed him by the arm. "Not so quick, buddy."

"I'm good." Maddock tried a few steps. "Yeah, I must have been breathing it. Bunch of nasty bad dreams. It's deadly. I thought I was a goner. Where's Sally?"

"Over here." Lyn waved at him from the edge of the pool. "She's breathing, but that's all."

Maddock knelt at her side. "Let's get her out of here, get her in the sunlight."

"I found a way to the top while you were drooling and mumbling," Bones said. "Up here, it's the quickest." He scooped Sally from the stony floor and started up a steep flight of stone steps. Lyn followed.

Each step was almost two feet high with only a sliver of tread, no wider than a man's hand. Above, daylight glowed from a narrow crevice. Maddock admired the stonework as they made their way toward daylight. "Whoever constructed this wasn't following any building code that I know."

With the young woman in his arms, Bones didn't look back. "The Lemurians aren't human. They're slender and very tall."

"They *aren't* human?" Lyn said. "Like you believe there's some weird skinny guys around?"

Bones kept climbing. "No. They left this place over ten thousand years ago. Sometimes maybe they visit, but most Lemurians have retreated to their Kingdom of Agartha, hidden beneath the North Pole."

Maddock waited, counting steps, but it seemed that Lyn was lost for a reasonable response to Bones' last statement. After about fifty of the tall steps all of them puffed and sweated as they climbed. By seventy-five, Maddock felt his thighs burning, but Bones just kept treading upward toward the daylight. At step one hundred and twenty-two, Bones hefted Sally up through a narrow stone slot and turned sideways to squeeze his own shoulders through. Lyn had a similar problem for a different reason. Maddock tried not to notice, but sometimes it couldn't be helped.

From the top, half the island stretched out before them. A strong trade wind swept down from the north, rippling the Philippine Sea far below. Lyn scanned the shoreline while Bones and Maddock knelt over Sally. The young woman was still breathing, but unconscious.

"Wake up," Bones urged. "Do it for Corey."

She twitched her foot. Maddock saw one eyelid flicker.

"Did that seriously work?" Maddock asked.

"Got to be coincidence."

"We need you Sally," Maddock said. "Wake up."

Sally sat up with a start. "The Lady. I have to get to the Lady. It's already too late."

Bones held her back, but Sally struggled to stand. "She's dying and there is no one to replace her. Let me go, I've got to get back."

"Easy." Maddock took her arm and steadied her. "Tell us who you saw. Why did you go in there?"

"I followed the Lady to her garden." Sally closed her eyes. "Greenery everywhere, with flowers that bloomed like the world had been made anew. Then the snakes came, thousands of them." Sally opened her eyes again. "They just swarmed all over the poor Lady. They pulled her down. It was horrible, her face screaming from a writhing ball of scales, with a hundred snakes springing from her hair." Her voice lowered to a whisper. "That's when they came for me."

Bones grabbed her by both shoulders and stared into her eyes. "There was no lady, no snakes. Where do you think we are right now?"

"I'm, I'm…" She looked around. "God, I don't know. Where are we? How did we get here?"

"Mama Lani, remember?"

Sally stared off at the sparkling horizon. "Oh my God, I've lost my mind."

"No," Maddock said. "You just misplaced it for a while. What you saw was an illusion. You've suffered from hallucinations, but it's temporary."

Sally visibly relaxed, closed her eyes, and let her arms sag. And then her eyes shot open.

"What is it?" Maddock asked. Sally looked down and he followed her gaze to where she held her hand pressed against her shorts pocket.

"It's here," she whispered.

"What is?"

"The Lady couldn't have been an illusion. She gave me this." Sally dug into her shorts pocket and pulled out a carved figurine. "She said it's the 'key to Maug,' whatever that means."

Maddock accepted the small statue and held it up for Bones to see. Clearly female in every way, it featured large pendulous breasts, wide hips, and exaggerated pudenda. Its legs tapered to a single point and its bulbous head bore no trace of eyes or mouth.

"Venus figurine," Bones said. "Can I take a look? There was this hot anthropology professor I dated for a while. Even took one of her classes. She didn't look like this, though." He turned the figure over, inspected the legs, and handed it back to Sally. "This one is carved from ivory or bone. It could be as much as thirty thousand years old."

Lyn stared at him for a full five-count.

"Don't look so surprised. He's much smarter than he lets on," Maddock said. "And he loves doing that to people, so don't give him the satisfaction of acting too impressed."

"Screw you, Maddock."

Maddock turned to Sally. "Where, exactly did you find this?"

"The Lady, in the pool, she called, and I just stepped in. It felt like—like falling for miles." Sally grinned at Bones. "You'd have jumped in too if you'd seen her. She gave it to me."

"I did jump in, but I didn't inhale."

"Well I inhaled," Maddock said. "Whatever is in there, it's a powerful hallucinogen."

Lyn looked over the statuette, examined Sally's face, and said, "The oracle at Delphi. She was young, virginal, and she smoked some weird stuff down in her cave. At least, she was in this romance novel I just read."

"Volcanic cave," Maddock answered. "Just like this one. It makes sense, but back there, you said you've seen something like this before?"

"A few years ago, I delivered some cargo to the Island of Pohnpei. Its capital is Kolonia, the only real town on the island. A couple of guys in this bar, we got to talking. One of them, a big guy like Bonebrake there. I kinda liked him. Well, this guy starts going on about these ancient ruins, lost city and all."

"I've heard of it," Maddock said. "Nan Madol, mostly a tourist trap."

"That's the one. People come there every year looking for alien astronauts. But this guy, his plane leaves in the morning and he's all fire-ants to see the place before he goes home. So this is in the evening, midsummer night. We'd had daylight well past nine o'clock, still the shadows started growing longer. There were mentions of ghosts and no one wanted to take us out to the ruins."

Lyn glanced at the rolling hills and jungle below them. "Speaking of growing shadows. We better head back to the boat. There's a long haul ahead of us and I can finish the story then."

16

Bones stood on the weathered ledge and stared down into the tangle of vines and undergrowth over two hundred feet below. *Someone had cut and set the stones beneath his feet, but who?* Long and irregular, they did resemble pictures of the Nan Madol ruins, but these stones were set with more precision. He turned to Lyn, standing several paces back. "This rock pile was built by some fine engineers."

"Great, just tell me how we get out of here."

"The same way we came in. I think we should circle down and cross that ridge to the south. There's a stream on the other side. It will lead us back to the shore."

Maddock joined him, glancing down for a moment. "Where's the boat from here?"

Bones pointed out their best route. He figured Maddock already knew where the boat was. That was just his friend's way of giving him the lead. "Those steps are gonna be tougher going down than they were coming up. Why don't you and Lyn go first, and I'll follow with Sally?"

Lyn started down immediately, but Bones saw his friend hold her back. Always cautious, but it had saved their necks more than once. Sally had regained her feet, but she was still wobbly. Down, one step at a time. Sally turned and used her hands, descending like on a ladder. Once at the bottom, Bones steered her well away from the glowing pool.

He watched Maddock retrieve the pack, not letting Lyn out of his sight. Once beyond the net of vines, Bones searched out a path, little more than a cleft in the vegetation, that circled below the looming stone edifice. Lower still, they broke into a clearing of tumbled rocks and scrubby brush. "Must have been a landslide here or something." He called a halt. "I don't like the looks of this field, too open."

Maddock agreed. "Then we cut over there and cross the ridge higher up."

Climbing to the ridgetop, Bones dodged around a maze of large boulders. Lyn said, "These stones have been cut and squared off." She gazed back at the stone fortress above. "There must have been an entire city here at one time."

Bones didn't stop. "Lemuria. It came to a bad end."

Crossing the ridge, Bones located the small drainage he'd seen earlier. Animal trails paralleled the trickling stream. He followed deeper into a green maze of underbrush. A little farther, the stream broke into a rippling cascade that plunged fifty feet to a pond below. The game trail they'd been following veered off to the south before angling back to rejoin the stream. At the foot of the falls, Bones halted them once more. "Let's take ten here. I want to refill our water supply before we go much further."

Maddock shrugged out of the pack and dumped a half-dozen two-liter bottles at their feet. Sally helped him fill them from the pond. She surprised them all by slinging the loaded pack across her shoulders. "Look, you guys do the fighting. I'll do the carrying."

Maddock tried to argue her out of it, but to Bones, she made sense. After a few words, Maddock gave in. She wore a smug look as they trooped down the mountainside, despite lugging a twenty-five-pound pack.

They hadn't traveled for twenty minutes before Bones heard the first shots. Still far off, they were answered by a half-dozen others. Maddock said, "I think Willis and Matt found your arsenal, Captain."

Lyn halted and listened. Four more shots, then two answering. "Damn," she said.

"We'll be expected, now," Maddock said. We've got to get back to the boat. I'll lead. Keep it quiet everyone."

Bones watched the tree line for birds or anything else that might reveal the other's movement. He checked his pistol. "I've got one round in the chamber, and seven in the mag."

Lyn gripped Maddock's shoulder and pointed to a gap between the palms. He nodded and led them that way. A narrow path, it ran past a row of huts. Maddock halted.

Bones moved up, he didn't care for this setup at all. One pistol against however many rifles was a bad hand to play but walking through the enemy camp was just stupid.

He shook his head and pointed off to the right. Maddock led them into a maze of palm trees and underbrush. The shots continued. Intermittent fire.

Their trail returned them to the stream, a broad meandering waterway by now that glided beneath a tangle of fallen trees and overgrown banks. It led to an opening in the underbrush where the jungle met the beach. Bones signaled the others to stop. On his belly, he crawled out to look.

A hundred yards south along the narrow beach, *Lark* sat right where they'd left her. Willis and Matt had managed to raise the landing ramp and now crouched behind it, firing at someone further down the beach. Bones returned and explained the situation.

"Did you see Corey?" Sally asked.

"No, but I'm sure he's fine."

Maddock said, "We need to find and eliminate the shooters before they find us."

"Then what?" Lyn said. "Usually about six guys hang out here. If you figure two waiting at the lava tube, that will leave at least four with rifles on the beach."

Maddock flashed a wolfish grin. "It's what we're trained to do."

"That sounds awfully boastful, coming from you," Bones said.

"Fine, you tell them."

Bones shook his head. "No, you stole my thunder. Anyway, the two of you stay hidden. Get as close to *Lark* as you safely can and wait for the signal."

"What's the signal?" Sally asked.

"No idea. I'll figure something out."

The two men split up. Bones moved silently, invisibly, toward the nearest shooter. He'd learned woodscraft from his grandfather, uncle, and mother, but refined it in the SEALs until he could move like a ghost under the right circumstances. And here, under the cover of lush tropical growth and the sounds of gunfire and the roaring sea, it was child's play to move toward the sound of the nearest shooter. He only hoped he wasn't struck by a stray bullet fired by one of his crew mates.

He crept up behind a dark-skinned man who held a rifle trained on *Lark.* The man never saw Bones walk up behind him and club him on the back of the head. He relieved him of his rifle, ammunition, and knife. The latter he used to make sure the man didn't follow them or anyone else ever again.

A shot rang out from *Lark*. Nearby he heard a grunt and a cry of pain. He followed the sound and was pleased to discover that one of his crewmates' bullets had found its mark.

The gunfire was abating. Obviously, Maddock was holding up his end. Grinning maniacally, he moved on, eliminating another target with ease. Footfalls crashed through the undergrowth nearby, headed away from the shore. The bad guys, what remained of them, were in full retreat.

He broke through the tree line to see Willis and Matt had swarmed ashore and established a beachhead at the jungle's edge. Bones saw smoke in *Lark's* stacks and Corey at the helm. He waved to Corey, who waved back and sounded three long blasts on the horn. *That should do as a signal.*

He heard the sound of running nearby. Lyn and Sally were making a mad dash for *Lark*. Bones fell in behind them.

While Willis and Matt laid down some random fire, the others sprinted for the water. Maddock climbed the boarding ladder and took up station behind the bow ramp. He covered the others with shots from his World War II relic while Willis and Matt crossed the beach and scrambled up behind him.

Bones followed, firing his last rounds. He waved an arm over his head and Corey reversed engines. Willis and Maddock bent their backs to the anchor line astern. Hand over hand they pulled, guiding *Lark* into the swell and holding her off the rocks.

"So, what exactly happened back there?" Maddock asked as they headed for open water.

"Matt told me there were two guys. They'd started unloading Lyn's Spam, but then they got nosey and started rummaging around the boat. Corey asked them politely to leave. One of them got mouthy and made the mistake of shoving Willis. Willis threw him over the side and that's when all hell broke loose."

"Well, we got rid of a few of them," Maddock said.

"Yeah, but some got away," Bones said.

Willis ducked in through the cabin door, followed by Corey and Matt. "Lyn's got the helm. Not sure if she's ticked that I played with her guns, so to speak, or if she's glad I did."

"She's more interested in playing with Maddock's gun, I think," Bones said. "I just wonder if she set us up."

"I don't think she did," Sally said. "She went along with your bonehead plan to climb that pit."

Maddock nodded. "You two acquitted yourselves well, back there."

Sally nodded. "I know. Now, how about a beer while we digest everything that's happened?"

"First I want to talk with Lyn," Maddock said. "Let's go up and ask our good captain what else she might have on board. I've got a few other questions as well."

Lyn looked up when they all piled into the wheelhouse. She shook her head. "No bourbon, no bitters. I've got vodka; we could make very, very, *very* dry martinis."

"That works." Sally said.

"Beer for me," Willis responded. "Y'all?"

Maddock nodded. "Beer's good, and I'm ready."

Matt made the run. Willis followed saying, "A little

squirt like you couldn't hardly carry enough for me, much less the others."

Bones positioned himself near the wheelhouse door where he could watch body language. Lyn had put the auto-pilot on while she hunted up the vodka. The woman seemed a little jumpy. *But then*, he figured, *it could just be that she'd had a rough day.*

Corey seemed antsy as well. He prowled the wheelhouse fiddling with various bits of equipment. Every so often he'd fuss with an old radio set bolted to the far bulkhead.

Lyn returned with two tumblers and a half-filled bottle of Moskovskaya. Corey said, "If you've another glass, I might join you."

She found a coffee mug and poured him a generous slug. "This'll have to do."

He clinked glasses with her and Sally, and said, "I'm curious. This looks like an old single side-band. Does it still work?"

Lyn tipped her glass back and poured herself another. "Need to phone home, ET? I use it for long-range communication. You have to switch the power over from the marine radio, and it's a bitch to tune."

"So, is that how your 'boys' knew we were coming?"

Bones saw the woman's back stiffen. Still, she grinned. "You got me. I called them before we left Guam. Had a swap all set up."

"Product, right?" Maddock said. "You brought food to swap for a load of weed."

"Something like that, but I can't figure out why the dirty little bastards double-crossed me. We've had plenty of dealings."

"Maybe they had a better offer," Bones said. "Maybe

they talked to someone else."

Lyn nodded, then that grin again. "The market's been in the crapper for the past two years. Spam for weed, and I hardly break even these days. Used to be, the Navy guys took all I could give them. Now some international consortium brings it in by the boatload. You want to know the worst? I don't even smoke the stuff myself."

Bones didn't take his eyes off her. "So, I want to know. Did you get a better offer, too?"

Silence. The grin vanished. "No, but I could have. That little worm Jungle Jim tried to call me after we left Saipan. I didn't pick up."

Bones glanced at Maddock and said, "I'll buy that for now."

"So, we cool?"

"We're cool." Bones opened his beer and took a long swallow.

Sally tipped back her glass and held it out for a second splash of vodka. "What was with those giant crab things?"

"Coconut crabs. They're usually nocturnal, and never aggressive. I swear Mama Lani must have a way of calling them."

"I don't know," Sally said. "Assuming for argument's sake she could do that, she didn't seem hostile when I talked with her. Maybe they were just, like a demonstration or something?"

"What else did she tell you?" Maddock asked Sally.

"She said she was *makana*, one of the old ones, a thousand years old if you believe her. She said she speaks with the *taotaomo'na*, the spirits."

Lyn said, "Here have another shot, then you can go

sleepy time. But first, what did she say of Maug?"

"Ma'óghe, 'the Eternal One.' Three islands, west is land, east water, north sky. Secret fourth island is fire. She said it will consume the world one day. The Ma'óghe dwell there and they eat ships."

Sally took Lyn's advice and tottered down to her bunk in the doghouse. Maddock said, "Pour yourself another slug, Lyn and get some rest if you can. It's been a long day for all of us." He opened a second beer, disengaged the auto-pilot, and took the helm.

Willis said, "Leave some for us, boss."

"You and Matt get some sleep as well. Bones, spell me in four hours."

Bones let the others thump down the outside ladder after Sally, then opened another beer. Corey sat at the single side-band with headphones on, fussing with the Vernier tuning knob.

Maddock glanced his way, then turned to Bones. "You look like you've got something on your mind. You make this pained expression when you're trying to think."

"Do you think Pym was behind what happened back there?"

"I don't know. Seems unlikely. He'd have had to know where we were headed, then make contact, bribe the locals, make a plan. It's a lot to do."

"Unless the connections are already there." Bones said. "You heard Lyn. Boatloads of weed sold by some international consortium. It wouldn't surprise me if more than one hedge fund didn't indulge in a little off-the-books trading."

"Could be," Maddock agreed. "But why let us see Mama Lani? Why not just kill us?"

"I don't know. Maybe we arrived sooner than they expected. Or maybe they're just not very good at what they do."

"Not as good as us, anyway," Maddock said, gazing back in the direction of the island.

Bones cleared his throat. "Listen, Maddock. About the thing with Angel…"

"Forget about it. It was a no-win for you. I don't know what I'd have done if the shoe was on the other foot."

"Thanks, man. You going to talk to Matt?"

"Yeah, but not until I no longer feel like stomping a mudhole in his ass."

"Hey, guys?" Corey straightened in his chair and pulled his headphones off. "I just learned there's a typhoon headed for Guam. No one will be traveling there for a while. Maybe that will slow down pursuit?"

"Maybe," Maddock said, "but I have a feeling we haven't seen the last of them."

17

True to his word, Bones clunked up the ladder and slipped into the wheelhouse. Maddock heard him coming and pulled in the auto-pilot.

"Nothing much on the radar. We'll be passing Agrihan in another hour or two. Keep it off to starboard and correct to three-five-eight degrees when we pass. Lyn should be up by daylight to take the next watch. Oh, and keep an eye on that port engine. The tach has been jumping all over the place."

Maddock didn't want to admit to himself how tired he was, and the problem of Pym, or whoever was dogging their heels, just wouldn't leave him alone. He clambered down to the doghouse and collapsed in a vacant bunk. Willis' snores rivaled the growl from the engine compartment aft, and Maddock couldn't help turning the same problem over in his head. *If some of Pym's men were following, what kind of boat would they have?* Eventually, exhaustion overtook worries and Maddock sank back into the arms of the deep.

He awoke to a ray of morning sun that danced about the interior of *Lark's* doghouse as she wallowed through a long series of waves. A different sound came up from the engine compartment. Muted, not the growling roar of twin supercharged diesels. He climbed up to the cabin and found Sally fussing with the galley stove. She didn't look up, but said, "We lost the portside engine last night. So, say bye-bye to one-ten power, microwave, refrigeration, and electric skillet. This brontosaurus," she kicked the stove, "runs on diesel, if I can ever get it lit. Hope you got good and tired of my coffee in the morning, 'cause you're not likely to see too much more of it."

Maddock retreated to the wheel house. He found Lyn at the helm, watching compass and gauges like a momma alligator watching her nest. He noted the radar turned off and the auto-pilot disengaged. "What happened?"

"Matt says the port blower froze up and broke the drive. We get a little juice from the starboard generator, but not much."

"How fast can we go?"

"I'm babying the engine. Sixteen hundred revs gets us about seven knots, give or take. We've got limited twelve-volt power for radios and such, but that's it."

Maddock stared out at the horizon ahead of them. A faint gray smudge showed just off the starboard bow. Lyn saw him look and said, "Asuncion. Last bit of land before we see Maug. Still want to go?"

"Right now, there's nothing I want more. I want to beat Pym and find the treasure, but more than that, I sense there are some deep secrets here that I really want to unravel."

Bones nodded. "And we'll deal with whoever or whatever stands in our way, be it Pym or the Moogly-Woogly."

Sally appeared, balancing four mugs of coffee. "This is squid barf, but don't expect much better." She handed one to Bones. "And you, Mr. Bonebrake, need to show some respect. It's the *Ma'óghe*, and if we expect to get out of here alive, we're going to need its cooperation."

"Relax," Bones said. "Just making a little joke. If anyone on this crew respects legendary creatures, it's me."

Maddock took a swallow of coffee and said, "This is several cuts above what we had in the Navy."

Bones sipped from his mug. "We still need a better understanding of what happened back there on Pagan. I mean that pool of green goo, what entered your mind?"

Sally stared into her cup of swirling black liquid as if it held the answer. "I don't know. It called—she called. It was as if I had no choice. Do you believe in destiny, Bonebrake?"

"Not really. I think destiny is a concept we use to explain past behavior, or to justify what we've already made up our mind to do."

Sally nodded. "I always thought the same thing, but now I'm not so sure." She shrugged. "It's not easy to put into words what happened."

"We have another unfinished story as well," Maddock said. "Lyn, this seems like as good a time as any to tell us about Nan Madol."

"Fine." The woman reached down and pulled in the auto-pilot. She checked the compass again, then drew a water-stained roll from the chart rack overhead. "This is Pohnpei. You can see Kolonia here on the north. Nan Madol is right on the coast, about fifteen to twenty miles southeast by boat."

"It's another volcano, like Pagan," Bones said.

"Yeah, but a lot older. Pohnpei has been sinking into the ocean for the past million years. They say some of Nan Madol's largest temples are now fully submerged."

Maddock had heard of this ancient complex of temples and palaces. Built of basalt blocks, it once covered most of an extensive coastal lagoon. Magazine articles likened it to a Micronesian Venice, but he'd heard other tales as well. Stories of a city with gardens and broad avenues slowly flooded by the invading sea.

Lyn continued. "Like I'd said, this guy and his buddy were hot to go visit the ancient temples. Well we were all three pretty messed up, a little gin, maybe we did some kava, too. Anyway, no one would take us there, even with big-guy waving bills around."

She went on to tell how the bartender had sent them to a small hut of tin and thatch. An old man lived there that just might take them. "Filthy old bastard," she said. "But he had a decent canoe with an outboard that worked."

It took them almost two hours to reach the site. "Big-guy had a bottle of schnapps that we shared around. It was a regular pleasure cruise." By the time they'd motored through a labyrinth of islets and mangrove-choked canals, the sun had slipped behind the hills and the sky lost its color.

"I hadn't a clue where we were, but this old local guy, he just kept smoking cigarettes and motoring along." Lyn told of staring up at the enormous piles of basalt blocks as darkness fell about the lagoon. "All overgrown and dripping with vines, they were huge. The big-guy, he wanted out so bad. I knew what he was thinking. 'I can go home now and say I've been here.' But our guide was having none of it."

He took them up a long narrow canal, almost a tunnel between the stones and overhanging weeds. "I saw mangrove crabs on both sides that were bigger than serving platters. Now those things are aggressive, they'll take your finger off right at the knuckle."

Finally, the old man stopped at a random flat stone lying half submerged. He tied his canoe to a mangrove branch and signaled them to follow. "Now the big-guy's friend, he's pretty excited. Me, I'm too messed up by then to be making any decisions. And big guy himself, he's kinda getting cold feet. But we all followed the old man through the bushes and up a steep hill."

Lyn described the long blocks of basalt, laid flat like logs. She told of standing on top of the edifice and staring out at nothing but an endless lagoon of crumbling islets. Every one of them had some kind of structure. "Then things got weird."

Their guide had insisted they see something more. "*Amazing secret of Nan Madol*, he'd called it. But big-guy was getting the willies, if you know what I mean. He'd have gone back to the canoe if his buddy wasn't so keen on seeing the rest." Lyn added that their guide had the only flashlight. "Without a light, I doubt any of us could have found that canoe."

Lyn told of their trek through the undergrowth. "No sign that anyone had been here before." They stopped at a vertical wall of stone. "You know what's coming next. An entrance, a high chamber, and this glowing pool of green."

She paused her story to check their compass bearing. A particularly long swell passed under *Lark's* keel and everyone grabbed for support. Lyn corrected their course and peered out to the side. "We've got some deep ocean waves coming up from behind. I hope everyone has their sea legs by now."

She glanced over at Sally. "You've got some strong allies, here. My team wasn't so lucky."

The old man had held back, standing at the entrance

smoking a cigarette. "Now big-guy is fascinated, entranced you could say. He walks right up to the rim. Me, I'm having trouble walking at all. Hey, don't judge me."

"Not judging," Maddock said. "I think we've all had those moments. Just tell us, what in blazes happened?"

"Well I'm sitting on this rock—in the dark. I couldn't see that well, but for a moment, it seems that big-guy's buddy, the one all eager to get here, pushed his friend into the pool. I'm like jumping up and doing this number." Lyn staggered around the wheelhouse. "But by the time I reached the pool, they'd both disappeared. Now, I wasn't about to go in looking for them. Not really that messed up, but I called for the old man and his flashlight. I waited. Nobody. The old bastard had slipped off and left me."

Lyn told of fleeing to the entrance and waiting there all night. When the sun came up, she tried looking for the canoe. "The rock was there, the mangroves, but the old bastard had ditched me."

She tried walking inland. "With the sun at my back, I knew I was headed the right direction." She'd had to swim between islets. "I wasn't afraid of sharks, but those lousy crabs were everywhere." Eventually, she reached a strand of shallow sand bars and open water. "I could see the mountain poking up into the morning clouds. All I had to do was swim."

About half way across, an open launch swung by to pick her up. The morning tour, they'd spotted her wading across the lagoon. "I got some looks, I'll tell you." She made up something about a lost kayak. Twenty minutes later, they passed through a regular channel and tied to a little wooden dock. "This place was all decked out with a footpath and signs. I expected a concession stand. When everyone else got off, I stayed in the boat, you betcha."

Four hours later, Lyn arrived back in Kolonia. She found a different bartender on duty. He didn't know anything. She checked the old man's shack. "I mean empty. Not like in be-back-soon empty. Nothing there but rats and stray chickens empty. Didn't look like anyone had lived there since the last typhoon."

She asked around. No one seemed to know of an old man with an outboard-powered canoe. "I almost went to the local cops, then it occurred to me. No way I'd ever find that islet again. No way anyone's going to believe my story of a glowing green pool. Nothing but a bad ending in that scenario. So, I split."

"And that's it?" Sally said.

"That's it until yesterday. I never told anyone because, come on. No way they're believing me."

Sally shook her head. "That seems like the kind of thing a person might want to know in advance. You got any more of these little revelations?"

"Nope, I usually try to stay away from that sort of thing. Like staying away from Maug, if any of you would listen to me. I've still got half a mind to break our agreement, but where would we go, with this Pym and a typhoon behind us?"

"Glad to hear you're still on the team." Maddock rolled the chart back up and stowed it away. He glanced out the forward window and looked at a different chart pinned to the back bulkhead. "Destiny or just dumb stubbornness, we're not going back." He pointed to an island off their starboard bow. "If that's Asuncion over there, it looks like we've got seven or eight hours to go."

Lark took another lurch and veered off to the west before Lyn could wrestle her back on course. Maddock scrambled down to the lower deck where he found Willis, Corey and Matt crawling out of the engine compartment. Corey shook his head.

From the aft deck, the four of them scanned the ocean. Their wake disappeared into the empty horizon. A few birds passed, heading north. An occasional flying fish broke the surface and went buzzing off across the oily wavetops. Other than that, Maddock saw nothing but a silver line where sky met ocean. "We've got eight hours, guys. Anyone bring playing cards?"

"C'mon, man," Willis said. "Lose that sour look. We're treasure hunting, maybe get a dive in tomorrow. That always cheers you up. What do you say we break out our gear and start rigging up?"

Corey said, "I want to see this drone toy that Doc packed away for us."

Matt and Willis dragged a Pelican case from beneath the settee and popped open the lid. Corey lifted out a smooth shape that looked like a fat, six-armed starfish. Below that, six extensions were nestled in a foam cutout. Each one had a two-bladed electric rotor. "These must plug into the body, and look, there's a controller in here, and something else." He pulled out a rectangular box with an antenna and computer ports.

"That's a processor unit." Sally had been watching over his shoulder. "There should be a thumb-drive and connection cables to go with it, if you haven't lost them already."

Corey held up a plastic bag. "A few playthings for the princess?"

"I don't know if that was supposed to be naughty or

misogynistic," Sally said.

"It's his attempt at naughtiness," Matt said. "Corey hasn't had a lot of practice flirting."

"Maybe you could coach him," Maddock said.

Matt's eyes narrowed but he didn't reply.

Corey began to protest, probably to break the tension, but Sally cut him off.

"Don't mind them," she said to Corey. "They're just jealous of our Geek love."

While Corey turned several shades of red, Sally opened the bag. "Looks like instructions in here too. I doubt any of you *men* ever thought to read them."

Willis said, "Instructions are for fearful men. Just push the buttons and wait for something to happen."

Sally had already stopped paying attention. She scanned the manual, then went back to the beginning and flipped through the pages. Maddock watched her dissect the instructions, then pick up the controller box and re-order them in her head.

"I think we've found our pilot," he said. "Corey, you'll be ground crew for this thing," he continued over the others' protests. "Willis, your job will be to keep Bones from fiddling with it. Ever."

"That's an impossible task," Corey said. "Bones never stops fiddling with it."

"Neither does your mom," Bones replied.

"If anyone is interested," Sally began loudly as she connected the processor unit to her notepad computer and loaded up the driver software. "This is sweet." She showed them a blank screen with a few random colored numbers. "As long as the water is clear, we can get a bottom profile to centimeter accuracy." She turned the starfish body over, revealing rows of plastic lenses on each arm. "It uses a multi-spectrum laser array to correct for distortion and scattering."

Corey looked closer at the notepad screen. "How do you tune the laser spectra?"

"Ha, there *is* intelligent life on this barge. Fair question. Turns out, you don't have to. The processor unit controls it. Oh, oh... I've got to try this." Sally punched a series of keys, and her computer played five notes in slow succession.

Maddock thought he recognized the tune but couldn't quite place it. A moment later, the processor unit repeated the same five notes and suddenly the cabin blazed with colored lights as both notebook and processor wailed out a fugue based on the five-note sequence. *Close Encounters?* He let out a tired sigh. *Maddock, you've been hanging around Bones altogether too long.*

Once they'd finished examining the drone, Matt climbed up to relieve his friend at the wheel. Corey had just replaced everything in the Pelican case when the big Cherokee came in, flopped on the settee, and began snoring like a spring bullfrog. Sally folded her oversize purse in half when she saw him and tucked it under her arm. "I think I'm going to lie down too," she said. "This constant bobbling is getting to me."

Maddock knew he was immune to any kind of sea sickness, yet he could sympathize with her. "Somehow, we'll struggle along without you."

While the others rested, he dragged everything out of both large plastic cases and took inventory of what Willis and Matt had packed. Side-scan sonar, data recorder, and satellite uplink were stowed with the drone. The other case held masks, fins, com gear, buoyancy compensation vests, and four neoprene wetsuits. "Impressive," he said to no one in particular. It had all been packed so tightly that little else would have fit.

He slipped out the cabin door and worked his way around the outer deck. Some time ago, their doghouse had been welded into a portion of the cargo well. He held on to a rail as he walked further forward. The remaining well was filled with fifty-five-gallon drums of fuel, a few remaining cases of Spam, and twenty large scuba tanks. *Lark* lurched to port and rolled. A sheet of spray caught Maddock in the face, but he never took his eyes off the cargo. Wedged against the inner hull, the drums didn't move.

"Maddock, a word?"

Maddock froze at the sound of Matt's voice. "What?"

Matt moved to stand beside him, but both men kept their eyes locked on the sea.

"You know what." Matt's voice was heavy with the burden of the secret he'd been keeping.

"So, talk."

"I could blame it on the liquor, but that wouldn't be the real reason." He paused but Maddock was not about to fill the silence for him. "Look, a few of us were hanging out a few weeks back when she was in town."

That stung. Maddock hadn't even known she'd come for a visit.

"Anyway, Willis went home, Bones passed out, and she got talking about you. About how she'd messed things up and now she'd never get you back because deep down you're made of stone. I put my arm around her and told her that wasn't true. That your nature is very different from what people see on the outside."

Maddock huffed a forced, scornful laugh.

"I'm not saying that to manipulate you. It's what I said. And then, next thing I know, well, it happened. And I didn't try to stop it." His voice grew hoarse. "And I have regretted it every moment since."

"I'm more bothered by the fact you didn't tell me. We're brothers on this crew."

"No. You and Bones are brothers. Willis is the stepbrother. Corey's the family dog. I'm the annoying neighbor kid you keep around because even though he's a pain in the ass, he's your pain in the ass."

"That's not true."

"Of course it is. Three of you served together long before you met me. Hell, even Corey's been part of the crew longer than me, but he fills his own niche. I'm the extra muscle. I'm the redshirt who won't die. And I think that's why I did it. It was so flattering that Dane Maddock's ex, Bones' sister, wanted me. I guess I wanted to feel like the hero for once." He hung his head. "That's the worst analogy I've ever come up with."

"Sounds like you've been reading the advice column in *Cosmo* again." Maddock forced a smile. "Hey, at least you didn't hook up with another cousin, right?"

"She wasn't a…" Matt stopped, a cautious grin creeping around the corners of his mouth. "Are we okay?"

"We're going to be. Just give me some space."

"Thanks." Matt turned to walk away, but Maddock grabbed him by the shoulder.

"However you might see it, we really are a family. All of us."

Matt nodded. "It's good to hear."

Maddock chuckled. "You're just going to be the red-headed stepchild for a while, until I say otherwise."

By late afternoon, a gray smudge on the horizon resolved itself into a cluster of cliffs and low peaks emerging from the ocean. Maddock once more stood at the helm. He glanced at the chart behind him; three islands guarded a circular lagoon. The only safe entrance faced due south. He headed *Lark* straight for it. A large rolling wave rushed up from astern and shoved them forward like a giant's hand. Maddock fought the wheel as they slid down the face, then set them back on course as the wave joined ten thousand of its brethren headed north. He could hardly believe they were so near their goal. They could take a quick survey of the lagoon before dark, three times around the perimeter at least. Then he'd let the sonar do its work.

Willis joined him after an hour, took a look at the looming cliffs and shuddered. "Man, if I was shipwrecked here, I might consider just walking back into the sea."

Lyn got up when she heard Willis talking. "You got that right. I've only been here once before, and I swore I'd never come back. Place gives me the creeps." Maddock wondered what would tempt someone like Lyn to come this far north, but before he could ask, she said, "Resupply for an archeological dig. Seems there were Chamorros here for thousands of years. A small group lived on the East Island. Spooky damn place, wind howls all night. Brrr… not for me."

"How long was the team on-island?"

"That was five years ago. I never heard anything more about them. Maybe they're still there, all weird like zombies or something."

Willis let his head loll to the side. "Brains!"

"Laugh if you want, sailor. I just hope we score a pile of loot and make-wake the hell out of here."

By the time Maddock could see individual waves breaking against the cliffs, all seven of them had jammed into the wheelhouse. Lyn took the helm saying, "This entrance is trickier than it looks. The middle is deep enough, but waves tend to build up on both sides."

He craned his head around, trying to get a general idea of the local geography. With three separate islands, the perspectives shifted every time he looked. Lyn held back, let several waves pass, then pushed the throttle all the way down. Their one remaining engine howled, and *Lark* surged forward, gaining speed on the face of a wave. In a moment they were past the inlet, all staring up at the surrounding peaks.

"Holy crap," Bones said. "This must have been a gigantic volcano that blew itself all to hell."

Corey nodded. "You're right. It's a caldera. The thing must have gone off like Krakatoa."

Bones turned to Sally. "Okay, chick. We got you here. Now where's the treasure?"

Maddock had experienced withering looks before but hoped never to be on the receiving end of the one she gave Bones. "Check your shirt pocket, Bonehead. Or did you forget, *you're* the treasure hunter."

18

Lark **began her** third circuit of Maug Lagoon, following the hundred-foot depth contour in a clockwise pattern. Thirty yards behind them the sonar tow-fish followed on a cable. It bounced high-frequency sound waves off the bottom that Corey recorded on a small unit in the cabin. He watched an orange donut begin to form on the screen.

Sally peeked over his shoulder. "This is kind of primitive," she said. "Wouldn't the drone give us a better image?"

"Too slow. We can map the lagoon tonight and pick the choicest spots before we fly them tomorrow. Look here; we're getting something already." Corey zoomed in on a wrinkly smudge, and it expanded to a cigar-shaped pile of clutter. "Wreck. Wreck right there. And there, just north of us, I'll bet that's another one."

Maddock heard the excitement in Corey's voice and leaned over to look for himself. No question. In the narrow path they'd traced already he could see five promising hits. "What is this, the graveyard of ships?" he said.

Sally slumped and let out a sigh. "It's real. I was so scared. I thought we were chasing a data fluke, but it's real."

As they continued circling, more and more smudges appeared on Corey's sonar screen. Willis and Matt joined them as darkness fell. They all stood around, hypnotized by the widening ring of data. They'd hit the seventy-five-foot contour when Bones climbed down from the wheelhouse. "You've got to come see this," he said.

Sally didn't move. Willis didn't even look up. Maddock nodded and followed Bones back up the ladder. Lyn stood in the dark, watching her fathometer and GPS unit. "Look, look out there," Bones said.

Bathed in starlight, the lagoon rippled in the evening breeze. Quiet, black, a sleeping animal heedless of the fleas that circled its back. As *Lark* plowed through the water, swirls of phosphorescence followed in her wake. Bones said, "Wait, it'll come back."

Moments later, a scatter of green lights spread across the waves. Like a cascade of tiny sparks, they flickered and vanished. Then another, red this time and further away. Streams of blue shot in all directions. A few more flashes, then the lights disappeared. Lyn said, "In all my years at sea, I've only seen this once before."

"Last time you were here?" Bones said.

Sally slipped into the wheelhouse. "What's so interesting?"

Lyn said, "Watch."

The flashes started again on the far side of the lagoon. Mostly greens and blues, a few sparks of yellow and red flashed through them like lightning on the far horizon. Sally watched in silence. A different part of the lagoon lit up, then all went dark. No one spoke and only the low murmur of their engine could be heard outside.

Maddock was about to remark that the show was over, when all about their boat, ten thousand colored lights flashed and danced and spun like an undersea carnival. He felt *Lark* shudder.

Moments later, Willis poked his head in and said, "The tow-fish is gone. Line snapped, just like that."

Anchored in the lee of the East Island, *Lark* rolled softly to the waves entering from the south. Corey tinkered with the temperamental diesel stove trying to heat an enormous frying pan.

Corey didn't straighten but kept peering beneath the stovetop with a lit splinter in his hand. "If I got the uplink going, could you actually use your connection at Columbia to process some of the data we've collected?"

"It would be slow." Sally thought for a moment. "Yeah, doable. But wouldn't it just be better to go back tomorrow and recover your instrument from whatever it snagged on?"

"There was no snag," Lyn said. "I told you, no snag, no rock, no damned sailing ship mast or anything else. Anything like that, I'd have seen it on my own depth recorder."

"Couldn't have been a snag." Willis said. "We were running that fish on the surface. Any snag, we'd have hit it first."

"Well if we didn't snag the tow-fish," Maddock said, "then what happened?"

They sat in silence until Bones heaved a tired sigh. "Are you really going to make me be the one to say it?"

"The monster," Lyn whispered.

"You believe in the witch woman's voodoo?" Willis asked.

"I do. This place is messed up. Always has been. You'll see tomorrow. We'll go ashore and look for the archeologists' camp. It wouldn't surprise me if they stumbled across something that scared the crap out of them and they all just took a hike."

By ten o'clock, they'd finished eating and Corey had the uplink on the after-deck with a clear shot at the southern sky. "I'm drawing power off the port battery bank," he said. "Should last until morning."

Sally plugged into the uplink, logged on, and tapped the screen with impatience. Eventually a dialog box appeared. Maddock left her at her work and walked aft to check their anchor line. It bumped back and forth in its chock as *Lark* swung between wind and current. A minute later, Bones joined him.

"So, what do you think really happened to our fish?" Bones asked.

"I don't know. A really big shark?" Maddock offered.

"Could have, I suppose. Our tow-cable broke just behind the shackle. If it was a shark, wouldn't we have seen it on the sonar log?"

"Not if it was following us."

Bones scowled. "Guess that leaves out night dives."

The next morning, Maddock found Sally back on deck, logged on through the uplink. "What did you find out?" he asked.

"I'm pulling a concert grand piano through a half-inch keyhole here, Skipper. It'll be another two hours at least."

"We're going to change positions then. Reset the antenna after we move."

Willis and Matt had already started the anchor winch. Lyn cranked up their engine and a few minutes later, *Lark* crossed the lagoon and crunched against the stony beach of East Island.

With the bow-ramp down, Bones strode ashore and

said, "Maybe this sounds nuts, but I kind of hope Maug is real. Imagine the look on Grizzly Grant's face when I discover a cryptid he's never even heard of."

Lyn pushed her way between them. "I'm the one who's nuts for even coming here. Follow me and I'll show you where the archeologists were working."

Maddock came ashore last. He followed them up a steep path that climbed north from the beach, then angled inland. About eighty feet above the water they reached a broad plateau. Maddock looked down at their boat. Sally remained bent over her notepad, and Corey was fussing with the uplink.

Lyn said, "They had pitched their camp on the field here, but I don't see a trace anywhere."

"Over here." Maddock stood at the edge of the plateau. "Your guys were definitely excavating something." He pointed down at a large rectangular stone bearing weathered inscriptions. "Any ideas what that means?"

"Sally might could figure it out," Lyn said, "but damned if I know."

Maddock knelt beside the stone. It bore the same circle within a triangle that he'd seen at the temple on Pagan. He brushed sand and dead vegetation from its surface. "Look at this, Bones. See anything familiar?"

His friend crouched down and blew more dust from the markings. "Lemuria. This was another outpost." He wiped his hand across the incised circle and then puffed again. "Hand me a stick or something, this one has a hole in the center." Bones poked around until he'd loosened more dirt and blown it from the hole.

Maddock oriented himself with one corner of the triangle. "Hold that stick upright, Bones." He squinted past the stick. "I think some kind of gnomon went in there. That way is due south. Each of these other markings could indicate a place or maybe an astronomical feature."

Bones stared at the rock for a moment, then crossed the field and gazed out over the Pacific. He crossed back and peered at the lagoon. "And you think that people lived here?"

"Yes, pre-contact Chamorros," Lyn said. "I think they were all *makana* like Mama Lani."

"Nut jobs, then." Willis said. "So, no one home. What now?"

Bones stood at the edge and looked down at *Lark* resting against the beach. "I think Sally should look at this before we split." He whistled and waved his arm.

Willis had trotted down to show her the way. Less than five minutes later, Sally came steaming up the trail, with Willis in tow. "This better be important because I've got data coming back any moment now."

"Isn't Corey minding the store?" Bones asked.

"Yeah, but then he'll get to see it before... Never mind. What do you need?"

Maddock stepped away to let her inspect the stone. "There must have been more to this at one time. Any idea what it means?"

She stopped in silent awe upon seeing the graven stone. No one spoke as she slowly walked around it. A flight of seabirds passed, heading north. Finally, she stooped and touched the center.

"The Eye of God. This symbol depicts an eye in the midst of a mountain or a pyramid. The triangle is the mountain, a symbol of Heaven."

She glanced up at the others. "What? My father was a

professor of Medieval literature. I know these things. As ancient symbols, they were universal east and west." Passing her hand over the markings, she examined them from every angle. "There should be a square surrounding this, something aligned with the cardinal points."

Maddock said, "What about the stone itself?"

"Of course, the alignment is right. Look, the four corners symbolize the four pillars of wisdom. The square stone represent the physical world." Sally got down on her knees and examined the engraved glyphs. "This hole must have had a purpose. Look, it's tapered like someone jammed a giant pencil into the rock.

"But what does it all mean?" Bones said. "Is it some kind of Lemurian map or did they use it as an astral compass?"

Sally continued her inspection. "I've seen some crazy things lately, so you guys will have to cut me some slack. But I think I can guess what this is." She stood up and dusted the sand off her knees. "I'm betting this stone is pre-Chamorro. If we knew what went in the center hole there, I could tell you for sure."

Lyn said, "Stop with the tease girl; that's my arena."

"It's a communication device. Like the Ouija Board, or a deck of Tarot Cards, I think it was used for communicating with the... spirit world for lack of a better term."

Willis frowned. "Are you sure all this Maug talk isn't just messing with your head? Or maybe the green fog?"

"No. I'm not hysterical or under the influence or anything like that. I don't even believe in this stuff but somehow I just know." She sighed. "Ever since we left Pagan, everything's been messed up." She glanced down at the lagoon. "Damn. I've gotta go finish parsing that data. You guys knock yourselves out up here, okay?"

Matt had kept silent throughout the exchange. Now he knelt at the stone and ran his finger around the triangular pattern. "Strange that so many of those sacred mountains were dormant volcanos."

"Not so strange if this rock is as old as Sally thinks it is," Lyn said. "Back then, most of those mountains were spitting fire and scaring the hell out of everyone."

Matt stood up. "I guess this place was all done with the fire and brimstone before anyone showed up. But what's that up there?" He pointed to a pile of rusty debris further up the slope.

"The Japanese outpost. Plane spotters. Sometime during the war it was abandoned, but no one knows quite when. They cut a tunnel into the rock. Must have been a damn lonely outpost—and no, you're not getting me to go up and check it out."

Bones waved his arms from the cliff edge and said, "Sally's signaling to us. Either breakfast is ready, or she's finished her computation."

Maddock lingered as the others filed down the path. He tried to imagine what this barren field would look like with any kind of dwelling or village. Minutes later, he gave up and followed the others on board.

He found Sally on the back deck, still bent over her notepad. She brushed the hair from one eye and said, "If you want breakfast, you better go help Bonehead. I'm busy. Oh, and I like my toast dry, light brown, with two eggs over easy. And tell the geek to hurry up with that coffee."

"It's not nice to call people names," Corey said, handing her a steaming mug.

"Names? I promise, that's the highest compliment I

can pay a man." She said the last in a whisper and punctuated it with a wink. Corey blinked twice, then turned and hurried away.

"Poor thing," Lyn said. "I really think he needs my advice."

Maddock and the others made themselves scarce while Sally focused on her data. Finally, she proclaimed herself ready to share what she'd found. They gathered around her computer.

"First thing I did was to run a wave response model of this lagoon. It's got some pretty weird internal reflections. Short answer is, wave action is going to have shredded anything shallower than fifteen meters, say fifty feet."

She flicked the display and a bright orange ring formed on the screen. "Normal storm event, those are two-meter waves. They'll stir up the bottom down to fifteen, twenty feet." She flicked the screen again. The entire circle turned orange with a broad violet ring around the outside. "In a normal typhoon event, we'd see internal waves up to five meters. They'll mess up the bottom fifty feet down."

"What about an *abnormal* typhoon?" Bones asked.

"Most deep-water storm waves come every sixteen to eighteen seconds. A super-storm can produce waves that arrive over twenty seconds apart. I modeled Maug lagoon with a twenty-two second natural eigen-frequency." She tapped a key. "Twenty-two second waves, this lagoon's a hyperactive five-year-old in the bathtub."

Maddock said, "That's good to know, but how does it help us?"

"I'm getting to that. We covered the zone from a

hundred and twenty-five feet to just inside seventy feet before we lost the tow-fish. Figuring you're not going to get much bottom-time below a hundred and fifty feet, and knowing that nothing from fifty feet to the shore will be worth looking at, we're damn lucky to get what data we have." She pecked away at the keyboard and spun her screen around for others to see. "Voilà."

Maddock counted dozens, perhaps hundreds of yellow dots that now littered a region between fifty and one-hundred and fifty feet below the lagoon's surface. "Those can't all be shipwrecks," he said.

"They are, all hundred and eighty-seven of them. I ran a simple pattern comparison with images of known wrecks and filtered for a seventy-five percent confidence interval..."

Bones interrupted. "Can you enlarge the image? Show me this dot right here." He pointed to a marker very close to where *Lark* hung from her anchor.

Sally dragged a small red box around the area. After a moment the screen went blank and then refreshed itself in a series of stripes. The fan in her notepad began to whine. "It's a little processor-intensive," she said.

A grainy image formed on the screen. Roughly rectangular, it occupied the center of a large debris field. "Maug or no, I'm going swimming," Bones said.

Corey stared at the screen a moment. "Lots of targets here. Shouldn't we fly a few of them first?"

"I've come this far, I've been shot at, and sat through your technobabble. I've earned a dive."

Willis said, "We're in seventy-five feet. You gonna free dive? I'll come with you."

Before Maddock could get a word in, they both bolted for the stern deck, mask and fins in hand.

Both men floated on the surface, adjusting their snorkels, clearing their masks, and inflating their lungs. As one, they doubled over, pointed their fins skyward and headed down.

Lyn stood on the deck, watching the two men disappear. "Seeing all of those shoulders and abs makes me just want to jump in after them."

Maddock rolled his eyes. "No one's stopping you,"

"How long?" Sally asked.

"Bones can do three minutes easy," Maddock said. "Four in a pinch."

He knew better than to count seconds but found himself at a hundred and twenty before he realized it. At a hundred and eighty-five, two heads cleared the surface about thirty feet astern. Maddock reached down to help Willis aboard and the two of them yanked Bones out of the water.

"She nailed it," Willis said. "There's a wreck down there!"

Bones caught his breath. "Sampan hull, wood, maybe forty or fifty years old. Looks like a Japanese fishing boat."

"So," Corey said, "do you two plan on knocking your heads against every ping on Sally's screen?"

Willis held his shoulders and shivered. "No, man. It's nasty cold down there. Next trip, we suit up and blow tanks."

"How about we fly a little recon first?" Corey suggested.

"Recon?" Bones said. "We got wings?"

Sally nodded. "Yup. I'm pilot. Corey is ground crew, and Bonehead here is security."

Bones looked around and said, "Security? Security

against what?"

All eyes turned to Bones and Maddock grinned at his look of bewilderment. "Not that you've been known to break things before, old buddy. We're just not taking any chances on this one."

"What the hell is it?"

"Drone," Corey said, "equipped with Light Detection and Ranging: LIDAR. With the conditions here, we should see bottom detail in a hundred feet of water or more. We've lost the SONAR tow-fish, so this is the best we got."

Sally pointed out a cluster of yellow dots just north of their position. Lyn nodded and took the helm. Willis enlisted Bones to help with the anchor, while Matt and Corey assembled the drone.

"The processor will take some time on these," Corey said, "but we should be able to map out at least five per hour."

Two hours later, their drone continued hovering and scanning the bottom. With three battery sets they could charge two while flying on the third. With some reluctance, Sally let Bones watch the display. "Just keep your hands in your pockets."

The images appeared almost like an old-style radar sweep. First passes showed a vague outline, then successive passes filled in details until a sharp picture of broken hulls and scattered superstructure filled the screen. Bones shook his head. "Looks like Maug chowed down on half the world's fishing fleet here." He fell silent for a moment, then bent forward. "Wait, oh wait… there's masts, there's ribs. Check this out you guys. I think it's time for me to suit up."

19

Like fratboys at spring break, eager to hit the beach, Bones and Willis scrambled for suits and tanks. Maddock said, "Matt, you may as well get your own gear organized. We'll go second jump."

Lyn ran out the anchor. A bump and rattle of chain, then the howl of rope passing over the davit. She snubbed it off and let *Lark* swing before the southeast breeze. Corey ran up and checked their GPS readings. "We're just about over it," he called down.

Maddock stayed glued to the LIDAR screen. Something just looked strange. Sally had returned their drone to the deck. "You look like a big yellow tabby watching a mousehole."

"I think we're missing part of the picture here. Can you run another scan just to the north?"

"Aye aye, Skipper. We've got enough juice for another flyover." She launched the drone and circled it once, then started a rectangular pattern just off *Lark's* bow.

Willis and Bones returned to the deck in neoprene suits, carrying tanks and buoyancy compensators. Unlike their free dive earlier, they each wore full-face masks with integral radio communication equipment. Matt helped them with the gear.

Maddock toggled the talk switch on their communication unit. "Coms working?" When both men nodded, he continued, "We've got a hundred and ten feet of water under us. Watch your dive computers and save enough air for a safety stop on the way up. I'd say you've got no more than twelve minutes on the bottom, so be careful. If you get the bends, you'll just have to tough it out. Matt and I will go next."

Maddock knew he didn't have to tell them, it just made him feel better. He heard a gush of air on the com-set and both men disappeared over the side. For the next three minutes there was nothing but breathing, then Bones said, "Come to papa."

Maddock and Lyn sat at the com-set. Matt watched over the side. "The water is so clear, I can see them down there."

At that moment, Willis' voice came over the set. "We got us a good one. Seventeenth century for sure. I see ballast stones, ribs and a row of cannon."

The com-set whooshed and hissed with the men's breathing. Maddock heard Bones say, "Stern broke off, it's back here."

The breathing became heavier; rapid puffs and grunts. Maddock thought he heard Bones say, "Help me with this," then, "stand by, we're coming up."

Matt turned and said, "It looks like they're both headed back to the boat."

Sally landed the drone and left Corey to deal with it. She rushed to Matt's side and said, "Are they okay?"

A surge of bubbles boiled to the surface. Bones' voice came through much clearer. "We're on a five-minute safety stop. Ask Sally if she has lunch ready."

"Why don't you tell him… ooh, just wait 'til he gets up here, I'll tell him myself."

Lyn said, "Spam and cheese subs for everyone, coming right up."

Two heads bobbed to the surface, ducked under, then reappeared. Sally said, "They're struggling with something. We need to help them."

Maddock toggled the talk button. "You guys okay?"

"Thought we could handle bringing this up on our own," Willis said. "It's heavy."

Maddock leaned over the side and grabbed the rough gray brick they handed up. Between them, he and Matt hauled the two divers on deck.

Sally pushed between them and helped Bones with his mask. "That was awful deep," she said, "and you were down a long time. How do you feel?"

Willis looked at Maddock and raised his eyebrows. Maddock shrugged back.

Bones had slipped out of his buoyancy compensator and tank. "We do this all the time." He knelt on the deck and hefted the lime encrusted brick. "The wreck is too deep for much coral growth, but it's been down there a long time. The worms and bugs have had a field day."

"So, what's that rock you dragged up?" Sally asked.

Maddock grinned. "My friend is just stringing us along. Show her, Bones."

At that moment, Lyn poked her head out the cabin door and said, "Lunch break."

Bones tucked the brick under his arm and said, "We should all see this."

Corey joined them in the cabin. Bones set the crusty wet lump on the dinette and drew out his dive knife. "Lyn," he said, "you should see this too."

With the others looking on, Bones rapped the brick with the butt of his knife, then inserted the blade in a crack and twisted. A large flake broke off, revealing a glistening surface of yellow gold. Maddock knew what to expect, yet he too gasped at the find.

"Gold, my friends," Bones said. "Bars of gold down there, maybe silver too. Sally, you are truly a genius. I bow in awe of your noodle network."

Corey said, "That's not all. While you were diving, we scanned a little further north." He set the LIDAR processor unit next to Bones' gold bar. "Look at this."

Not a hundred yards off their bow, a similar wreck lay at about the same depth. Three more like it were scattered nearby. Maddock said, "A fleet. An entire treasure fleet lies just beneath our keel."

Lyn finally spoke. "Manila galleons. They brought gold and silver from New Spain and traded for Chinese porcelain and Indonesian spices. This one must have been on the westward leg. I can't believe it! We actually found something."

"Well we just brought up our gas money," Bones said. "That should earn us lunch."

Willis and Bones had slid out of their neoprene suits, still they both perspired from their recent exertion. Bones wiped his face and said, "I wish we had a boarding ladder."

"For a bunch of smart guys, you sure can find the hard way to do things." Lyn said. "Why don't you just lower the bow-ramp and dive from there?"

Matt blinked at her. "You mean, like a ramp, in the water? Just walk on, and walk off?"

"I was going to suggest that," Bones said, between bites. "I was just about to say 'We should lower the bow-ramp,' I really was."

"Well I'm thinking of our next jump," Maddock said. "Matt and I will take crowbars and bags. We'll need a line to get whatever we find back to the surface."

This time, it was Bones' turn to deliver the stern lecture. He focused on Matt, "When Maddock says time's up, it's up. Got it?"

The two had each clipped an orange, mesh-bottomed bag to his belt, marched down the bow-ramp, and sat on its lip to don their fins. Now, swimming along the bottom, they listened while Willis guided them over the com-set to the galleon's stern. Maddock trailed a length of half-inch line behind him. He kept an eye on Matt, swimming at his side. The ex-Army Ranger was no novice, but there remained a world of SEAL dive training that he never had.

"Here, I see it," Maddock said.

A scatter of unidentifiable debris lay around them, but a compact pile of fist-sized lumps looked different from the ballast stones and other remains. Matt signed okay with his thumb and forefinger, then said, "Yeah, roger that."

Maddock pried loose a few lumps. Matt struggled with a large cluster, then managed to break it in half. Between the two of them, they filled one bag, then the other. "A hundred and fifty pounds per bag," Maddock said. "Time's up. We've got to go."

He clipped the bags to the line at his waist and told Bones to haul away. Above, he knew that his friend had fed the line through *Lark's* anchor davit and looped it over the windless. The heavy bags began to drag along the sand. Matt fended them away from the mounds of ballast stone and coral debris until the rope went vertical and their haul cleared the bottom.

Maddock followed the bags up until they neared the surface and then hung at depth for a five-minute safety stop. Above, their bubbles trailed away to the silvery water's surface. Something swam by. He caught it out of the corner of his eye before it vanished behind him. Then two more shadows passed, not three feet away.

"Did you see that?" Matt said.

"Squid. Big ones, longer than my arm."

Lyn came over the com-set. "What are you seeing, guys?"

"They look like Humboldt squid," Maddock said. "Three, four feet long… here come some more."

Matt swung his head around. "Holy crap, there's hundreds of them. No, thousands…"

Maddock felt something on his leg, tentacles covered his mask, and suddenly he felt their beaks tearing his suit and ripping into his flesh. Matt started to scream. Maddock tore the obstruction from his face, only to see his friend nearly enveloped in a writhing mass of eyes and tentacles. They had shredded his buoyancy vest. Head down, Matt spiraled back into the depths.

Maddock dumped his own air and kicked downward in pursuit. When he caught up with Matt, he was doubled over, wrenching the squirming bodies from his legs and streaming blood from a dozen wounds. Maddock grabbed his friend by the vest and dumped his ballast. He flipped the weight belt buckle and watched it disappear below.

Ignoring the searing pain as scores of sharp beaks tore into his own arms and legs, he held fast to Matt's vest. Maddock ditched his own weights and kicked for the surface.

"We've got trouble, guys. I'm going to need some help here."

His com-set remained silent, and he heard a loud rasping on his dive mask. Matt kicked and thrashed before finally straightening and swimming toward the surface on his own. A mass of gray suckers affixed themselves to Maddock's mask. Just in front of his eyes, a black parrot's beak began to attack the plastic itself.

Another squid clung to his neck. Within seconds it had chewed through one of the straps holding his mask in place. Water began filling beneath his chin and he tasted a stream of salt coming through his regulator. A mass of wriggling tentacles pushed their way beneath the neoprene seal and crawled like an army of worms across his face. Maddock tried to inhale, but drew only salt water.

Something gripped him about the ankles and wrapped his legs, drawing him down. He kicked and twisted, his lungs burning. His buoyancy vest wrenched and tugged as if it were being torn from his back. One last regret passed quickly through Maddock's fleeting consciousness. Matt! He hadn't saved his friend.

20

Sally followed Maddock and Matt's trail of bubbles as they descended into the tourmaline-blue lagoon. Bonebrake padded along the deck watching his friends swim for the bottom. He fed out coils of half-inch line and walked it to the stern. Sally let her gaze linger on his broad back and muscular legs. She didn't hear Lyn step up behind her. "That's a lotta man in those trunks, hey sister?"

Sally nodded without looking back. "We're surrounded by a sea of men, Lyn. How do you do it? You whistle, and they run to you like puppies."

"A man has two brains. You've just been talking to the wrong one."

Unaware of their attention, Bonebrake bent over the side, watching the two divers cruise along the bottom. Sally found a seat on the engine hatch and listened to him directing them to the galleon's broken stern.

Lyn continued, "Take my advice girl. Forget that one. He's got more women in his wake than most men have on their horizons."

"Oh, I'm just looking. He's not the one I'm actually interested in, but he's not bad to look at. Just don't tell his cocky ass that I said that."

Willis strolled past them. He looked over the side and watched a moment.

Lyn said, "Now he's not bad."

"Yeah, but I don't have anything in common with

him. I'm more into geeks and nerds."

"You could do worse."

Willis raised one arm and said, "Ready to come up. Haul away!"

Corey started the windless and Willis slipped the line over the anchor davit, giving it three turns around the capstan head. "Argh, Billy Bones, we've a pretty sack of loot to bring aboard."

Sally watched the line go taut and thrum as it passed over the davit. She had to go and stare down into the crystalline blue depths. Indeed, a compact mass rose from the bottom. A school of fish darted past the ascending package, and then another crossed her vision just beneath the surface.

Bonebrake said, "Look at the lagoon."

As far as they could see, millions of tiny ripples danced along the surface. A moment later, the blue, transparent water turned sickly green and from the com-unit, Sally heard Matt's cries of pain.

Willis snubbed off the line, leaving the two gear bags hanging from the stern. Bonebrake didn't look back. He stepped out of his shoes and dove over the side. Sally took two steps toward him, then remembered something she'd read. She ducked into the deckhouse and returned a moment later with a large plastic bottle from their laundry supplies.

Sally grabbed a rope from the deck, knotted two loops around her ankle, and passed the coiled line to Lyn. "You'll know when to pull me up."

Before Willis or Corey could speak, Sally shrugged off her shirt and dove over the side, bottle in hand. She saw Bonebrake right beneath her, struggling with something. Twisting the lid from the bottle, she swam down, deeper than she thought possible. Bonebrake held a squirming mass and already dozens of tentacled cylinders had attached to his body. Sally squeezed the jug around him and watched as the animals fell from his torso and jetted away.

Matt, Sally recognized Matt. *But where in all this hell is Maddock?* A trail of bubbles—she looked below and saw a vague shape descending into the shadows. Something inside her said, *too deep, too late.* Her lungs burned from the exertion and she knew that if she didn't surface, she'd never make it back.

Sally plunged deeper. Maddock had showed her the secret of exhaling in order to sink. It was her last trick and she played it. The line on her ankle pulled tight. *No, no, not yet.* So close. She could see him, he struggled upward and in a last effort Sally grabbed the tank and buoyancy vest that floated over his head. The line grew tighter until it felt like it would rip the leg from her hip. Something dragged them both toward the bottom. She pulled herself to him, circled him with her arms and crushed the bottle against her chest.

Sally felt her consciousness drift away in a sea of white speckles that converged from the sides. She clung tighter, but knew it was only a matter of time before Maddock would slip from her arms. *A sea of men and she couldn't even hold on to one.*

Semi-conscious when she broke the surface, Sally didn't mind the indignity of being hoisted by the ankle. Nor did she notice that it was Bonebrake who held her in one massive fist while swatting her back with his other hand. Hacking, choking, each gasp felt like a throat full of razor blades. Each cough threatened to split open her head. She vomited, and it felt like saltwater sprang from every orifice.

"Are you all right?"

Sally recognized Corey's voice and mumbled something. She opened her eyes to find herself lying on the deck with Corey and Bones leaning over her. She reached out and took Corey's hand. It was warm and dry.

"Matt, did you get him?" she said at last.

"Yeah, he's in rough shape, but he'll live," Bones said. "Those Army Ranger guys are like kudzu; useless and impossible to kill."

"Maddock?"

Bones managed a grin. "Lyn's cleaning him up. He looks like he picked a fight with a gang of bolt cutters. I don't know what the hell we ran into down there."

Sally felt the warm solid deck plates vibrate beneath her with the reassuring grumble of *Lark's* engine.

"Can you move?" Corey asked.

In reply she pushed herself to her feet and grabbed his arm for support. He pulled her close and she rested her head against his shoulder.

Sally realized that Bonebrake wore a hundred small lacerations of his own. "You're injured," she said.

"And you're not. Chlorine bleach. You may be completely nutso, but that was a genius move."

"Thanks. I want to see Maddock and Matt."

They found Matt stretched out on the cabin settee. He was swathed in bandages, mostly around his arms and legs.

"I'd give you a hug," he said, "but, well, I'm kind of tied up right now."

"I've never had a mummy fetish," she said.

"You think this is bad, you should see Maddock."

Maddock still remained in the cargo well where they'd dragged him from the water. Lyn had bandaged him from head to foot. Sally found him stretched out on the shady side of the well.

"He's resting," Corey said. "I don't think we should move him until he recovers a little more."

Willis sat on the bow ramp, shotgun in hand. "I'm waiting for the bastards to bring it on. Let's see how they like it in *my* world."

"Has anyone checked our haul?" Sally asked. "I'd hate to see all of this go for nothing."

Corey nodded. "All secure on the poop deck, admiral."

Maddock stirred his limbs and blinked. He looked up and met Sally's eyes.

"Do I even want to ask for a damage report?" Just then, Matt shambled out of the cabin and made his painful way into the cargo well. "This day keeps getting better and better." Maddock said.

"At least I can stand up. You look like archaeologists just opened your sarcophagous."

"If I look worse than you, I don't want to know about it."

Matt leaned against the bulkhead. "I feel like I've been hunting with Dick Chaney."

Maddock forced a smile that didn't reach his eyes. "I'm thinking that whatever else is in those wrecks is just going to have to stay there."

Bonebrake climbed down and sat next to Maddock. "Are you sure? I don't disagree based on what we just encountered, but maybe we should gather a little more intel before we make our final decision? Maybe there's something we could do?"

"That's a lot of squid, and angry ones at that. I'd hate to leave, but we did recover some valuable pieces. It wouldn't be the worst thing in the world if we were to make wake south, and soon."

Bones glanced up at the sky. "It's going to be dark in less than an hour. Let's secure ship and make our decision by morning?"

"Agreed," Maddock said, closing his eyes and drawing a tired, ragged breath.

Sally had been watching the lagoon change color as shoals of squid crossed its surface. "Do we have to keep the welcome mat out?" She pointed to the bow ramp. "I don't want Cthulu paying us a visit."

Willis held a finger to his pursed lips. "Shh. I'm on guard duty."

Bones stepped over to the port-side winch and started cranking its wheel. "Come on Willis. They took one look at your ugly mug and ran home to their mammas."

Sally watched the two men work the winches for a minute. Matt and Maddock were safe. No question, they would recover. Corey bent to help Maddock stand up. She realized she now felt a strong connection to this team. It would have broken her heart to have lost any one of them. She scrambled out of the cargo well and made her way to the stern deck.

Lyn climbed out of the engine compartment as she arrived. "Checking on that starboard power unit," the woman said. "We can't risk losing it too."

Inside the cabin, they found the floor littered with half a dozen pulsing gray squid carcasses. Lyn made a face. "We had to rip and cut those disgusting things off Matt. I think some of them are still alive."

Sally picked one up by the tail. "Not for long," she said. "You wouldn't happen to have a mallet and a cutting board, would you?"

Knife in hand, Sally went to work. She'd finished most of her prep when Willis burst into the cabin.

"Anybody seen our loot?"

Bonebrake came in right behind him. "They're gone. Everything we recovered." He cursed. "That freaking Maug must have slithered up onto the deck and snagged them."

"Snagged what?" Maddock asked from the doorway.

"You better sit down," Bones said. "We've lost our treasure."

Sally kept her back to them. She felt sick; she felt tears that no one need see. She wielded her knife and mallet like a vengeful goddess. Rubbery slabs almost an inch thick yielded half-inch steaks, yielded large, chamois-soft cutlets. She dredged them in flour, pepper and parmesan cheese before frying them in oil and pushing them between toasted bread rolls with basil and onions. She slammed a platter of sandwiches on the dinette and said, "Here. Eat these, maybe you'll feel better."

Sally shoved in next to Corey and slumped, head hung low. Corey gave her shoulder a squeeze.

"You okay?" he asked.

"I'm a jinx, a Jonah. Bonebrake walks into my café and he gets the whammy. You guys come to our rescue and what happens? Whammy on everyone. I'd say just throw me over the side, but I've been over the side and I don't want to go back."

Corey slipped his arm around her waist and said, "We chose this life. We've all been here before. Hey, c'mon don't cry. You just made it into the club."

From the corner of her eye, Sally watched Bonebrake taste one of her sandwiches. He gave it a puzzled look and took another bite. Maddock sniffed a sandwich and tasted it. "Lobster?"

Corey tried one, "I swear I've had this before, I just can't remember."

Bonebrake shoved half the sandwich in his mouth. "It ain't Spam!"

Lyn banged in from the back. "I've searched the boat. Our loot is gone." She paused a moment. "Say, that smells good. What is it?"

"Just eat one," Sally said. "Everybody's gotta eat one to get the jinx off, then I'll tell you what it is. Just humor me! I'm feeling superstitious."

Lyn picked up a sandwich and tasted it. "I know what this is," she said, grinning, "but I'm not telling."

Sally glanced at Maddock. "You don't seem as glum as I'd have expected."

"Just wanted to remind everyone we've still got this." Maddock reached behind him and set a crusty lump on the dinette. "I figure about fifteen pounds of gold that Bones and Willis brought up on that first dive."

Lyn narrowed her eyes. "I'd forgotten about that. Nearly three-hundred grand just sitting here."

"It'll fix your *Lark* for you," Bonebrake said. "Maybe even get you another tank of diesel and a bottle of vodka. Now spill it, Long Tall Sally. What are we eating?"

Sally grinned. "Fillet de Ma'óghe. Truly hair of the dog that bit you."

Matt spat out the bite he was chewing. "Are you crazy? What if it's like a puffer fish or something?"

"It's just squid," Sally said. "I wouldn't have served

them to you if I wasn't certain. Lyn identified them, too."

"Calamari," Bonebrake said. "So, do we think this army of squid are Maug's foot soldiers, or is Maug a name for the phenomenon we just witnessed?"

Maddock nodded, thinking. "Their attack seemed organized. And I'll tell you, something much bigger than these oversized appetizers had me by the legs. If Sally hadn't…"

"Maug and her minions?" Willis asked.

"I don't know," Maddock said. "If I'm correct, then the big one was intelligent enough to steal back its treasures. We've been doing this for how long and I can't remember a time an animal has stolen artifacts from under our noses."

"So we discovered an actual giant squid." Bones pounded his fist into his palm. "That rocks! I mean, except for the part where she tried to kill us."

"This could go a long way toward explaining the aura of fear that surrounds this place," Maddock said. "The Ma'óghe takes down every treasure ship that strays into the lagoon, leaving no survivors to tell the tale. Pretty soon, all the disappearances begin to add up, and no one goes near the place."

Sally glanced out across the stern. "It's dark now. What if they come after us?

Lyn turned around to look. "Holy crap, would you look at that lagoon?"

The others filed out on deck. Sally climbed the wheelhouse ladder to get a better view. All about them, the lagoon surface blazed in a living mosaic of colored lights. Streaks of blue and red shot across the water, faster than any single organism could ever have moved. Rills of light converged and spread, then turned and formed patterns, only to explode into pulsing stars.

Matt climbed up next to her. "It's like, I don't know, almost like visible music, like we're watching a brilliant composer at work," he said. "We should crank up the classical music and sample some of Lyn's weed. Who's with me?"

No one paid attention. They were too focused on the incredible sight.

"Matt's right. There's an intelligence here. It is like music." Sally paused a moment, then said, "Where's Corey? I want to try something."

Back on deck, Sally rounded up her ground crew. Maddock watched her from his seat on the engine hatch. "Do you think it will really work?"

"Not much to lose at this point." She plugged cables into her notepad and connected it to the drone controller. "A neural network is mostly a pattern recognition machine. It will identify music, or pick faces from a security cam feed. If I'm right, this thing uses bioluminescence to communicate."

Maddock finished her thought. "So, our drone should pick up light flashes and detect patterns. But what will it be looking for?"

"Universals, memes and phonemes. My father was a linguistics expert. He taught me about the basic underlying structure in all language."

Bones sat next to Maddock. Sally noted that for once he was more interested in what she had to say, than in the toy that Corey was assembling. "Your father said something about that. In translating Beowulf, he had to use the language structure as much as the words themselves. I was more interested in the monsters and dragons of course…"

"There was something more," Maddock said. "Something old Mama Lani said about the Ma'óghe somehow *knowing* us."

"Bingo, Skipper. So, what's it going to be talking about? Us. And who has our food questionnaires all categorized and scrutinized and tucked away in a neural network? Us. We'll just let that same network connect the dots, and we should know what this thing is saying."

Corey interrupted and said, "Ready to launch, Commander."

She lifted the drone into the air on six whirring blades and positioned it just forward of their bow. Corey watched her computer screen. "We're getting a signal. I just don't know what it means."

"We won't know anything for an hour or so, but as long as these things keep putting on a show, we'll keep getting data."

Ten minutes later, Sally brought the little drone back to the boat for a battery change. Bones picked it up. "Hey, mind if I try the next flight?"

"What could it hurt? Sure, just don't go provoking any dragons."

Sally was pretty sure he'd be careful. To emphasize the point, she handed him the controls and walked away. Corey had their uplink connected. "I'm tracking three satellites. We should get a decent signal."

Sally logged in and began uploading their data. Maddock and Matt had already retired to the cabin for some rest. Willis prowled the deck, shotgun in hand. Lyn said, "It's a nice clear night, lots of radio-bounce. I'm going to try to get something on the single side-band."

While the powerful Columbia University computer system gnawed on their data, Sally perched on an engine hatch and watched the lightshow. Soon the whir of blades told her that Bonebrake was returning the drone. "We've got one more battery pack charged. Want to burn it?"

Sally thought for a moment. "No, if we're going to learn anything at all, we should have enough data."

"I'll stash this up in the wheelhouse then. Don't want any curious little tentacles getting ahold of it."

Willis said, "They seem content to stay in the water now. Must have been mighty ticked off we boosted a bit of their swag."

Sally just sat and watched the lights. Almost mesmerizing, just on the edge of her consciousness, they seemed to have meaning. Patterns developed, dissipated, then reappeared on the other side of the lagoon. Some rare instances, one complex mosaic of color would surround them from shore to shore.

"What do we do now?" Corey asked, "play cards 'til dawn?"

Sally studied the monitor for a moment. It had a dashboard that tracked progress of the network training and validation. "I think we'll see results in a few minutes, if there's anything to see. What's Bonehead doing? He's been gone quite a while."

Willis laughed. "I think he's on the bridge with Lyn, giving her a hand—so to speak."

Sally blushed in the darkness and wondered, just wondered for a moment. Then Corey said, "Bingo, toast is up."

The monitor blinked and began displaying rows of text. Sally watched them fill the screen and then scroll upward. A minute later it stopped. "Whatever this is, we've got it," she said. "I need a little quiet time. When

Bonebrake returns to earth, give him that shotgun and get some rest yourself."

Sally sat in silent contemplation of the lines of gibberish before her; they teased her with some hint of meaning. Still, no conversation, no dialog emerged. Like stream of consciousness from a madman, it all seemed to stem from some common core. She parsed the words into multiple clusters, she tried her password decryption algorithm on various snippets. Ma'óghe, the eternal one, the Eternal *One*. And in a flash, she understood.

21

Maddock lay flat on his back in the semi-darkness trying to find sleep. *Lark* rolled and tugged at her anchor line. Normally the gentle motion of a ship on the water would send him to dreamland in seconds. This night, the angry red wounds that covered his legs and torso burned like a thousand wasp-stings. *There's something else*, he thought. *A toxin or something.* It made him feverish and dizzy. Matt's snores came from the opposite bunk. *At least he can sleep.*

Deep down, he believed they'd be better off cutting their losses. They'd leave in the morning. Averaging five knots, it would take them four days to reach Guam. *I'll recover by then*, he thought. *I can deal with the mess when we get back.* A little light filtered down from the cabin above. He heard Sally rustling around up there. *Crazy chick*, he thought. *She should be sleeping too.* Moments later he heard the cabin door open and Bones' voice.

"Yo, Maddock. I've got some good news and some bad news."

That was enough to rouse Maddock. Stiff with pain, he nonetheless stood and steadied himself against a stanchion. The bunks around him wavered; Maddock climbed six steps to the cabin. "What is it?"

"Got the radio working. Weather report is not looking good. They're calling it super typhoon Chaga. It missed Guam and flew right past Saipan. Looks like it's we're right in its crosshairs."

"When will it make landfall?"

"Maybe twenty-four hours out. It's nothing we could outrun in this tub."

Lyn followed him a moment later, tucking her shirt into her shorts. "We'll batten everything down and put you all ashore. Then I'll ride it out with *Lark* and hope we don't turn turtle."

Maddock said, "Put Matt, Corey and Sally ashore. Matt is in bad shape. Willis should go with them. Bones and I will stay to help. You can't single-hand this thing in a typhoon, and I sure as hell don't want to lose our only ticket out of town."

Lyn shook her head. "You're more than a little banged up yourself, big boy. Or are you too scared to go look in the mirror?"

"Don't worry about me, I'll be fine. Just start thinking about what we have to do before the storm hits."

"We should pump all our fuel into the tanks and lash those drums tight in the cargo well," Lyn said. "God knows, we'll need all the flotation we can get."

"Everybody pack a bailout bag. Essentials only. We'll bring our food ashore as well." Maddock said.

Sally dragged a Pelican case from under the settee. "I want the electronics. I want our drone, the computers, the uplinks and batteries from the port engine to run them. And I want my purse."

Maddock said, "You get some rest. You've been up half the night and we'll need you at a hundred percent tomorrow." Sally began to object but Maddock said, "That's an order. You too, Lyn. Tomorrow will be a long day. Willis, give me that shotgun. I'll take night duty.

Bones, relieve me in two hours."

Maddock knew that his friend could pack more sleep in two hours than most men could get in a full night. He stepped out on the aft deck, twelve-gauge pump shotgun in hand, *four rounds in the magazine and one in the hole, number two buck shot, high-base, an efficient load.* He checked the safety, *no use blowing out* Lark's *windows.*

Sitting on the engine hatch, Maddock watched the lights play across the lagoon. They hadn't diminished since evening, but whatever was down there had done nothing to attack their boat. *Save filching our loot*, he thought. Something big, something powerful had held him by the legs. Something big enough to move two bags, weighing a hundred and fifty pounds apiece.

But why hadn't they come back? There was enough sheer mass in the lagoon to overwhelm *Lark* and carry her to the bottom. Sally slipped out the cabin door and sat beside him on the hatch cover. "I know. I'll go get some sleep in a little bit. But I've learned a few things you need to know—before it gets crazy here."

When Maddock didn't reply, she continued. "Mama Lani isn't as flaky as she seems. This Ma'óghe thing is real."

"Thing?"

"One organism, made up of billions of individual entities. *Cephalopods*, squid, they have lived on earth for over four hundred million years, Maddock. They don't communicate, like we'd assumed. They are more like neurons or co-processors in one enormous creature."

"You mean this Ma'óghe is a swarm of some kind?"

"Something like that, but it functions as a single animal. From what I could tell, it is nearly immortal and has a memory that stretches back to the dawn of time.

The Ma'óghe lives in an eternal now, almost a Buddhist nirvana state… until it's disturbed."

"And we disturbed it with our LIDAR scan."

"Exactly. That's how we're going to get our treasure back. I won't say we can control this thing, but with the proper signals, we can, um… manipulate it."

"Wait, what?" Assuming Maddock accepted her hypothesis, why would they try and mess with the thing? "You want to manipulate its brain, and you think I'm going back down there while you're doing it?"

"If you won't, then I'll go. One to beam down, Scotty."

"Two. We dive in pairs with a support team on the surface. No dead heroes on my watch. So, what makes you so sure we'd be safe?"

Sally tossed her head to one side and peered back at him between strands of hair. "Don't think I'm crazy for saying this, but Maddock, I can feel it talking to me now. Some connection to what happened in the green mist How can I explain—it's almost subliminal, like a conversation in another room. It wouldn't hurt me, I just know."

Maddock sat in silence for a moment. The rising wind blew salt spray across their stern, peppering his face. *Would he dare dive on Maug Lagoon again?* "Let's see if we live through the typhoon first. Then we can decide what we want to do."

By dawn, long rolling waves entered the channel from the south and a pall of dark clouds marched its way across the Philippine Sea. Lyn brought *Lark* around to the same beach they'd landed earlier. Willis led Sally,

Corey and Matt ashore. Maddock watched them go. "They won't find much shelter up there, but it'll be better than here."

Lark surged and banged against the beach. Lyn backed her off and headed into the lagoon. "We'll ride it out under power," she said. "If it starts getting hairy, life vests are in the cubby just behind me."

Lyn tuned the single side-band radio, trying to catch a signal. A few squawks, and then silence. She buttoned the mic and gave their position. Nothing came back, not even static. "I think we're on our own for this one," she said.

Maddock watched the rolling waves pour into the lagoon. Just inside the entrance, a gray rectangle cut the water's surface like the fin of some gigantic shark. Bones followed his gaze. "What the bloody hell is that?"

Maddock shook his head. "I'd been wondering how long it would be before our friends caught up with us."

"Pym?"

"Pym riding a submarine. Dive planes on the bow and no vertical rudder, Kilo class if I had to guess. Soviet cold war relic." Maddock grabbed a pair of binoculars and stared at the approaching craft. "Diesel powered and built like a tank. Some Asian countries still use them. Lyn, meet your competition."

The tall woman stood at her helm and said nothing for a dozen heartbeats. Then she cursed and said, "I'll be damned. They're shipping product by submarine."

"You didn't stand a chance," Bones said.

"Yeah, and now *we* don't stand a chance. What's your plan?"

Maddock said, "We've met the enemy, and they aren't ours, not yet. We surrender."

"For now," Bones added.

The gray submarine cruised up to *Lark* and nosed its bow against her side. The little landing craft listed hard to port, throwing all of them against the wheelhouse bulkhead. A swarm of men poured out on deck with ropes and grappling hooks. Moments later, Maddock, Bones and Lyn faced the worn muzzles of a half-dozen Kalashnikov AKS carbines.

Below them, black clad figures swarmed over *Lark's* deck and rifled her cabin. Bones said, "You know, if you wanted to borrow a cup of flour, you could have just asked."

The wisecrack wasn't quite worth the rifle-butt to the face he received. A few orders, waving of guns, Maddock got the picture. Bones struggled to his feet and wiped his bloody nose. They all marched down the ladder and made their way to the submarine's deck. Just behind the bow, a hatch stood open. Maddock didn't look back, but scrambled down a steel ladder to a grating below. A glance around revealed stacked boxes in racks where torpedoes would normally be stored. Another ladder led through an internal hatch to a lower passageway.

A little prodding and the three of them were shoved into an empty compartment. Seated on a row of utilitarian chairs, they were bound arms and legs with zip-ties. Two men remained on guard. *Russian mercenaries*, Maddock thought. A third man stepped into view. Heavily built, no fat, his black eyebrows met just above his nose. *Mako.*

With little more than a twitch, he struck Maddock in the chest. The blow knocked him to the floor. The force of the blow stole his breath and opened one of the bandaged wounds. Hauling him back upright, Mako tore open Maddock's shirt. Like a curious child, he pressed a finger on one of the festering lacerations, his eyes alight with malice.

Maddock winced, but uttered only a grunt. But Mako knew how to inflict pain. It wasn't long before Maddock couldn't contain his cries of pain as the big mercenary pinched the wound and squeezed it between thumb and forefinger.

"I waited for this day. We have fun, *da*?"

At that moment, a tall man entered. Dark, square jaw, he would have been handsome had it not been for the cruel squint in his eyes and a chunk of an ear missing. Augustus Pym, Junior!

"Where's the girl?" Pym asked.

"We left her on Saipan." Bones said.

"Wrong answer." He gestured toward Bones. Mako administered two quick jabs, just below the sternum. Bones grunted. "My friend Maksim here is a *kuntao* master. They call him Mako in the islands, he knows more ways to hurt you than all of your ex-girlfriends could ever dream up in a year."

"She was with us," Lyn said. "We put her ashore on the East Island ahead of the storm."

"Now finally an answer I can possibly believe. Information on these two has proved strangely difficult to come by, but you, *Lyn Askew*. I know all about you. I know your names, I know where you came from, I know your bank accounts. It's amazing what a person can learn these days. All it takes is a little money, properly applied—for people who have money, that is."

Lyn grinned and said, "And you know we have none, so it must be something else you want. How can I be of service, Mr. Augustus Pym?"

"I think you just have, lady. At least for now. We'll descend a few hundred feet and let nature take her course. If things get boring, maybe I'll let Mako play with Mr. Maddock over there. There's apparently bad blood."

Lyn quirked an eyebrow. "Yeah, my former client. I think he's tapped out. Let me know if you think of anything else you need from me."

"Oh, I certainly will, but right now the three of you are nothing but ballast." Pym turned and spoke with someone just out of Maddock's vision. A few words, which sounded Slavic, then he grabbed Maddock by the hair and held a rough gold ingot to his face.

"So now you have a choice. You can tell me where this came from, or you can be the latest subject in Mako's research into how to inflict pain. He's studied the topic in depth."

"Don't waste your time. He'll just give you a load of crap," Lyn said. "They found a wreck on the east side of the lagoon and brought that coin up just before the storm arrived. We were planning to go back for the rest after things settled down. It's about a hundred feet down. I can take you right to the spot."

"You know what I love about a person who can be bought?" Pym straightened and grinned at Lyn. "You can always trust them to act in their own self-interest." He tossed the lump of gold to Mako. "Go make sure the airlock is ready and bring all the dive gear over from that tin can of theirs."

Maddock watched the big mercenary pad aft and he saw the look in Bones' eye. Someone was going to die that day. He just wasn't sure who to bet on.

Pym smirked and said, "Oh, I think Mako is going to have fun with you. I've had a special airlock built into this sub for transferring cargo underwater. You'll see it in a few minutes. But here's what I'm wondering. How long could you spend at a depth of a hundred feet before you got the bends? I hear they're excruciating. At that point, a person's best hope is for a nice aneurysm to end things quickly."

Clanking, voices, and footsteps forward. Pym's men were busy loading scuba bottles onto the sub. Moments later, Maddock felt the air pressure change, the hatches had closed. He kept his head down and didn't need to feign exhaustion. The attack, the toxins, the beatings, and now the creeping infection spreading from each laceration. They sucked the strength from him like nothing he'd felt before.

Pym said something to one of his mercenaries, and then smiled down at Lyn. "I think it's time you got acquainted with your new business partner. Ever ridden a big long submarine like mine? It's called the *Pale Horse,* and you are going to love it to death. Now come show me where this wreck is located, and maybe I'll show you a few things as well."

Lyn studiously avoided Maddock's gaze as she left. Though he should probably feel a sting, Maddock found himself utterly unsurprised by her betrayal. A leopard couldn't change its spots so easily.

22

Rushing waves surged knee deep as Sally waded ashore. The wind tugged at her bundle of gear and howled to rival the retreating whine of *Lark's* engine. She tried not to think of what Maddock and Bonebrake would be facing for the next few hours.

The towering wall of clouds, once only a line on the horizon, now bore down on them like an advancing army. Rain squalls cut across the lagoon, outriders of the storm. She climbed from the beach, noting that the coral stone had been cut into crude steps. Corey and Matt had preceded her, and Willis followed, carrying his own gear, as well as the marine battery she had insisted they bring.

The path ended in a flat shoulder. Bonebrake had described it as a meadow, but to Sally it looked more like the blasted heath of a Victorian novel. Willis thumped the heavy battery down behind her. "No way I haul this damn thing another inch higher," he said. "If you want it so bad, it's all yours."

Sally tried her sweet smile. It seldom worked but she'd run out of bluster. Pointing to a low bluff where Matt huddled out of the wind she said, "Please? Just over there." She didn't look back, but the grumbling told her that *sweet* had worked for once.

The rain, at first a fine mist, now fell in sheets that swept the East Island. Sally crouched next to Matt. He trembled, and his forehead was hot to her touch. "We need to find shelter," she said.

Willis looked up the hillside. "There was that Japanese outpost right above us. I'll see if there is some place up there we can take cover." Moments later he returned. "C'mon, there's a bunker up here."

Corey and Willis helped Matt climb. Sally waited for a heavy squall to pass, then clambered up after them. A gray cement wall had been constructed against the hillside. Its rusty steel door hung open like the flaccid jaw of a drowned man. Sally glanced back at the lagoon before entering. Across the water, another band of rain swept toward her. In the momentary clearing she saw a huge gray form slide beneath the waves.

She called to the others. Willis was first to poke his head outside. Sally could only point. He watched for a while. "It's only *Lark* down there."

Corey came out and Sally tried to explain. All three stared across the lagoon. The little boat swung and plunged in the waves below. "I see it, something's wrong. She's adrift with no one at the helm."

Sally tried to convince them. "I saw a whale or a huge shark, it was gray with a fin like an orca."

"You mean like a sail?" Corey said. "Like a tower in the water?"

Willis stared at her. "Did you see a submarine?"

"It could have been. There was this gray shape with a huge fin."

"They call that a 'sail.' There's a con in the top that's manned when they're on the surface." The advancing wall of rain had crossed the lagoon and blotted everything from sight. "We better take cover," Willis said.

Sally had feared the bunker when she first set eyes on it, but now she retreated inside to escape the pummeling rain. Dark and filthy, it stank like the latrines of hell. Corey and Willis ducked in after her and Willis repeated his question. "Was it the sail of a submarine?"

She squatted near the door and thought for a moment. Her head filled with a flood of impressions. She felt something alien, something dispassionate but curious; it left a word in her mind—a non-verbal word like the egg of a parasitic wasp, part of her, yet not. She shivered and looked up. "It was Pym. He has us right where he wanted us all along."

In the dim light she saw Willis nod. "I can't figure how you know, but I think you're right. That man is beginning to irritate me."

"He's got Maddock and Bones now too." Corey said. His voice was almost lost to the howling wind. It slammed the rusty door shut and they sat in a moment of darkness before another blast wrenched the door open and tore it from its hinges.

"We probably ought to move a little farther inside," Corey said. "Where's Matt?"

Willis raised his voice. "Matt, where are you man? C'mon, sound off."

Sally fished around in her purse. "Am I the only one who thought to bring a flashlight?"

She panned the interior. Rats had built a huge midden heap of trash and bones along one end of the narrow bunker. The remains of cots, and a scatter of aluminum cookware littered the other end. Directly before her, a square black tunnel had been cut into the hillside. *No Matt.*

Willis said, "He was loopy, but no way Matt would have crawled in there."

Corey dug out a flashlight of his own and peered

into the tunnel. Low, narrow, Sally wondered how Matt could have even found it in the dark. She examined the rat's nest. It consisted mostly of brush and flotsam, but slender bird bones had been interwoven into the pile. Something caught her eye, a button. She looked closer and discovered a crumbling human rib cage buried beneath the trash.

Corey came over at her shout. "Must have been one of the Japanese spotters. Just didn't make it, I guess."

"Well it sure ain't Matt," Willis said, "and we know he's not outside…"

Sally didn't let him finish. "I'll go in there." Before Willis could object, she said, "Dude, with those shoulders, you'd get stuck and I'd have to pull your ass out anyway. And I need you to watch my purse. Don't either of you think of touching it, or I'll break your fingers when I get back."

Sally had to duck as she entered the tunnel. The stench almost made her back out. Bent at the waist, she retched and gagged as she followed the flashlight's yellow beam. A bend in the tunnel took her deeper into the hillside.

Her wet shoes squelched as she walked. Something crunched beneath her feet. She stumbled. Catching herself against the walls, Sally focused her light on a broken skull. Bits of hair clung to one side and a set of porcelain dentures grinned back at her from the ruined mouth.

A short distance further, she met a cross-tunnel. The darkness in either direction swallowed her flashlight beam and Sally continued straight ahead. Something moved in the far shadows. Still crouching, she inched closer. Matt lay on a pile of debris. He'd been swathed in strips of rotted cloth like some obscene chrysalis.

Sally paused a moment, then something caught her about the knees and threw her to the floor. She yelled and kicked but whatever held her had a wiry grip that she couldn't dislodge. She felt sharp teeth sink into her calf and the pain gave her the frantic strength to pull one leg free and kick out at whatever held her.

It squealed like an injured dog and she swung her flashlight around. Just at her feet, two maddened eyes glared from beneath a mane of filthy hair. Its naked body was covered in sores and as Sally cringed back, she saw swarms of parasitic insects clinging to its skin.

At first it scuttled back under the glare of her flashlight, but moments later it began crawling toward her. On fingertips and calloused knees, the thing resembled nothing more than a giant coconut crab stalking her in the shadows. Once more on her feet, Sally groped around for something to use as a weapon. Her hand fell on the smooth curve of a bone. A human femur, she wrenched it free and swung at the glaring eyes. The thing bounced back. Agile, wary, it scuttled into the shadows, then sprang out.

Stumbling back, Sally swung with all her strength. Her blow caught it just behind the cheekbone, knocking it dazed to the floor. She stepped forward to finish the thing, but it retreated into the darkness, chittering and blinking. She didn't dare follow.

Sally backed toward Matt, flashlight fixed on the bestial eyes that glared from the shadowy passageway. He had freed one hand. Sally helped him shed the coils of fabric from his other arm.

Matt said, "Where's Willis?"

"Holding my purse. Can you walk?"

"Yeah, think so. But how do we get past Gollum there?"

She handed Matt the leg bone. "Fire Team A, Fire Team B, Ranger boy. I'll go first. If he jumps me, you beat on him."

As Sally advanced, her flashlight flickered and dimmed. She shook it and thumped it, still the beam faded to a yellow glow. "Really?"

"Just go, go," Matt said.

Sally rushed forward in the near darkness and felt the clutch of scratching nails. She brought the flashlight down on the raddled face. Matt barreled into her back, knocking them both sprawling in the darkness. She heard the crunch of Matt's club striking something and the teakettle scream of her assailant.

On her feet again, Sally had lost her flashlight. She reached out to find the walls and felt the rough vertical edge of an entrance. *The chamber? The branching tunnel she'd passed?* Head brushing the ceiling above, she groped at nothing but darkness in all directions.

Sally called out, and she heard Matt answer, but the echoes bombarded her from everywhere and nowhere. In the ensuing silence, she heard a soft scratching and chittering noise. "I need you, Fire Team B," she whispered.

Like a spider with strength far out of proportion to its size, the thing landed on her back and drove Sally to her knees. She managed to throw a hand up to block its stranglehold, yet still the thing crushed her neck beneath its arm. She kicked and thrashed, trying to roll it off her back, but the pressure on her throat just tightened with every move.

She could barely breathe, and flashes of light crept in

from the periphery of her vision. The flashes converged into a single bright glow that filled her consciousness and stole her will. She felt something tugging, tugging her. It grunted and cursed.

Sally thrashed and kicked. Willis said, "Damn, do that again and I'll leave you here."

"How did you find me?"

"Heard a bunch of yelling and screaming. Crawled in, just about beat to death by Matt. He's gone loony, babbling about spider man or something. I sent him out with my light. Then I see this weak-ass yellow glow, figured it was your flashlight. Next thing I know, I get jumped by Spidey himself." Sally felt Willis' hands on her shoulders. "Here, go this way."

"That thing, it's behind us." Sally struggled down the passage.

"I hit it good. You don't need to worry right now."

Willis guided her to the intersection of tunnels and indicated a passage to the right. "Ladies first."

"Just watch our backs."

A bend to the right and she saw the dim glow of their bunker refuge, and again heard the roar of the storm outside. Corey helped her from the tunnel and Willis emerged behind her. "Look what the cat dragged in," he said.

Matt stared at Sally as she straightened. "You saw it, you saw it. Tell them you saw it."

She nodded. "Something lives back there, look." She held out her leg and showed them a nasty bite that bled down her ankle. "It jumps and pounces like a spider. It would have eaten Matt and tried to eat me."

Corey inspected the wound. "The bite mark looks human." He crinkled his brow in concentration. "I've heard of Japanese soldiers who never surrendered. Maybe?"

"Too long ago," Sally said. "I'll bet it was the last survivor of Lyn's archeology expedition. But what happened to him?"

Matt said, "If we don't leave soon, we're all going to be like him."

"We got bigger problems, man," Willis said. "Pym showed up in a freaking submarine. He's got Maddock, Bones, and Lyn."

Sally didn't add …*Assuming they aren't already dead.* She knew it was on everyone's mind. The typhoon continued to rage outside, blowing a horizontal cascade across the bunker entrance.

Willis said, "Matt, you need to rest. Sally, you too. Corey and I will take watch. If that spider-looking thing shows his bootleg ass out here I'll stomp him good."

Sally slumped against a concrete wall. She rested but couldn't sleep. Something didn't add up. The Chamorros had lived here for centuries. *Why did the Ma'óghe spare them while driving others insane?* She recalled Mama Lani and her strange affinity for the coconut crabs of Pagan.

Willis came and sat next to her, never taking his eyes off the dark tunnel entrance. "You need to sleep."

"I can't help thinking," she said. "This Ma'óghe being, could it be trying to communicate with us?"

"How? By biting our asses?"

"I don't know. Maybe it reached out to us and we didn't reply, so it got more aggressive. Maybe it gets lonely. Maybe it's trying to talk with us by some kind of telepathy."

"Now you sound as looney as your friend Mama

Lani."

"Maybe she's not all that looney. Maybe it messes with us because it's trying to communicate and we don't respond. Or it misinterprets our lack of responsiveness?"

"Messing with us like Spidey in there?"

She shrugged. "And you don't feel this place is getting to you? It's getting to me."

"So, what are you going to do about it?"

"A great man once said, 'When your mind plays tricks on you, play tricks right back.' I'm going to talk to it."

23

Bones watched his friend haul himself aft, prodded in the back by an AKS carbine. He eyed the weapon, and the man holding it, each a model of lethal efficiency. Bones had trained with the AKS as a SEAL. A short-range weapon, its 7.62 millimeter round packed a wallop. The merc wielding it seemed at ease, his trigger finger pressed lightly against the receiver, just above the trigger guard. *He'd shoot us soon as he'd scratch his nose*, Bones mused.

He knew that behind them a second guard followed, an arm's length back. Maddock paused at a hatchway. He hoisted one leg over the coaming, then the other. Bones watched the guard's reaction, patience, no anger. *Damn good bunch of pros*, he thought. *I'll almost hate to kill them.*

Bones followed. Barking his knee on the coaming, he cursed and stumbled. No use looking too agile. They reached a wide spot in the passage with an open hatch in the deck. Two tanks and a stack of gear lay next to the hatch. When Maddock began suiting up, Bones got a good look at his shredded legs and torso. *The man's running on nothing but stubborn will*, he thought.

For the first time, Bones saw one of the mercs display a trace of expression, a fleeting glance of respect followed by a face of stone. Bones donned his own gear, slinging the huge tank over his back. One-hundred thirty-three cubic feet of life-giving nitrox mixture, compressed to three thousand pounds per square inch. About thirty minutes before they drowned, twenty minutes before they'd get the bends for certain.

As Bones adjusted his mask, he felt pressure on his left leg. One of the guards had shackled a light chain to his ankle. Maddock got one as well. Maybe fifty feet long, it draped down into the airlock where it had been attached to the ladder. *So much for Plan A*, he thought.

They were each given a canvas sack and invited to climb into the airlock chamber. As the inner hatch closed, Bones switched his com on. "Hear me?"

"Oh, I hear you loud and clear Mr. Bonebrake." Pym's voice came back over the radio channel. "You don't think I'd go to all this trouble without proper communications." He was interrupted by the burble and rush of water entering the chamber. It came in fast and compensating for the pressure was all they could do for several minutes. "Now listen up," Pym continued, "we're sitting right on top of the wreck. You each need to fill your sack and bring it over to the sub. If you do well, I might let you live and dive again. Mako is just waiting for one of you to fail."

A green glow lit the bottom of their airlock as Pym activated the outer hatch. "Twenty minutes, gentlemen. Work quickly."

A familiar scene presented itself, the same wreck, but now the water surged like a laundry tub, stirring sand and silt into a maelstrom of confusion. Maddock began by jamming random lumps into his sack. Bones grabbed his friend by the shoulder, but then looked at him, mask to mask.

Maddock switched off his com. When Bones did the same, he spoke by direct mask contact. "Fill your bag,

I've got a plan."

They both switched on and the first thing Bones heard was Pym's voice. "What's happening out there?"

"Com cut out," Bones said. "We're about done." He wondered what Maddock was up to. He'd just have to follow his friend's lead.

"You've got almost ten more minutes, gentlemen. Make them worth my trouble."

Maddock shook his head and made a slashing motion across his throat. Bones watched the pantomime for a moment and then said, "Maddock's having problems with his gear, we're going in."

"Damn you, I'll have you both sitting in that lock until you're sucking dead air."

Bones didn't bother responding. He followed Maddock with his bag of ballast rock and coral debris, hoping the plan involved something more than divine intervention. Once inside the chamber, they pulled bags and tether chains in after, and waited.

Nothing moved for several minutes, then an interior light came on and the outside hatch slowly closed behind them. Maddock gave him a smile and a wink, and then his head slumped. As the water receded, he collapsed beneath the weight of his scuba tank. Bones understood and played along. He did what he could to support his friend, stripping off his mask in the growing pocket of air. Shortly, he felt his ears equalize as the air pressure fell to surface normal. Maddock hadn't moved. He didn't appear to be breathing.

"You'd better be acting." When the inner hatch opened, Bones shouted up, "We need some help! He's not breathing."

No reply.

Gripping Maddock by the vest, Bones tried to boost him, but the limp man only doubled over and wedged against the side. "I can't believe I have to carry your fat ass," Bones grumbled. Climbing higher, Bones still clung to his vest. Arms reached down and pulled them both free. They dropped Maddock on the deck where he lay crumpled on his side. His jaw hung slack and water drained from his mouth. Bones stripped off tank and weights. He'd long ago slipped out of his fins. The same two mercs guarded them. One had set aside his carbine and was checking Maddock for a pulse, the other looked up as hurried footsteps sounded in the corridor.

In the next instant Maddock's eyes opened and he slammed the kneeling guard's head against the open hatch. Bones already had kicked out, knocking the other man's legs from under him. His next move reversed the carbine and discharged a 7.62 millimeter bullet up through his opponent's jaw.

"Back in the airlock." Maddock yelled.

Bones went in headfirst as a spray of shots ricocheted off the deck and pinged about the interior. Maddock slipped down right after him, then popped up to return fire. Silence followed. "You got 'em all?" Bones asked.

"Not hardly. There are at least six at the aft end of the passage." Maddock fired another short burst.

"Why aren't they shooting?"

"Just cover your ears, this is about to get crazy."

Bones saw his friend turn around and face forward. He fired a single shot, and in that moment, Bones remembered the stack of ten fully charged scuba cylinders that remained beneath the forward ladder.

The resulting concussion blew Maddock back down

into the chamber like a cork pushed too far into a wine bottle. Bones could hear nothing. From above, a spray of seawater grew into a torrent that rushed down about their heads. Maddock, now unconscious in truth, lay in a heap at his feet. Bones once more grabbed his collar and hoisted him up. Maddock's eyes flickered and he struggled to get his feet back under him.

"Come on, dude," Bones said.

Maddock nodded and placed a hand on Bones' shoulder. "Let's go."

The passageway lights had gone out, replaced by red emergency illumination. Forward, a chaos of spray, churning water, and debris filled the corridor. The sub tried to rise. Pitched bow down, it backed toward the surface. It took Bones five shots to sever their chains. With Maddock wobbling along behind him, he worked his way forward. Four men lay in the next compartment, stunned by the shock wave. Taking no chances, he dispatched the four with a knife, then searched them for weapons.

Maddock had regained his balance and his wits, so Bones gave him a Makarov he'd recovered from one of the fallen men. Maddock inspected it, then chambered a round. Then he frowned. "Do you feel that?"

Bones nodded. The submarine shuddered, fighting the rising tide in its forward compartments. Then a different vibration, a whine he could feel beneath his feet. Bones glanced up the corridor to confirm what he already knew. The watertight hatches had closed, trapping them in the doomed bow section. He turned back to Maddock.

"This day just keeps getting better. I think…"

Suddenly, Maddock raised the Makarov and fired it

at Bones.

"What the hell?" Bones said. A heavy thud behind him told the story. He turned to see one of the mercs lying on the deck, a pool of blood around his ruined head. A knife lay inches from his limp hand. With a shudder, Bones stepped back into the compartment. *Careless.*

"I'm your huckleberry," Maddock said with a grin. "Sorry. I've always wanted to say that."

"Normally I'd come back with a Wyatt Earp quote, but I'm busy trying to decide whether or not to punch you."

"No time to warn you," Maddock said. "Now, let's think. We've got four men on the deck here and that guy in the corridor." He pointed to the fallen man.

Bones nodded. "Where's the sixth man?" He could feel his ears pop as the pressure in the forward compartment increased with the rising water. Maddock held his hand flat beneath his nose. They'd wait until it equalized.

Bones mouthed, *Forward hatch?* Maddock shrugged. *Divine intervention after all. Wonderful.*

By the time the water had risen to waist level in their compartment, Bones felt the submarine begin to buck and lurch in response to the typhoon-driven waves above. A great rolling surge of water would begin at the forward end of the dim, red corridor and slosh toward them like a charging hippopotamus, drenching everything before retreating in a cascading mass of bubbles and debris.

At the fifth such cycle, Bones saw something different, almost human in the rush. Maddock gasped, seized the door frame, and then was dragged wide eyed underwater. Bones dove after him, slammed up against a floating table, and then flew backwards as the next surge caught him. A floating hand, a dead face, one of the mercenary guards glided by. Bones surfaced for air and saw his friend thrashing, struggling with something in the eerie red light.

Another surge and Bones ducked under, expecting to find a nest of tentacles wrapped about his friend's legs. Instead, it was Mako. The big merc gripped Maddock by the neck, knife in hand. Bones let the rush of water carry him like a human torpedo straight at the struggling pair. Heedless of the knife, he slammed into the attacker, breaking his grip.

Faster than Bones had expected, and twice as strong, Mako spun away from him and returned with a fist rather than the knife. Even underwater, the blow to his ribs knocked the air from his lungs and left him seeing flashes. Still, years of SEAL training and street reflexes told him where the knife would strike. It nicked his chest, flashing by. Bones trapped a sinewy arm beneath his own. He thrust his other palm beneath the man's chin and wrenched his head back.

A knee in the abdomen finally forced Bones to let go. For the first time, he caught sight of his adversary's face. A flash of hatred, then the next surge rolled past carrying chairs and boxes and even an intact scuba tank. Bones lost contact and surfaced.

Maddock swam up, relief on his face to see his friend alive. Bones shook his head and pointed down the corridor. The man was still in there, hiding in a compartment, somewhere. The rising water and the confusion rendered guns mostly useless. Besides, Bones knew that Mako himself was probably the deadliest weapon on the sub. *Second deadliest*, Bones thought, and grinned.

Maddock pointed to himself and mouthed *airlock*, making an opening gesture with his hand. Bones nodded. The thing should have a manual actuator on the inside. He drew his hand across his throat and pointed forward. No words needed. Diving into the churning water, he'd hunt, one compartment at a time.

Bones surfaced for air, then pulled himself forward. A glimpse of movement. Mako had allowed himself to be seen. Bones pulled back just as a knife blade streaked up from behind a coaming. The big mercenary followed, filling the doorway. Bones blocked his rush, then withdrew.

Mako lunged forward and Bones jammed a hatch against his knife arm. Held this way, he couldn't retreat and couldn't surface. Mako tried a few blows to the neck and sensitive spots of the abdomen. Water slowed him, and Bones absorbed the pain, knowing that each lunge cost his opponent breath.

With a wrenching movement, Mako dropped the knife and pulled his arm free. Bones seized the knife and followed, grabbing the big man's ankles. Still, he couldn't prevent him from reaching the air pocket.

Now it was Bones' turn to retreat. Air, air... even a navy SEAL needed air sometime. Bones rode a wave of debris aft, gasping in the maelstrom of floating trash. He slammed into Maddock. A grim look and shake of the head. *The outer door must be locked.* They were trapped, and the devil was still loose. Something smacked into his leg. Scuba bottle, intact and full. He scooped it up... something from BUDS, Basic Underwater Demolition School... something about incompressible water, and a tank with three thousand pounds per square inch pressure.

His friend nodded when Bones held up the tank, but no sign of comprehension reached his face. *Maddock must be fading fast,* Bones thought, *or he would have figured this one out first.* Still his friend followed as they worked their way back to the airlock. He opened the tank valve and dropped it into the open airlock. Maddock finally caught on and helped Bones close and dog the heavy inner hatch.

A hunch made Bones signal *halt* with clenched fist as they were about to resurface. Both held on to the closed hatch and let another wave build, then carry them back aft. As they surfaced, the rattle of gunfire was followed by a spray of bullets that peppered the water behind them. "This is getting tiresome," Maddock said.

"I hear you. I can hear you, buddy."

"My ears are working too. So, what do we do about this joker? I'm out of ideas."

Bones drew his stolen combat knife. "Let's just go stalk him and kill him. You hold him down, I'll rip the crap out of him."

Moments later, the sub rung like it had been struck by a giant hammer. Maddock said, "I think you just blew open the gates of hell, my friend. What say we fly out of here, instead?"

Bones led the way, pushing through a wall of debris. The submarine pitched, stern up, and all the water rushed to the bow. "Now for it," Bones said.

When they reached the airlock, the hatch had been opened and a pool of greenish water glowed before their eyes. Maddock jumped in first, Bones followed, a quick swim and they found themselves less than thirty feet below the surface of the lagoon. As they rose, it became very clear that super-typhoon Chaga had arrived in force.

24

Waves broke over the submarine, rushed along its sloping deck, and poured across its submerged bow. Maddock and Bones swam for the stricken sub, their only refuge in a chaos of wind and spray. Thrown against the starboard dive-plane, they crawled up its forward deck and found shelter behind the high gray sail. The wind screamed past them carrying a torrent of rain and spray. Maddock dragged himself to his feet and clung to a handrail. "He's out here too, isn't he?"

Bones ducked to let a great hissing wall of green water pass over his head. "Only Mako could have opened that inner hatch. He's here somewhere."

Like a djinn summoned from the underworld, the *kuntao* master appeared from behind the sail holding a deadly Makarov pistol.

Maddock saw him first and said, "Speak of the Devil and he shall appear."

Bones looked up. "Oh, is that the best you can do? After all we've been through together, a pistol? Come on. Are you really going to kill me straight out and miss the chance to hurt me a little bit first?"

Before his friend finished, Maddock released his grip and slid back into the churning water. A bullet zipped past his face leaving a tiny streak of bubbles in the chaos about him. *Fifteen-thousand, sixteen-thousand, seventeen-thousand*; Maddock surfaced to see a giant wave wash past the sail. The big mercenary hardly flinched. Knees bent, he slid forward squeezing off two more rounds in Maddock's direction.

Once more under water, Maddock struck his head against the dive-plane and grabbed blindly at its trailing edge. The smooth metal bucked beneath his outstretched arms, then carried him clear of the waves. Crouched on the deck, Mako took aim at Maddock, then spun around to face Bones scrambling up behind, knife in hand.

At that moment, they all pitched forward as the *Pale Horse* plunged bow-down into the lagoon. Maddock was dragged once more under water. Nearly exhausted, he worked his way towards the hull and crawled to the deck. It shifted beneath him. Up, up, the water rushed back and Maddock found himself once more in the air.

Not three yards away, Mako clung to the forward hatch, his legs wrapped around Bones' neck. His friend stabbed at the man with no effect. Summoning the last of his strength, Maddock sprang up and slammed his elbow down on the big merc's right collar bone. Like a trodden snake, Mako released his grip on the hatch and struck Maddock in the neck. The next wave swept all three over the bow.

Gagging in pain, Maddock swam to the surface. But the sea, normally his refuge, now fought his every move. Huge and gray beneath the water, like a curious orca *Pale Horse* once more swept him up on its deck. Gasping, flat on his back, Maddock could only stare at the cloud-studded sky above. A breeze, a glimpse of sunlight, rain forgotten, if not for the pain in his throat and the deck vibrating against his back, it all could have been a dream.

A spray of gunfire against steel tattooed his arm with bits of paint and shrapnel. Maddock's reverie broken, he rolled to his feet and leaped for cover at the base of the sail. Someone had spotted him from the con above and opened an upper hatch. *The storm's eye, of course.* He knew they had about twenty minutes of calm before Super-typhoon Chaga redoubled its fury. Twenty minutes for Pym's men to shoot him where he crouched.

Willis heard it first. Sally watched him raise his head, and then stand in the half-light. "What's up?"

"Storm's letting up, listen…"

The incessant wind had roared and whistled around their bunker for hours. Sally concentrated on the sound. There was a difference. "Wind's changed directions, that's all."

"I'll take a look," Willis said.

Sally stood. "Let's go."

Corey eyed the two. "Be careful out there."

"We'll be fine. You keep an eye out, too." Willis handed him a length of rusty pipe. "Spidey comes back, wallop him good for me."

Sally ducked her head and stepped outside. She was greeted with a face full of warm rain sheeting down from the north. Still, it beat the bunker's fetid stench. Willis followed her out; his shirt plastered itself to his broad chest and a small torrent ran from his chin.

"Wind's changed," he shouted. "Look out there."

Sally flattened herself against the concrete bunker and worked her way toward the lagoon. Far across, on the west side, she saw a smudge of yellow sunlight breaking through the rain. "Eye of the storm," Willis said. "It's moving northeast now, be here any minute."

As Sally watched, the rain let up and the wind died to a fresh southerly breeze. Willis put his hand on her shoulder and pointed further north. *Lark* lay run aground upon a gravely beach. Waves broke against her stern. They surged through the cabin to burst foaming from her empty wheelhouse windows.

Almost two miles off, a gray cylinder bobbed and rolled in the waves. Willis cursed under his breath. "Son of a... That's got to be Pym."

Sally watched the ungainly shape. Its sail rose like a fin from the water, dipping and swaying in the heavy seas. For a moment, the propeller broke clear of the surface, only to slam down again in a shower of spray. "Why doesn't he dive?" Sally asked.

"There's damage. Pym's boat is a wounded tuna. Look at it. Bones must have gotten loose. He's been known to have that effect on machinery."

A squall line crossed the lagoon, blotting everything out in a curtain of gray. Sally clung to her position and let the rain and wind whip past. When the last drizzle fled off to the north, the submarine had moved much closer to the east island. She made out its forward diving planes and two figures crawling across the bow. Maddock and Bones! They were alive! But what were they up to?

Sally jumped up. "C'mon, we're launching the drone. We're going to provide them with reinforcements."

They grabbed Corey and Matt and hurried down to the plateau, closer to the water. Down to the spot where the strange, carved stone stood.

"I don't know how well this is going to work," Corey said, looking out across the lagoon. "It's still awful windy."

Sally ignored him. She knelt next to the glyph-covered stone and set up her little notebook computer.

"Batteries, check. Controls, check. Multi-spectrum squid-squawker, up and flashing. *Give me warp three Scotty.*"

Willis stood and shaded his eyes. "Hurry up! Our boys are about to get slaughtered."

Corey stepped back. The drone buzzed into the air, banked hard, and whined down to the water below. Sally headed it straight toward the men pouring from an aft-hatch. She held it just above the water, skimmed it past their heads and hovered off the port bow.

"You making a kamikaze run?" Corey asked.

"Don't distract me. Just shut up and plug me into the data unit." She bent over her computer. Sally's fingers danced like Michael Flatley. Almost crying, she whispered, "Be there, be there…"

Willis had the binoculars out. "You better move it. They're shooting at your toy."

"Better at the drone than at Maddock and Bones," Matt said.

Sally veered the drone behind Bones and Maddock. *I'm here guys, I'm here. Just hang in there.* From their spot up on the bluff, she could hear the shots.

Two men approached the sail. Willis said, "Bones has his knife out, but I don't see a gun. Two seconds, they're both dead."

Sally did the only thing she could. She swooped her drone around and crashed it into the nearest attacker. It caromed off and struck a second man before spinning into the lagoon.

"Two down, nice flying," Willis said. "Now what?"

"I hate this," Matt said. "If we had weapons, we could take action, but now we're stuck waiting to see what the geek squad has rolled up their sleeves."

"Working on it, dude. Working on it," Sally said. Something… something else she needed. On impulse, Sally dug into her shorts pocket. The familiar little goddess practically burned in her hand. She pulled it out. *The legs. The tapered legs!* Sally jammed her ancient figurine into the conical stone socket. As one, her computer lit up and all of the symbols surrounding the Eye of God responded with a blazing array of flashing lights.

"We got a signal," she cried out. "Oh God, I can feel it, I can feel it. *Ma'óghe* is with us."

Sally no longer had to read her computer screen. She knew, she knew… it was with her and she was part of something. She felt the ocean about her like a cloak that spread from her shoulders to the horizon. She felt the grip of ten thousand arms on the steel intruder below. She would shred them all and send their carcasses to feed the millions…

They were in deep trouble. Aft, past the sail, where waves had once crashed unabated against the submarine's hull, Maddock saw another hatch open and a dozen armed men swarm on deck. They fell flat as something like a bird swept past. Six of them knelt and opened fire at the thing while the others advanced toward Maddock's position. Flying low over the water, it buzzed around the sail. Sally's drone. It hovered for a moment and Maddock could almost hear her voice say, *I got your back, big guy.*

The drone tilted and bore down on the advancing men. Its whirling propellers sliced into the face of one mercenary. Caroming off the deck, it slammed into the back of a second, before spinning into the lagoon. There it floated in the chop and flashed like a defective neon sign.

A hand on Maddock's shoulder slammed him to the deck as a burst of gunfire rattled off the sail above. Bones. "Keep your head down, buddy," he said.

"Where's Mako?"

"Last I saw, he was swimming for the island. Willis is going to be busy."

Another spray of gunfire from the con, but nothing struck nearby. Maddock looked at Bones. "What's he shooting at if not us?"

Already up on one knee he said, "You aren't going to believe this, look."

Just behind the sail, a dozen black-clad mercenaries rolled on the narrow deck struggling beneath hundreds of pulsing gray squid.

"Holy crap!" Bones shouted.

Maddock's eyes went wide. "It's the Ma'óghe!"

Bones darted from cover. He grabbed a carbine off the deck and spun, firing a burst up at the sail. "C'mon," he yelled. "The aft hatch is open."

Maddock felt something latch onto his left leg. With a shudder, he kicked it off and ran across the deck. Bones dropped down the open hatch. Maddock followed.

A powerful arm wrapped around Sally's waist and lifted her off her feet. She gasped and blinked her eyes. Where was she? What was happening?

"What are you doing?" Willis hissed. "You just gonna fly off that cliff?"

She fought a moment, then the sunlight and smell of wet earth brought her back. "I don't know, I was… what's happening down there?"

"Didn't you see it? Tentacles! Just did a Pirates of the Caribbean on that bunch. Pulled 'em down under the water. Next thing I know, you're about to do a swan dive off the cliff."

"And Maddock? Bonebrake?"

"Down the hatch. I mean below deck, they made it inside and battened down tight."

"So, they're inside of Pym's sub. I don't know if that's good or bad."

"Don't worry about them. It's the kind of thing we do and they're the best. Besides, we've got problems of our own. Look over there!" He pointed toward the horizon.

Charging up from the south, a black precipice of cloud swept toward them. "It's the eyewall," Willis said. "Gonna get twice as hairy when that thing hits."

Sally watched a new set of waves surge into the lagoon through the south channel. Long, low rollers, they mounded up and poured over the rocks on either side. Like watching some enormous pride of lions rushing a herd of antelope, Sally couldn't look away. "I'm already soaked. I think I'll stay for the show."

"I'll stay with you," Corey said.

Willis shrugged. "Suit yourselves. Me and Matt are going inside 'til it's over. And try not to jump off any more cliffs."

Sally retrieved her carved Madonna, now a cold lump of bone. She and Corey helped carry the equipment back beneath cover, then found a sheltered overhang in the outer wall. Sally had entrusted Matt and Willis with her notepad, but kept her purse clutched to her side. Corey wrapped his arms around her and they snuggled close. The concrete bunker offered some shelter from the onslaught of the storm, but the windblown spray still managed to soak them in a matter of minutes.

A large wave grew and crested as it bored down the lagoon. *One one-thousand, two one-thousand...* she reached twenty before the next one shouldered its way between the rocks.

"What's with that look on your face?" Corey asked.

"Remember the data? This lagoon's going to resonate like crazy!" She watched the next set arrive. "Twenty-two second waves and all hell is going to break loose."

"The sub!"

They moved forward for a better look. Sally tried to make out the submarine in the chaos below. Sometimes it looked like the bow or the stern danced vertically below her. Other times the entire craft was lost beneath the churning foam. *Nineteen-thousand, twenty-thousand, twenty-one...*

The lagoon exploded into a cauldron of insanity. From the south, a chain of impossibly huge waves blasted through the channel entrance and washed high up the opposite cliff.

The waves reflected and merged with a new set of rollers. Like colliding armies, they ran back and crashed together again. By then another set had entered and added its energy to the boiling mass. Exactly twenty-two seconds later, yet one more mountain of foam added to the fury. Still more waves kept arriving.

Within minutes, Maug Lagoon looked like a nuclear test site. Green water surged up the cliff and over-washed the small plateau below. A great leaping tongue of seawater sprang into the air before Sally's eyes, drenching her in salt spray. And out in the lagoon, she watched the submarine rise from the water like a conjurer's trick. Supported by six enormous gray arms, it swayed almost thirty feet above the surface before plunging into the maelstrom.

Sally let out a shriek. Corey pulled her close and she let her head sag against his chest and wept as he guided her back to the bunker.

"They're dead," she sobbed. "They are all dead. I saw it. Oh God, it's horrible! I think Ma'óghe crushed the submarine. Maddock, Bonebrake, Lyn, they're all dead."

She let Corey hold her, sobbing into his rain-soaked shirt. "It's my fault. None of this would have happened if Bonebrake hadn't wandered into the diner that day. Everything that's happened is because of me."

Corey said nothing, but she could feel the tension in his arms and the trembling in his chest.

Matt came over and sat next to them. He said, "Hang in there. We don't know what actually happened." His hollow tone told a different tale.

They all waited in silence while the wind shrieked around their cramped shelter. Typhoon Chaga raged over Maug Lagoon for most of that afternoon. Peeking outside, Sally watched wave after enormous wave leap high and spill across the flats below.

For a moment, the westering sun broke from behind the banks of swirling clouds and curtains of rain. In the shadows below, Sally made out a dark shape. Gray water surged around it. She gasped and pulled back; the thing moved.

"Ma'óghe has come," she cried. "My God, it's coming for me."

Willis looked out. He stood while the rain streamed

from his face. Finally, he said, "Nothing out there except a butt-load of nasty weather."

"I saw it, some big thing has crawled up from the lagoon."

Willis muttered a curse and stepped back into the bunker. The doorway darkened and a shaggy figure pushed its way inside. Large, human, it held a twelve-gauge shotgun.

"Mako." Willis said.

25

"**Close the hatch** now!" Maddock ordered. Gunfire rattled above. The submarine shook. The very air seemed to vibrate.

Bones didn't hesitate to reach up, draw the heavy steel door over his head, and dog it shut. They descended a vertical cylinder and slid out through a second hatch.

"Escape vestibule," Bones said. "We practiced with them in BUDS, but I've never used one. Look, it's like an upside-down airlock." He frowned. "Of course, we're back inside. This is where my plan ends. What now?"

Maddock bared his teeth in a wolfish grin. "We take out Junior. Then we drive this thing back to Guam and let the Coasties take care of it."

Bones said. "Okay, get Junior first. How we gonna do it?"

"Shut her down. I lost the Makarov when Mako jumped me, so you'll have to cover me," Maddock said, pointing at the Kalashnikov Bones had snatched up. "I'll go in and pull the panic-dampers, kill the engine."

Maddock pushed open a hatch and crawled through. Four crewmen sat at consoles in the next compartment. One stood and reached for his pistol. Bones took him out with a well-aimed shot.

"Don't be shooting up the equipment," Maddock said. "We'll need it."

Following the fleeing crewmen, they entered a long gallery housing the engine. Maddock could hear nothing over the howling superchargers until three bullets pinged off the deck. Bones returned fire as Maddock bent double and crossed a steel grating. One, two, three, four gray steel levers, he slapped them down in sequence and the howl died along with the engine.

"There, nice and quiet," Maddock said.

A burst of automatic weapon fire from the forward end of the gallery sent them both flat on the deck.

Bones yelled, "Ivan! *slooshey. Nikureet*, comrade. *Nikureet*." Silence followed. He grinned at Maddock. "I just told them not to fire."

"I think what you actually said was, 'No smoking,' but it worked."

"Looks like you'se all done w' crewing ol' Lyn here," someone yelled out.

It took Maddock a moment to recognize the voice. "Jungle Jim. So, you found a new master."

"Yep, one that pays. So you're gonna put that gun down now. Better give it up, or I'll pull the fire suppressor and gas you both. Gas the girl here, too."

"That's not going to happen, and you know it," Maddock said. "We'll just retreat back a bulkhead and wait until this thing runs up on the beach."

"We got us about two days of battery power. Think you can last that long?"

"Bring us our gold bar," Bones yelled back, "then maybe we won't flood another compartment."

"What about your lady friend? My boss made a good start on 'er. How 'bout I just let Mako finish it?"

The engine room lurched and rolled. Odd bits of equipment slid across the deck, rattled on the grating and fell clattering below. Bones had handed him the rifle and disappeared during the exchange.

"Your buddy Mako is nothing but squid poop by now. You want to join him?" He punctuated the question by firing off a single shot.

"That was foolish, Maddock. You wasted your ammunition and might'a hit your pretty girlfriend here. Say something for the boys, Lyn."

Maddock heard a muffled scream, and Jungle Jim said, "Oh wait, I done forgot to remove the tape." A second later, the gallery echoed with shrieks and sobs. "She's got a surprisingly high tolerance for pain, but we got there in the end. So, you ready to do a little trade? Say the weapon for the lady?"

The deck heaved and rolled beneath Maddock's feet. Maybe it had electric power, but this sub wouldn't dive again without major repairs. He crouched to steady himself and tried to figure what Bones was up to. *Likely he was weighing the odds of jumping an armed man before being shot.* Angling for time, Maddock said, "How do we know you won't kill all three of us if I give you this gun?"

"You don't. Either way, you're probably dead."

"I'll lay it on the deck. You send Lyn to get it. The deal is, she comes back here after she gives it to you."

"Eject the clip and put it where I can see it."

One round left in the chamber, she gets one shot. Maddock hoped Lyn understood. He ejected the clip and made sure the safety was off. Hiding behind a gray steel cowl, he pushed the carbine out, barrel first. Footsteps on the steel grating, but instead of Lyn, Jungle Jim appeared, pistol in hand. "Never, ever give up your weapon. Didn't they teach you nothin' at school?"

Pale Horse rolled, then pitched forward. Jim grabbed a bundle of conduit for support as the Kalashnikov skittered down the deck. Bones rose from behind an air duct, snatched the carbine, and put a ragged hole where Jungle Jim's third cervical vertebra had been. "And never turn your back on the enemy," Bones said.

At that moment, *Pale Horse* put its bow to the air, rearing like its namesake. Maddock clutched the deck, then fell tumbling backward. Bones came crashing down on him. Duct-taped to a chair, Lyn slid screaming past, little more than a falling projectile.

She bounced off a cooling pipe and hung in the air as the sub toppled like a felled tree. The lights flashed, then dimmed to orange as emergency lamps came on. Maddock slid forward, skidded across the engine grating, and collided with Lyn's chair. He hung on as once more *Pale Horse* pitched on its stern.

A loose carbine bounced past. Set on full automatic, it fired random bursts that pinged and whined about the compartment. This time, the sub rolled as it came down. The canted deck turned until Maddock and Lyn slammed together against the engine. A shower of debris, bilge and loose furniture cascaded around them. Maddock called out for Bones and his friend answered from somewhere in the chaos. Another roll and the submarine heaved up, then slammed down hard.

Someone grabbed Maddock's leg. He looked down and Bones grinned back at him in the dim red glow. "Hang on buddy, this tub's coming apart."

"I've got Lyn, but she's strapped to a chair."

"Got Mako's knife right here." Bones dragged himself along the engine and slashed away the woman's bonds. "Back, everyone back aft," he yelled.

Lyn didn't move. Maddock slung her across his shoulder and worked his way along the canted deck.

Between the two of them they carried her through a hatch into the next compartment. More shots pinged off the bulkhead as Maddock scrambled after. He shut and dogged the hatch. *Pale Horse* rolled to her starboard side and shuddered. "We're on the bottom, Bones. What in hell is going on?"

"The curse of Maug. We need to get the hell out of here before this thing floods."

Maddock paused to get his bearings. In the red emergency lights, he made out an open hatch behind them. At that moment, a loud horn began to sound. "Too late, the batteries are on fire and someone has pulled the halon gas system."

"Mako," Willis said. His voice betrayed neither surprise nor fear.

"Maksim, Mako, *da*. Is perhaps unfortunate for you I find shelter in boat. Is uncomfortable ride, but have useful weapon. Ha?"

Matt moved slightly to the left, as Willis crouched. Sally clutched her purse and retreated into the shadowy bunker interior. Mako grinned. "Do not do stupid things. Have four targets and five shots. I think is advantage mine."

Willis said, "Shoot me, and see if you can move before Matt brings you down."

"Is not a problem. See? I take New York City girl instead. Come, boss wants you. Makes Maksim very rich *cheloveck*."

"Your boss is dead, smart guy. His sub is a debris field right now."

"You are ignorant. Boss has escape pod. Is not a

problem. Now move aside or I waste shot."

Sally said, "Move Willis, it's okay." She saw him glance over his shoulder and nodded. "Really, I'll be fine, won't I Maksim?"

Willis moved. A single shot blasted out in the cramped chamber. Mako recoiled a step, leveled his twelve-gauge; then a second shot spun him around. His shotgun discharged against the doorframe, peppering them all in cement and lead fragments.

Matt tackled him first, sending Mako to his knees. The big merc slammed the gunstock into Matt's face and racked another round. Willis lunged up with the iron pipe and smashed it down on Mako's shoulder. He grunted and gave Willis a shove. As Mako stumbled away, Corey dashed toward him, fists clenched.

Sally stepped up and thrust her purse in Mako's face. The next instant, Mako's head exploded in a spray of blood. The boom of the gunshot rang in their ears.

Sally pulled the smoking Smith and Wesson from her purse and held it out in a trembling hand. "A wise man once said, 'Whoever shoots first, gets to live.' That one was too stupid to live." Her brave words rang hollow.

Willis recovered his wits. "Damn. You packing heat too?"

"Bonebrake gave it to me. Thought it might come in handy." She paused and stared at the old revolver. "I just…"

She suppressed a sob, and Willis finished for her. "It's all right. You did what you had to do, but it ain't easy."

Sally turned pleading eyes upon Corey. "I had to. We've already lost so many."

"You did the right thing, the necessary thing," Corey assured her. "Now, it looks like the storm is letting up and Spidey is probably still lurking around here somewhere. What did Mako say about a boat?"

"I don't know. I was a bit distracted," Willis said as he dragged the ruined corpse aside.

Corey was first to duck outside. "Look, there *is* something down there."

Sally followed him out just as the rain squall passed. "Holy crap. It's *Lark* come to get us."

Matt pushed past her. "I've got to see this."

Willis had started down the slope, with Corey right behind him. Sally and Matt followed. They stepped over broken bits of steel and plastic all twisted up in great mounds of seagrass. The field had been stripped to the bare rock, with only piles of coral debris to mark the waves' passage.

Scattered clouds followed in the wake of Typhoon Chaga, but the rain had stopped. They all stood staring up at *Lark*. It sat perched on the hillside, trim and upright on its flat bottom. Sally stood back, clutching her purse. Somehow this apparition of a boat seemed ready to spawn yet more enemies.

Beaten and battered, *Lark* rested on the slope with its bow hanging out over a ledge like some huge seabird peering from its nest.

"We must be eighty feet up," Sally said. "I'd stay back. If that thing falls."

Willis ignored her. He jumped for a frayed line that hung from the port side and pulled himself up. "Engine compartment is flooded," he shouted down. "But the forward cargo well is dry."

Matt examined the stern. "We've lost both rudders

and the starboard wheel is pretzeled. Port side doesn't look too bad, a little dinged."

"Who gives a rat's ass about the rudders?" Sally asked.

Matt gave her a confused look. "Unless you plan on swimming to Saipan and get us some help, it's the only boat we got right now."

"That's not a boat. It's a wreck."

While they were bantering, Corey had climbed up the side. He stood conferring with Willis, then said, "C'mon up Sally. I want to show you something."

Wondering if Ma'óghe had already affected all of their minds, Sally accepted Willis' outstretched hand and found herself teetering on the aft deck. Hatches gone, she stared down at the engines submerged beneath three feet of clear water. "Are those fish in there?"

"Yeah, I think I saw a big eel, too," Willis said. "Look, Corey's got an idea. You explain, man."

Corey said, "Come up forward with me. Watch your step and hold on to the rail."

Sally did her best to give him the *don't patronize me* look, but Corey wasn't paying attention, and Willis didn't comment. Forward of the cabin, she felt a moment of vertigo, staring out across the lagoon. The setting sun painted streaks of red across the sky. From the south, a gentle breeze belied the storm that had just roared past.

"I'm somehow not feeling like 'king of the world' here, you know. Even though the context seems right."

Corey said, "Imagine what would happen if we pumped all of the water from the engine room, up to the bow."

"It'd run out the drains."

"We plug 'em."

"Then you'd tilt forward until this wreck goes over the ledge and sliding down the hill. Whoever is left on board better know how to fly."

"Okay, we jam our anchor into the rocks back there and let out the line slowly."

Sally thought about it for a while as darkness spread across the lagoon and climbed the hill below her. "I guess you couldn't make things too much worse."

Huddled together, they rested in the lee of the hull as the moon climbed above the east island. When it finally climbed high enough to cast dim gray shadows, they set to work. A hand pump built into *Lark's* deck drew from the bilge and discharged overboard. Matt used a length of salvaged hose to direct it into the forward cargo well. Flashlights in hand, Corey and Sally scrambled around stuffing rags into all the drains.

Willis unlashed *Lark's* heavy grapple and wedged its hooks beneath a slab of rock. He looped the anchor rope through an eye in the grapple and doubled it back to the deck. "I'll stand up here and pay it out slowly. We'll just cruise on down the road, all chill."

Matt started pumping. He and Sally took turns until the moon dimmed and the eastern horizon lit with a golden glow. Sally watched the cargo well fill with water until she felt a tremor in the deck and said, "I think I'll go ashore now. *Bon voyage*, boys."

Corey had climbed down ahead of her. Sally wondered if that made him the smartest person on the island. The sky lightened, and the first rays of dawn lit the hilltop in shades of yellow. Matt and Willis argued about who would ride down and pay out the line. Moments later, *Lark* lurched forward, and Willis jumped to snub the anchor rope around a deck-bollard. "Okay,"

Matt said, "I'll feed you the line and you pay it out. We both ride down."

Lark tilted and slid a little further over the brink. Sally watched Willis' muscles bulge as he eased rope over the bollard. The line ashore had pulled tight as a bulldog's leash. It thumped and vibrated every time *Lark* lurched forward. A few more feet, and the boat hung like a swimmer on the blocks, just waiting for the gun.

With a crack, the line broke, zipping past Sally like a giant rubber band. *Lark* lunged toward the water and disappeared over the edge.

26

Still unconscious, Lyn was nothing but dead weight across Maddock's shoulder. The submarine had stopped lurching and lay still, canted to starboard. Bones led the way aft, pushing debris as he went. "A little further," he said. "We'll have company pretty soon."

In the next compartment Maddock found a store of life vests next to the aft hatch. "This thing doubles as an escape hatch," Bones said. "We get in, close and dog the door behind us, then equalize pressure with the outside."

Maddock coughed at the acrid fumes that rose from the lower compartments. He passed the unconscious woman over to his friend and said, "Get her inside, I'll grab us some flotation."

Pistol shots. In the dim red emergency lights, Maddock could see flashes from the next compartment forward. Dragging three vests, he crawled into the escape chamber. "Close the hatch, close the hatch. I've got her." Bones said.

Maddock dragged the door shut and dogged it down. The last of their light vanished. The door squeaked; someone was trying to wrench it open. Maddock jammed a foot against the chamber wall and heaved at the handwheel. "C'mon, pressurize this thing, Bones."

He felt Lyn slide down and collapse across his back. Bones said, "I'm trying, I'm trying, but it's bloody dark as hell in here."

"Just open a valve."

"Give me a minute, I don't want to open the wrong one."

Maddock heard banging on the chamber and he felt the wheel start to slide under his fingers. Someone must have found a bar to lever the wheel around. He gripped with both hands. Lyn suddenly started struggling and kicking him in the head. She stamped down hard against his hands and Maddock released the wheel.

Nothing happened. The door remained dogged shut. No sound came from the compartment outside, or anywhere inside the submarine. Maddock suddenly realized that the smoke and halon gas must have snuffed out every other person onboard. Bones yelled down, "Hold on buddy. I think this is the one."

A gentle hissing, and Maddock felt water rising above his knees. Lyn wrenched and twisted. She cried out, "What the hell is going on?"

"Easy," Bones said. "We're just trying to get us all out of here."

Maddock found her hand and set it on a ladder rung. "Glad to hear you're alive. Now take these life vests and climb up to Bones."

The water rose above Maddock's waist and he climbed after her. "I'm letting the water in slow," Bones said. "We've got about five minute's worth of air, make it last."

Maddock wiggled into a vest of his own, and soon he was floating high in the chamber with the others. "What do you figure, three-hundred feet?"

"I'd say. Let's bail before we all get the bends."

Lyn said, "Wait, I just got to this party. What do you mean, bail?"

"We'll just pop the hatch and float gently to the surface," Bones said. "Just remember to scream all the way up."

Maddock added, "What he means is you've got to exhale as you go."

"Wonderful. And I suppose it's a day at the beach, topside."

Bones reached up and grabbed the handwheel. "Let's go find out."

Being right under the hatch, Bones was first to shoot from the escape-chamber. Lyn had no choice but to do the same. Maddock followed her out, propelled like a missile by the buoyancy of his vest. He blew a steady stream of air as he rose, but the ascent seemed to last forever.

The surface came as a surprise. The sky, so dark with rain and clouds, did little to illuminate the churning lagoon. He rose on a wave the size of a building and tumbled from its crest into a boiling mass of foaming water. The next wave broke over his head, followed by another before he could recover. Breathing was next to impossible, swimming out of the question.

No sign of the others, Maddock had all he could do to keep his head above the waves and air in his lungs. A blizzard of rain and wind-whipped spray fled above the waves. Maddock let himself be driven along, just another piece of storm-wrack.

He heard it before he saw it. The booming waves and shrieking wind battered themselves against land nearby. Maddock readied himself. Then something caught his eye. An orange vest… no, two orange vests bobbed and tossed in the surf, not a dozen yards away. Somehow, Maddock made his way over. Lyn and Bones. The woman struggled to keep Bones' face above the water. "He hit his head on the way out," she said.

Maddock seized his friend's vest just as the next wave picked them up and hurled them to the shore. Gravel under his feet, Bones' dead weight threw him over backwards. Maddock saw stars for a moment. He gasped a lungful of air as another giant comber tumbled them among the rocks. A brief pause between waves. Maddock dragged his friend higher, then crouched over him when the next surge of water swept over them.

"Up here, up here." Lyn called from somewhere above. She stood perched on a tiny ledge, clinging to the rocks as the waves washed over her.

Maddock caught Bones under both arms and backed away from the lagoon, letting successive waves batter them both about the rocks and carry them higher up the shore. Lyn climbed down and grabbed a limp arm. Maddock took the other, and together they towed Bones over the ledge and partway up the hillside.

"I don't know if he's even alive, and I'm not sure I am." Lyn said.

"A little bit higher and we'll find out. The storm is almost past, but we need to get above the water."

Maddock could find nothing like a path, but down the shore, a portion of the cliff had collapsed. "There," he pointed. "We've got to climb that."

Lyn crouched on a boulder and crossed her arms over her head. "I don't think I can move another inch."

As she spoke a wave swept up the rocky slope and surged over the three of them. Lyn sprawled flat and it was all Maddock could do to keep Bones' limp body from washing back into the lagoon. "You've got to do it, lady. C'mon you made it this far, one last push."

Another wave passed; Lyn struggled to her feet and hooked her arm under Bones' shoulder. "Okay, big fella. If I'm going to die, I want to do it with a friend by my side. Or you."

Together, they managed to wrestle Bones along the rocky beach and drag his body up the mound of fallen rock. Maddock rolled him on one side and removed his vest. Lyn began rescue-breathing while Maddock listened to the back of his chest. "The man's full of water, but he's still alive. I have no idea why."

Lyn stayed with it as the clouds blew off to the north, revealing a cherry red sun descending toward the western horizon. Bones coughed and gagged, then vomited up a heroic fountain of seawater. He shivered as he lay and hacked like he was going to explode. Maddock held his head up. Retching, Bones tried to sit, then collapsed, coughing up blood and phlegm.

"Well it ain't heaven, 'cause you're here," he managed to croak out, "so where in hell are we?"

"North Island," Maddock said. "Lyn's with us, so that makes you about as close to heaven as you're about to get."

Bones coughed. He retched again and spit up another wad of bloody mucus. "What about Willis and… and that girl?"

"Sally? Remember, we put them all ashore on the East Island."

"Yeah, the storm… the storm and a submarine. Did I dream about the submarine? Seems like I did."

"There was a submarine, Bones. It sank and you saved us all. Now flop down here on one of these life vests. We'll rest until morning."

Bones hacked and shivered where he lay. Maddock

spread the remaining vests over him and Lyn curled up at his side. "What about you?" she said. "You were in pretty rough shape when I last looked."

"I've had better days, but the toxin seems to have left my system. A little rest will help. How about yourself?"

"Not great. Sally's nasty friend is one seriously broken hombre; he's a monster, and I've known a few monsters in my life."

"Is? You think he's alive?"

Lyn kept her head down. Wet strands of black hair covered her face. "God, don't look at me. My face is on fire and my head feels like it's going to explode." She rocked, head between her knees. Maddock thought she might be crying.

"Yeah, he's still around," she finally said. "Pym gave me a tour of his little toy. Right behind the con station he had an escape pod, a lifeboat for one, thoughtful guy. Don't write him off yet." She hesitated. "You do know it was all an act? Yes, I was trying to save my own skin but I was also looking for any way to rescue you guys, too."

"We know," Maddock assured her.

After a while, they drifted off. Sometime after midnight, Bones stopped hacking, rolled over, and began to snore. Maddock nodded off and slept until the rising moon awakened him. Lyn had added her own contralto to Bones tenor snoring. *A pack of seals in fact,* Maddock thought. It occurred to him that at least one other might have made it to the North Island. Crawling a little higher on the rocks, he settled in to watch for movement.

He awoke a second time, sprawled on his side, his cheek in the mud. Pushing himself upright, Maddock shivered and glanced about. The moon had risen directly overhead and a field of tiny gleams reflected off the wavelets below. For the rest, the lagoon was quiet and dark.

Maddock looked for the Ma'óghe's telltale blaze of color. He saw nothing, nor did he see any sign of Pym. Waves lapped against the rocky beach, and a warm breeze blew in from the south. *Just another night in paradise.* Maddock scanned the other islands. To the west, a rocky crag rose from the lagoon. Bare and desolate by moonlight, it looked like something from an alien planet. He could see little of their refuge, North Island, but was certain that nothing could approach without attracting his attention.

Most of East Island remained in the shadows. He saw only darkness along the shore where they'd landed the previous day. Something caught his eye further up. Maddock felt certain he saw lights moving along the cliff top. He stood and shaded his eyes against the bright moonlight. Nothing, then another tiny glint.

Something moved in the darkness just below him. Bones climbed up and said, "If I'm going to have a headache this bad, I should at least have the memories of a night of drunken debauchery to go along with it. It's not fair."

"I'm just glad to see you standing, bro. Thought we'd lost you there."

"I was about to say the same. What about Lyn?"

"Pretty beat up, but she dragged your ass all the way here. One rough, tough smuggler chick, that one."

Maddock recapped the last moments of *Pale Horse* and how they made it to the North Island. "I don't like the idea that Pym escaped," Bones said. "How do you think Willis and the others are doing?"

"Up to something." Maddock squinted at the East

Island. The horizon beyond had lightened to a pale shade of pink. "I've seen lights moving over there."

Bones squinted that direction. "Looks like something on the hillside."

Below them, Lyn stirred. Maddock scrambled down and helped her sit up. She cursed quietly under her breath and said, "How's my mascara?" Blood had caked in her hair and run down the left side of her face. Lyn reached up and touched her cheek. "Damn that Pym. He didn't have to do this to me."

"He knew you'd bought us time," Maddock said. "As soon as we broke his little toy, he figured out your angle."

Bones came and squatted nearby. "Now I'm glad he survived." He felt around his waist. "Damn, I've lost my knife. That's okay, it gives me a chance to kill him with my bare hands."

Maddock eased the matted hair away from her left cheek. Her eye was swollen almost shut. "It's not pretty but you'll live."

"Pym wasn't concerned with whether I lived or died. My face is numb right now. It's not going to get better when the feeling comes back. So, what's going on over there?" Lyn pointed at the East Island. The sun had cleared the horizon and outlined a blocky shape on the hillside. "It looks kind of like *Lark* up there."

Bones stared for a moment, and then grinned. "That's just what it is. Good old *Lark*…" He paused mid-sentence. "Holy crap. What's going on up there?"

As they watched, the ship tilted forward and inched down the hill. About half way down, it cut loose and hurtled downhill.

27

"**I'd say the** East Island is a five-hundred-yard swim from the far end of this rock," Maddock pointed off to the other shore. "The chart shows a rock between the islands, but I'd want to stay well clear. Say figuring currents, a thousand yards of water."

Lyn kept her head down. "I'm not sure I'm up for that kind of swim. I don't have much left after what Pym did to me."

"You made it here, towing Bones, too. We'll put a life vest on you and stay with you all the way."

Maddock hung one of the bulky vests over his arm and led them down to the beach. The waves still surged around their ankles, but nothing like the evening before. Bones helped Lyn negotiate the rocky shore. She told them more of her time with Pym and what he'd done. "He'd have killed me if you two hadn't started messing with his engine room. How in hell did you get back there?"

As they picked their way east along the shore, Bones told Lyn of their fight on the submarine. "…Then that Ma'óghe came and ate all of them. You should have seen it."

Maddock had been watching the opposite shore. Figures moved along the beach but couldn't quite tell what they were doing. Something bothered him about his friend's story. "Sally's drone," he said. "Somehow, she called them. What I don't understand is, why didn't they just eat us too?"

Bones grinned. "They got a bite of you the other night and didn't care for seconds."

"Well they were gnawing on you too, buddy, and it didn't seem to leave such a pleasant taste either."

Lyn spoke from beneath a cascade of wet hair. "Haven't you noticed? Sally seems different now, like she hears things that we don't. I think that Ma'óghe thing senses her thoughts."

Maddock nodded. "She tried to tell me the other night. I didn't know what to think."

"Legend holds that Lemurians took up black magic, which is why the gods punished them by destroying their continent," Bones said. "Maybe this creature is a part of that."

"A squid that practices black magic?" Maddock asked.

"Or she's a product of black magic? Her behavior is hardly normal."

"Compared to all the other glowing giant squid you've studied?"

"Screw you, Maddock. You know what I'm saying."

"I do. And you might be right."

Bones looked around. A hundred yards farther, the beach ended at a jagged ridge. Bones pointed up a narrow cleft that climbed the headland. "You good for a bit of scrambling?"

Lyn sat on a rock with her hands on her knees. "I don't think so, Bones. My head is throbbing, and my face feels like it's on fire."

Maddock knelt next to her. "We can't stay where we are, and I'm not leaving you." He stared off at the East Island. "It's almost a half mile across, maybe a mile of swimming. We might make it from here."

"No way," Bones said. He crouched in front of Lyn. "C'mon, piggy-back time."

"I'm not going to ride piggy-back."

"It's either that or I go all cave-man and toss you over my shoulder. Which way do you want it?"

"Any other time big fella, over the shoulder cave-man style might get interesting."

She hugged him around the chest and Bones hooked his arms beneath her knees. "Oof! NO more Spam for you."

"I hope not—I'd be barfing it all up."

Maddock tried to ignore the banter; he was more concerned that Lyn would pass out, or that Bones would stumble. "I'll lead. Just be careful, Bones."

The cleft turned out to be an easier climb than it had looked. A few times Maddock turned to watch his friend negotiate a steep passage. Lyn wrapped her legs around him and clung like a monkey as Bones scrambled between the rocks.

Cresting the ridge, they were treated to a panoramic view of Maug Lagoon, and East Island. Beyond that, the Pacific Ocean sparkled in the morning light. Lyn regained her feet and stretched her arms. "Was it as good for you as it was for me?"

Bones' attention had wandered elsewhere; Maddock followed his gaze. Below them, the North Island ended in a series of terraces that descended to the water's edge. A narrow channel surged and foamed between the shore and a flat rocky islet. Another hundred yards and the East Island rose from the water in a line of cliffs and narrow gravel beaches. He watched the waves come surging up from the lagoon to rush in swirling eddies between the islet and the shore. "I don't like the looks of that current. We'll have to stay well clear of the channels."

Bones said nothing for several minutes, then pointed to the islet below. "Is that what I think it is?"

Maddock scanned the jumble of waves and rocks. One large gray boulder seemed oddly symmetrical. "Looks like aircraft wreckage washed up by the storm."

Bones didn't miss a beat. He clenched his fists in the air and said. "Let's go finish the job we started."

The passage took longer than expected. A strong current poured between the rocks, threatening to sweep the three into the open Pacific. Swimming side-stroke, he and Bones towed Lyn between them. Maddocks arms felt like cement bags when he finally waded ashore. "I feel like I'm back in SEAL school."

"You're getting old and fat and lazy. Next time, I'll make you carry the lady."

Maddock heard a soft click behind him and spun around. A familiar shadow stepped from behind a rock. "I'm afraid there won't be a next time, gentlemen."

Augustus Pym Junior didn't look quite as stylish as he had onboard the *Pale Horse.* His hair bristled around his left ear and lay plastered flat where his right one had been. His torn shirt hung over his slacks and he picked his way over the stony beach on bare feet. Maddock said, "A pity the captain didn't go down with his ship."

"Since one of you shot my captain, he had little choice. However, the *owner* never sinks with his ship. Isn't that right Lyn?"

When she didn't answer, Pym continued. "I am

surprised to see any of you alive, although perhaps I shouldn't be. Is there any reason I don't just shoot the three of you right now?"

"Because you'll need us to get you off this rock-pile," Maddock said. "In case you don't know, Captain Lyn's ship is still afloat."

If Pym was surprised, he didn't show it. Waving his pistol, he said, "Is that true bitch? Am I going to ride you back to Guam? That ought to be fun, but tell me why I need these two idiots?"

Lyn swept the hair away from her left eye, revealing her battered and bloody face. "You may as well shoot all of us Junior, because I'm not taking you anywhere."

None of them had moved, but Pym shifted from one foot to the other like a hyperactive six-year old. "Oh, this is good, a bargain truly made in hell then. Do you like bargains Lyn? Because here's what I have to offer; you and your crew will take me to Guam—and I let them live. How about that?"

Bones shook his head, "No way in this hell or the next one, assclown. Stop playing with your gun before you grow hair on you palm."

Lyn touched his shoulder and said, "Wait. I'll do it. Just no one gets shot."

Pym grinned and Maddock noted a strange glint in the man's eyes. He wondered, *a bit of the Maug madness?* Bones on the other hand, looked about to rush Pym, gun or no. Maddock clutched his friend's arm and dug his heels in. "We're all stuck on this island. If we work together, maybe we'll all make it off."

Bones tugged against Maddock's grip. For several heartbeats, the gun didn't waver from its body-center bead on his chest, then Pym said, "You know, I'd like to kneecap you, just to hear you scream all the way to Guam." He lowered the pistol. "But a bargain is a bargain. Oh, wait… darn, there's one more thing. The girl, you know, the one with the tight body and loose lips? Yeah, I like her, she comes with us too."

Maddock tightened his grip, but he felt his friend relax and go all cold, like a martyr walking to the cross. "If you touch Sally," Bones said, "there aren't enough bullets in that gun to stop me from tearing you to shreds. And that goes for the rest of our crew."

Pym's grin didn't waver. "You know, the only thing I need from you, big mouth, is your shoes. The rest I should just leave for the crabs."

"Easy Bones," Maddock didn't release his friend's arm. "We'll do this one step at a time. One step, Bones— give him your shoes."

Bones glanced at his feet, looked over at his friend, nodded slightly, and sat on the rocky beach to unlace his soaked sneakers. Maddock watched Pym fidget and realized that gun or no, the man was afraid of them. He made a note to himself, *all bluster and no guts.* Bones seemed to have the same idea. He glared up at Pym as he slipped out of his shoes.

"Now all of you step back," the man said, "back by those rocks."

Lyn started to sway, and Maddock found her a place to sit. Bones stood, a cobra unwinding from its basket. Pym shooed him back with the pistol and stepped up to slip into his size elevens. "That's better, much better. Let's all scurry along now, we don't want to miss the boat, do we?"

Bones led the way, supporting Lyn who sagged and stumbled at his side. Maddock followed, with Pym close behind. Maddock listened for the footfalls—perhaps eight feet back. Too far to try disarming him, too close to run for it.

Bones glanced back. Maddock nodded. He'd heard it too. Pym limped slightly on his left foot. He caught Lyn's eye and arched his eyebrows, questioning. She gave a tiny nod. She understood.

As they rounded a slight headland where the beach narrowed and a boulder field stretched from lagoon to hilltop, Maddock looked at Lyn and mouthed, *Distraction.*

Lyn collapsed sobbing at Bones' side. "I can't go any further. My head is killing me."

Pym raised his left foot and said, "Stop here all of you." He half doubled over to dig a pebble out of his shoe.

Maddock gave Lyn a nod and she sprang to her feet and ran for it, disappearing between the tumbled rocks. Bones hesitated only a moment before diving for cover. Maddock lashed out with a roundhouse kick aimed for Pym's head. Under different circumstances, the kick would have landed with devastating effect, but Maddock was injured and exhausted, and Pym was wary, and managed to move at the last second. The kick caught him on the shoulder and sent him staggering. One finger still in his shoe, Pym fired a shot in Maddock's direction, then he lost his balance and fell.

Maddock sprawled flat, flung a handful of gravel at Pym's face and sprang for the meager cover of a driftwood log. Two rounds smacked into the rotten wood, throwing dirt and splinters into the air. Maddock heard approaching footsteps and saw the nine-millimeter Glock 17 pistol, a finger of doom pointing down at him.

Pym grunted and cursed as a fist-sized cobble smacked him in the side of the face. He spun and fired three shots into the maze of rocks above. Maddock didn't wait to see the results but scrambled behind the nearest boulder, dodged to the side, and dove behind another. He waited out two shots that rattled between the stones like enraged hornets, then dodged and ran for all he was worth higher up the hillside.

Pym didn't waste any more rounds, and looking back, it seemed to Maddock that the man had slipped off between the boulders himself. The tiniest flash of movement betrayed someone hiding among the gullies and ravines. It came again. Bones, no one else could be that subtle and still that visible. Maddock worked his way closer but saw nothing of Pym. The man had disappeared.

To trail Bones, Maddock knew, a person had to think like Bones and to anticipate him. A broken stem, a scraped rock, too obvious, Maddock headed the opposite direction. A clear patch of sand. Bones would have stepped over it. He could move faster in bare feet than most men could run in track-shoes.

Another boulder, then another. Maddock stopped and listened to the wind hiss among the crevices and gullies. "Bones?"

The man in question stepped from behind a rock. "Here."

"Where's Lyn?"

"Up there somewhere, hunkered down, I hope. Where's Pym?"

"Lost him back there."

"Lost him? How could you lose him—I was counting

on you to take him out."

"You might have noticed that he was better armed. Nice shot with that rock, though."

"That wasn't me..."

Before Bones could finish, they heard Lyn scream. Maddock swung around. "It came from the beach."

Defying caution, Bones jumped from rock to rock headed toward the sound. Maddock followed, taking a somewhat more circuitous route. Another scream and then silence. Slipping out from behind a rock, Maddock came face to face with Pym.

His face bore three long scratches, but he had Lyn in a chokehold. She clutched something in her right hand, but it just hung at her side. Pym's pistol barrel pressed into her wounded face.

"Bitch just doesn't know when to quit. I'm just going to kill all three of you and take my chances on that boat."

Bones stood flanking the man. "You shoot one of us and the others will take you out in a second. I almost want to see you try it, asshat."

"Stop it, Bones. Can't you see what he's doing to Lyn." Maddock held his hands out, palms down and addressed Pym. "Just let up on her. We'll make this work."

Bones tried to inch closer, hands out to the sides. "Yeah c'mon, drop the girl. Let's settle this like men."

"Don't try it." Pym's finger twitched on the trigger. Before anyone could react, Lyn threw her head backward, crushing Pym's nose. Pym let out a shout of surprise and released her. A rock flew through the air, just missing his head. Pym turned and ran.

Maddock started to pursue the man, but a shot rang out. The bullet whizzed past his ear. So, Pym hadn't run far.

"We've got to get out of here!" he shouted.

Maddock dodged toward the water, then cut back up the beach. Lyn and Bones followed him around the headland as two more shots sizzled off the rocks. The woman stumbled as she ran. Maddock grabbed her around the waist saying, "C'mon, we're too exposed here."

Bones had his hand pressed against his left arm. He'd been clipped by a shot and blood streamed from the wound and ran off his elbow.

"Let me go back and kill him like we should have," Bones growled.

"Forget it Bones. Discretion is the better part of valor."

"You say that to me at least once a week and I still have no idea what it means. Nice job by Lyn, though. I think you broke his nose."

Lyn nodded, not looking up. "Just seemed like the thing to do. He had his arm around my neck, and I thought he was going to kill me. Might as well try."

Bones shook his head. "You should have just run."

"I just want him dead." She stumbled, fell to her knees and sobbed. "He's hurt me—he's hurt me so much I want him dead."

Maddock said, "Pym's not going to talk next time. He's going to shoot. We need to run."

A hundred yards farther, the beach ended at another rocky spit. Maddock was glad to put something substantial between himself and Pym's Glock. "How many rounds does he have left, Bones? Have you been counting?"

"Not really. Five or six, I'd guess. Let's just hope

there's some firepower left onboard *Lark*." They waded through the surf and rounded a narrow point. Bones stopped so quickly that Lyn stumbled into him.

"This day just keeps getting weirder."

28

Lark **actually looked** like a boat again. Battered and listing to port, she bobbed on the surface of the lagoon. Despite all she'd been through, the old craft was seaworthy.

"I think we're ready to fire her up," Corey said, wiping his hands with an oily cloth. "Let's give her a go."

Within minutes, the deck vibrated as the engine rumbled.

"We did it!" Matt said. "Now, to get the hell out of here without disturbing Maug."

"I don't sense anything," Sally said. "I think we'll be fine provided we leave the treasure alone. No point in going anywhere until Willis gets back."

They had heard gunshots in the distance and Willis had gone to investigate, reasoning that even if it were Pym or one of his underlings firing the gun, whomever he was aiming at was probably an ally. He'd been gone for a while, though. No more gunshots, but no Willis.

"I guess we should be ready to make wake as soon as he gets back," Corey said reluctantly.

Just then, someone called out from the shore.

"What did you do to my boat?"

"Lyn?" Sally cried. She ran to the stern and saw Willis, Lyn, Maddock, and Bonebrake boarding *Lark*.

"Oh my God! I thought you were all dead!" She hurried forward and embraced Lyn. "You're hurt. What happened?"

"Pym happened, but there'll be time to talk about that later."

"Pym is somewhere out there," Maddock explained. "And he's armed and nuts."

"In that case, let's cast off," Corey said.

While Sally tended to Lyn's and Bones' injuries, Willis stood guard, keeping watch for Pym.

As *Lark* whined and the engine noise rose to a throaty roar, the sturdy craft heaved itself through the lagoon, headed for open water.

Sally cut the sleeve from Bones' shirt and used it to bind his wound. "I'm getting tired of patching you up, Bonehead."

"Thanks," Bones said simply.

Next, she turned her attention to Lyn. "No mirrors for at least a month," she said as she cleaned Lyn's wounds.

"I'm just glad to see that Sally was wrong, for once," Bones said.

"What are you talking about?" Sally didn't look up.

"I heard you thought we were all dead."

"I feared Maddock and Lyn were dead. You, I was kind of hoping."

Bones mimed stabbing himself in the chest. "Ouch! That's just beyond the pale."

"Look, just shut up already," Sally said, laughing.

"Now," Sally said to Lyn, "tell me all about your adventure with Mr. Pym."

Lyn related the whole story, including Bones' account of what he and Maddock had been through. "So now, what the hell happened here?"

Sally told of their encounter in the Japanese bomb shelter and her run-in with Mako. "But seeing that thing, that Ma'óghe thing just drag the submarine down like it was nothing. That was the worst for me." She frowned. "I'm amazed *Lark* held together."

Lyn couldn't grin, but she nodded. "Her hull was built to survive a war; a little storm is nothing. I should ask how the engines are."

"Starboard engine is toast. It was idling when she flooded. Matt says he can put the starboard blower on the port side and get us one good motor. The wheel's tweaked and the shaft might be slightly bent, but Corey thinks it'll get us to Saipan."

Sally finished bandaging Lyn's face and sat herself cross-legged where the woman could see her. "I've got one more story to tell; one that Mr. Bonebrake would attribute to my noodle-network. I'd call it intuition and leave it at that."

Lyn said nothing, so Sally started. "There was this girl. I think she grew up in east Texas or south Louisiana. Tall, she was picked on when she was young. Maybe a stepfather didn't treat her too well either. Anyway, this girl might have hooked up with the fishing boats down there on the Gulf, or she might have worked some offshore oil. Men liked her, but never in a nice way. Smart girl. She saved her money, and when the time came, she got the hell out of Dodge. Sound believable?"

Lyn sat in silence, didn't even blink. Sally continued. "This girl grew up tough and smart. She bounced around a bit, maybe she's still got warrants out somewhere. One day, she was looking at a federal auction poster and saw an old landing craft for sale cheap in Guam. With the Marine Corps relocating from Okinawa, she spotted an opportunity. Like I say, smart girl.

"So, when times got lean, this girl found other

income opportunities, made new contacts. Still, she doesn't trust anyone. This tough girl grows up be a tough lady. Alone, she doesn't make friends. Everyone's either a customer or a competitor, *use 'em and lose 'em* she'd say. Years passed, and life got real lonely." Sally paused. "Just the noodle-network here telling me stuff based on what people like to eat, you know. But does this person sound familiar?"

Lyn twitched her head. A tear trickled from the corner of her right eye. "So what's your point?"

"I think this person saw another opportunity, a seven-figure opportunity. And later, things got hairy. Two guys who could have just lit out for the shore risked everything to drag her wounded ass off the bottom of the sea. So how do I end this story?"

Lyn shook her head slowly, but kept her silence. "I need to check on my girl."

As they made their way to the helm, Lyn took in the damage and shook her head. "How are we going to steer with no helm?"

"We rigged a drag," Corey said. "Pull it forward or let it out, we can keep her in a southerly direction. We're pivoting around the anchor now. Soon as the bow points south, we're going home!"

Shots, three in a row, pinged off the starboard rail and buzzed over their heads.

"Get down!" Corey yelled.

Lyn dragged Sally behind the cabin as two more bullets zipped past her ear.

Willis stepped out with the twelve-gauge. "Where is he? Bring her in close and give me a shot."

A ragged figure came running up the beach. *Pym.* Lyn pointed him out.

"Corey, bring us about!" Willis raised his shotgun. "Just get me a little bit closer and I can take him out."

Sally pushed the gun barrel aside. "Don't bother."

"What are you talking about?"

"Killing him ends his suffering quickly," Maddock said, stepping up beside them. "Wouldn't you rather just let him watch us leave? We cruise on out of here leaving him to his fate."

Willis lowered the barrel. Another bullet ricocheted off the steel cabin.

Standing waist deep in the water, Pym raged, shook his fist, and flung his pistol in the direction of *Lark*. It made a disappointingly small splash as it struck the water.

"Let's get the hell out of here," Maddock said. The remaining engine roared and *Lark* departed the lagoon and began her slow journey south. Moments later, all seven of them stood watching Augustus Pym jump and flail his arms.

"He'll have Spider Dude to keep him company," Matt said.

Sally watched until the tiny dancing figure was indistinguishable from the waves that danced in their wake. Without thinking, she touched a polished ivory statuette in her pocket. "And don't forget Ma'óghe," she said. "It'll be whispering to him for a long, long time."

29

With a bent propeller blade, *Lark* vibrated like an old pickup on a gravel road. Matt had found an engine speed that minimized their discomfort. A barrel, half filled with water dragged just off their stern quarter. Maddock could snub it closer to head east or let it out to go west. During the day, navigation was pure guesswork, based on the sun and the waves. After sunset, Polaris appeared low and pale in the northern sky. Maddock kept the star hovering right above their wake, dead amidships.

That evening as they sat on the deck and watched the sunset, Sally was quiet, contemplative. "I don't know what it is, but I think there's something of the Ma'óghe that I'm taking with me as well."

"That's actually a good thing," Bones said. "Corey's always been into tentacle monsters."

Corey sputtered a protest while the others laughed.

They swapped stories, filling one another in on the details of their exploits.

Bones said to Sally, "You shot Mako with that old Smith and Wesson? I thought we'd ditched it back in New York."

"A girl can't just leave weapons lying around. You taught me that, Bonehead. I jammed it in with our equipment—and your Glock, by the way."

"I've been wondering something," Lyn said. The side of her face had swollen and turned a nasty shade of purple. She looked at Bones. "What did you see when you dove on the wreck with Maddock?"

"Pretty murky. A typical wreck, you know; about the same as the first time I was down there. Why?"

Maddock straightened. "I think she's asking what we *didn't* see. Right Lyn?"

"I didn't see a monster, if that's what you mean."

"What else?" Lyn pressed.

A light seemed to go on behind the big man's eyes. "No lost treasure, no orange bags from the previous dive. We'd have spotted 'em for sure."

Lyn nodded. "That's what I meant, boys. They aren't down there."

Bones pursed his lips and made a face. "So...?"

"They aren't there because I secured them in a hidden compartment, just above the keel, forward of the engines."

"You were afraid Squidward would steal them?"

"No. No, I hid them to make sure you didn't try to rip me off. I don't know. I've got trust issues, okay?"

Bones gaped. "Are you freaking kidding me?"

"What are you so upset about?" Maddock asked. "If it weren't for Lyn, we'd be leaving with nothing."

"I know, but it's usually me who manages to surprise everyone with some purloined loot. She's horning in on my territory."

They retrieved the bags from their hiding place and brought them up on deck.

Sally opened the first bag and drew out a heavy sphere, the size of a man's fist. Bones scraped it with his knife, examined it under the light, and passed it to Lyn. "Here, part of your share."

She eyed the orange flakes Bones had scraped off. "Cannon ball, thanks."

Sally pulled out an irregular mass, covered with marine growth. She hefted it, then slammed it on the deck. The mass split into three small lumps. Bones picked one up and scraped it. "Silver, silver ingots," he said.

Next item from the bag was the size and shape of a hotdog bun. Sally hefted it. "I think this one will make up for the cannon ball."

Bones picked it up and grinned. "Oh, yeah." He scraped it with his knife to confirm. "Gold." Curling it like a dumbbell he said, "I think maybe eight pounds. What's that worth?"

Maddock said, "Figure twenty grand a pound, do your own math."

"Here, I got another one," said Sally. "Look! Two more."

Piece by piece, they sorted the junk from the bullion. Bones shoveled the miscellaneous cannon balls and coral encrusted lumps of iron off to one side. "I'll deep-six this mess."

All told, their haul tallied to over fifty pounds of silver and two hundred pounds of gold.

"You're lucky the Ma'óghe let you take it," Corey said. "Maybe because it was already bagged, she didn't recognize it or sense it, so she allowed the bags to be taken."

"What the hell are you talking about?" Willis asked.

"It's not that crazy," Sally said. "Gold has some unique properties when it interacts with certain wavelengths. NASA uses it all the time. Depending on the frequencies the Ma'óghe's colony uses, the gold might absorb or reflect it at an unusual rate, especially compared to the volcanic rock in the area. The Ma'óghe might be fascinated by it."

"It's more than that." Corey paused. "There's some things I forgot to tell you guys."

"Now's as good a time as any," Maddock said.

"First of all, do you remember when Matt compared the lights in the lagoon to 'visible music?' Well, that got me thinking. I started analyzing video of the lights with that idea in mind. I won't bore you with the details…"

"Thank God," Willis said.

Corey flashed him the middle finger. "Long story short, I eventually converted it to sheet music and discovered a form of musical cryptography."

"What's that?" Lyn asked.

"It's a way of using sheet music to embed hidden messages," Maddock said. "Composers have done it, usually as a lark. They'd hide the name of a friend within the composition." He turned to Corey. "So, what does it say?"

Corey's expression was grave. "Beware thief."

"Ma'óghe speaks English?" Matt asked.

"Oh, the analysis is ongoing, but so far I've found the same two words in Russian and Spanish. I'm sure all the others will simply be representations in different languages."

"So, the Ma'óghe tried to warn us," Sally whispered. "She didn't care what happened to us as long as we didn't steal her treasure."

Lyn shook her head. "But how could it do that? Know about this cryptography stuff, and different languages."

Sally shifted uncomfortably in her seat. "I imagine it looks into our minds."

No one knew what to say. Finally Matt broke the

silence.

"Corey, you said you had some other things to tell us."

"Heard from Jimmy. He says he's 'nibbling around the edges' of Pym's cyber network. Also, he says the FBI is sniffing around Pym, probably thanks to Maddock's call to Alex. Nothing's gone down, but Jimmy's glimpses into their network make him believe Pym senior and his company are treading cautiously at the moment." He suddenly sat bolt upright and turned to Sally. "Oh, and your uncle's alive. He's in San Francisco staying with a friend. "

"What!" Sally hugged Corey tightly then shoved him away. "Why didn't you tell me?"

"We've had a lot on our minds. Like, how are we going to move all this treasure?"

The blatant attempt to change the subject worked.

"I've got a connection who can move this stuff with ease," Lyn said. "He'll want a twenty percent cut, but he can sell it at full market value. He's the best."

"Is he trustworthy?" Maddock asked.

Lyn rubbed her chin. "Now that is an interesting choice of words. I guess it depends on how you define the term. I can tell you we can rely on him to do what he says he's going to do."

"Good enough for me," Bones said.

"What about Augustus Pym Senior?" Corey asked, flashing a nervous glance in Sally's direction.

"Daddy is crooked," Sally began, "but Junior is the crazy one. Like I said before, it wouldn't surprise me if Junior never even told his father about my program. I think as long as I keep a low profile and Junior never leaves that island, I should be safe."

"Just the same," Corey said, taking her by the hand, "I'd like you to be somewhere we can keep an eye on you."

"Oh, really?" Sally eyed him with suspicion, the ghost of a smile playing at the corners of her lips. "What did you have in mind?"

"We've got a friend down in Key West who runs an awesome bar but the food sucks. I'll bet she'd love to have you on staff."

Sally pretended to consider the suggestion. "Key West? That actually sounds pretty good, but where would I stay?"

"Um," Corey began, going from beet red to white as a sheet. He glanced at Bones who gave him an encouraging nod. "I've got a king-sized bed at my place."

"Now that's interesting." Sally stood and hauled Corey to his feet. "I think we should go somewhere private and discuss it at length."

As the two disappeared, Matt turned to the others, poleaxed. "What the hell just happened?"

Bones chuckled. "After all these years of studying at the master's feet, the young grasshopper has…" He paused, screwed up his face in concentration. "Do grasshoppers come out of cocoons?"

Maddock groaned. "Tell you what. How about you leave the entomology to others and instead concentrate on something you're good at?"

"Such as?"

Maddock laughed. "Such as helping us decide how we're going to spend our loot."

The End

ABOUT THE AUTHORS

David Wood is the USA Today bestselling author of the action-adventure series, The Dane Maddock Adventures, and many other works. He also writes fantasy under his David Debord pen name. When not writing, he hosts the Wood on Words podcast. David and his family live in Santa Fe, New Mexico. Visit him online at davidwoodweb.com.

C.B. Matson C.B. Matson has survived former incarnations that include mining geologist, commercial fisherman, civil engineer, mess-hall cook, surveyor, and international port consultant. He lived much of his life in Colorado, California and Virginia, but he has also spent considerable time in Moscow, Bogota, Dakar and the Pacific Islands. When he is not writing, he enjoys walking, tinkering, and "... simply messing about in boats." C.B. Matson and his wife live on the water in Hampton Roads, Virginia. Learn more about him and his work at cbmatson.com.

Made in the USA
Middletown, DE
03 November 2019

77874524R00177